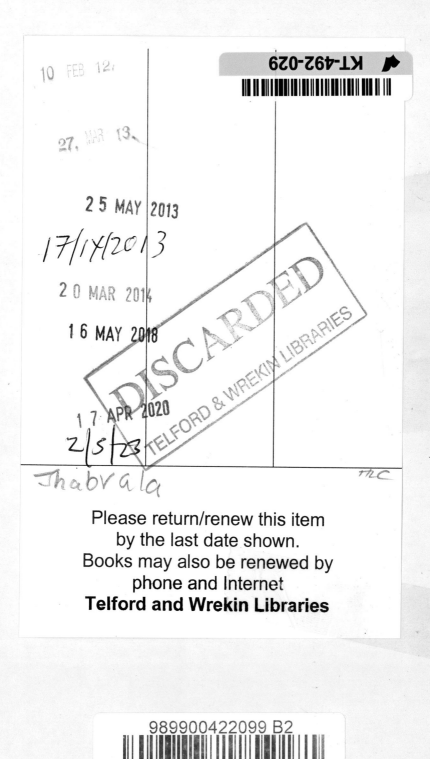

Please return/renew this item
by the last date shown.
Books may also be renewed by
phone and Internet
Telford and Wrekin Libraries

A LOVESONG
FOR INDIA

Ruth Prawer Jhabvala

Illustrations by C. S. H. Jhabvala

Little, Brown

LITTLE, BROWN

First published in Great Britain as a paperback original in 2011 by Little, Brown

'Innocence' and 'The Teacher' first appeared in the *New Yorker*
'Talent' first appeared in *Sisters: An Anthology* (Paris Press, 2009)

Illustrations © C. S. H. Jhabvala

A CIP catalogue record for this book
is available from the British Library.

ISBN: 978-1-4087-0354-0

Typeset in Goudy by M Rules
Printed and bound in Great Britain by
Clays Ltd, St Ives plc

Papers used by Little, Brown are from well-managed forests
and other responsible sources.

MIX
Paper from
responsible sources
FSC® C104740

Little, Brown
An imprint of
Little, Brown Book Group
100 Victoria Embankment
London EC4Y 0DY

An Hachette UK Company
www.hachette.co.uk

www.littlebrown.co.uk

A LOVESONG
FOR INDIA

Contents

INDIA

Innocence

Dinesh never became a famous writer, but he did become a writer and published several novels. I translated one of these from the original Hindi into English and tried to get it published here, but I was told that the background was too unfamiliar to be of interest to an American audience. Of course it was very familiar to me, who had actually lived in New Delhi and was not only a witness to the principal events but a part of them.

I was also a character in the novel, where I was called Elisabeth (not my name). Dinesh himself became D, and he was the narrator. The fictional Elisabeth and the real me had both come to India to absorb the wisdom of a woman saint who lived in a tenement building near the Old Delhi railway station. The building was very old and so crammed with tenants and subtenants that it appeared to be leaning sideways. It was also very noisy, but the two rooms our teacher occupied had a peaceful atmosphere. Her disciples sat crosslegged in a circle around her while she spoke of the Absolute, both in its aspect of the inconceivably immense, and also the tiny Person no bigger than a thumb within the human heart. The real Dinesh and the fictional D had the same attitude towards our absorption in this heady stuff. He said we lived in an India made up in the nineteenth century by German professors, and that in keeping our eyes fixed on mystical and mythical abstractions, we failed to look down at the earth and the people crowding it. It was only, he said, when something unpleasant happened to us, like a sickness, jaundice or whatever, or some fat shopkeeper cheated us, or some youth groped us on a bus, or a thief made off with our credit cards – it was only then that we recognised we were living in a real place, in a city like any other; and at once our noble, our spiritual India became degraded into a country of thievery and lechery. By the time he got to this point, the real Dinesh, like the fictional D, had become very worked up; but unlike D, he recovered himself immediately and said, 'Not you, of course, this is not personal,' and he flashed me one of his smiles in which both his teeth and his glasses participated.

Dinesh and I were fellow lodgers in the house of Mr and Mrs Malhotra, a middle-aged childless couple who looked more like brother and sister than husband and wife. Both were small, delicate, and with an ivory complexion much fairer than Dinesh's slightly pockmarked skin. They had one servant, Gochi, a very old and tattered woman sweeper who called her employers Sahibji and Bibiji – a respectful address that I too adopted. At first Dinesh and I were the only lodgers, though there was another room, which had not yet been rented. The advantage of the house was that it was centrally situated, but it was almost the only small domestic residence left here and was surrounded on all sides by huge commercial buildings. It was a tiny house badly in need of whitewashing and with many cracks that expanded during the monsoon; there was a central little courtyard with a series of little rooms opening out from it. In front, there was also a patch of garden in which a tree stood, with a single living branch and a few sickly leaves hanging from it.

I was glad to be living in an Indian household, for I had not received many invitations to local homes. At that time there were many Westerners like me in love with India, and people tended to laugh at us – maybe because those of us who wore saris sometimes tripped over them, and although we were rapt while listening to Indian music, we couldn't tell one raga from another. Also, some of the foreign girls got involved with respectable Indian boys, whose families then had hurriedly to find brides for them or send them away for higher studies.

There was nothing like that between me and Dinesh, though we became good friends. He was from Kanpur, the son of a poor widow; he had won a scholarship to Delhi University, and, after graduating, had got a job with All India Radio. He wanted to be a writer; so did some of his friends, while others were painters or art critics, all of them with very little money left after sending most of their salaries home to their families. Many of these friends were gloomy and bitter, but Dinesh seemed always to be in a good mood, though I noticed that this became exaggerated in times of stress. He had a very bony face, and his pitch-black oily hair was straight and lank; his teeth were too many and too large for his mouth, but he looked charming when he flashed them in one of his frequent smiles.

He and I walked around the public parks and gardens, taking shelter from the hot sun in a mausoleum or other pavilion to carry on our discussions. These were mostly about his writing. He had some strong ideas, principally that he could write in no other language but his own; for though his English was fluent, he said his thoughts could only be expressed by the tongue his mother had given him. But he laughed at my idea that it was

5

really impossible for anyone not Indian to understand India. 'Oh I see,' he said with the amused irony that was his favourite mode of debate. 'So it is your opinion that we are not like other humans but completely different, completely monstrous and bizarre? ... And by the way, what about you? What about this?' he said, though with a smile, indicating my sari. 'Why are you wearing it? Why are you loving our music, not to mention our food, our parathas and tandoori rotis and so on? And also, may I ask, why are you here at all? Isn't that bizarre?' He didn't give me time to answer – and anyway, what was there to say? We all of us here in Delhi, all of us pale foreigners, said it over and over, about what we were missing at home, what we were finding in India. 'Yes yes yes,' said Dinesh, still smiling with all his teeth, 'I've heard about it – our spiritual dimension – only where is it, can you tell me that? Can you show it to me? Never mind, let's speak about something more interesting, like for instance—'

'The Malhotras,' I said. 'Our landlords.'

Dinesh disliked gossip, but he had, reluctantly, filled me in a bit about them. They were obviously middle-class, educated people – both spoke good English, and he was, or had been, a lawyer – but marred by a scandal many years earlier. Dinesh briefly indicated that it was something to do with gold smuggling and that both of them had been involved. I was surprised: both of them? It was not impossible to believe about Sahib – there was something anxious about him, as if he wanted very much to be liked, or even forgiven. He was always eager to make conversation with us – when he was at home, that is, which was not all that much. He would leave in the morning, in his black tie and panama hat, giving the impression of going out to some business. However, one tended to run into him in a modest coffee house, sitting over a cup of coffee and talking to the waiter. One afternoon I saw him standing in a cinema line, and when he caught sight of me, he laid his finger on his lips, amused and tolerant of himself. He usually came home late at night, and then Bibiji would tell us he had been delayed in the office. She said it in a very serious tone of voice, giving no one grounds for suspicion that there was no office.

He liked to tell us how he had studied law in England and had eaten dinners at the Inns of Court. When he spoke about England, it was as if he were talking of a familiar friend. He mentioned Lord's Cricket Ground and Lyons Corner House and several other places that I, as an American, he added in a kind way, couldn't be expected to know about. He was interested in hearing about the States too – he had never been there but was hoping to go one of these days, as a tourist not as a student. What, he joked, was there left to study, at his age? Then he regularly asked me to guess how old he was. When I as regularly said thirty-five, which was at least ten years younger than he could have been, he smoothed his hair and chuckled that he had always managed to fool the world about his age.

Had he actually been in jail? He sometimes referred to his 'trouble', as though he expected everyone to know what this had been. Dinesh told me, after I persisted in asking, that he had done time as a prisoner awaiting trial. He had been at least partially cleared and placed on probation, though stripped of his licence to practise law. It was the two other accused in the case who had been given long jail sentences; they were more palpably guilty than he who had been their dupe, and one of them had a previous record. And what about her? Dinesh shrugged, said that she'd had to make several court appearances before the case against her was dropped. When I asked him how he knew, he said it had all been in the papers and everyone knew. After that, he wouldn't say any more but went on talking about our usual subjects, India and literature.

It was impossible to think of Bibiji's involvement in a criminal case. She was so proud and dainty, with the folds of her sari falling smoothly to her feet; her bangles were only glass, but probably they replaced some gold jewellery that was, due to circumstances, temporarily absent. Unlike her husband, Bibiji did not leave the house very often. Maybe she was afraid of meeting people and having to guess what they were thinking. In every exchange I had with her, she was scanning my face for information – not about me but about herself, how much I knew. But like her husband, though in a more guarded way, she seemed eager for conversation with her lodgers, Dinesh and myself. There were no visitors ever, though she was fully set up to receive them, in her living room. This was the front room, and it was furnished with a blue sofa, two matching armchairs and a carpet. She owned a china tea set and every afternoon she took it out and sat on the blue sofa to enjoy several cups of tea with digestive cookies.

Whenever I happened to be at home, she invited me to join her. She repeatedly impressed on me how Sahib had studied in England and was a professional person, and how she herself had been educated at a ladies' college where she had studied domestic arts and music. Sometimes she took out her harmonium and sat with it on the carpet and sang songs that may have been erotic or spiritual. She said she appreciated my love of Indian culture and that I wore the Indian sari. Here she rearranged its folds a little bit for me, and passed from talking about me to Dinesh.

She told me that she had first met him at a bus stop: on the arrival of the bus, there had been the usual rush in which she had been pushed to the ground. In the scramble to get aboard, only one person had bothered to help her up: yes, Dinesh, thereby missing the bus himself. But he didn't care about that, only wanting to make sure that she was unhurt. It was obvious to him at once that she was not the sort of person who would usually be found taking a bus; so that even before they knew each other, he had responded to something delicate in her nature, as she had to the same in his. When she said that, she looked at me for the first time directly and not, as usual, aslant with shyness and anxiety.

Dinesh was very attentive to her. He took care that the water buckets were kept filled during the hours when the municipal supply was turned on (six to eight in the morning, six to nine in the evening – I remember it so well!). He noticed whenever she was running short of tea leaves and filled her little canister, buying tea with his own money, though of course she always paid him back. Neither of them could afford to be as generous as they may have wanted. But she took care of him as he did of her – she said he was like a younger brother to her. When his glasses broke, she mended them with tape; or she cooked a little more of the dish she prepared for herself and her husband for their evening meal.

This meal she and Sahib always ate alone in their bedroom. Usually the door was kept shut and no sound came from behind it. It was only when I came to read Dinesh's novel that I learned how they did not eat in silence but amid fierce and bitter whispers, in which each blamed the other for what had happened. This too was revealed to me not by Dinesh but by scenes in the novel narrated by D.

It was D who described how Sahib had first met their two fellow conspirators. This had been in the same sort of coffee house where he could still be met – the same stains of ketchup on the tablecloths – but at that time he was part of a very jolly group that included freelance journalists, a doctor who had lost his licence and the younger son of an industrialist. This last was trying to start a business of his own, and he introduced his prospective partner into the circle of friends – a different type from the rest, with cruder jokes and more oil on his hair. A businessman, he called himself; eager to ingratiate, he stood treat for a round of chicken kebabs.

Sahib had completed his studies several years before but had not yet rented an office – he intended to do so the moment he had some clients; so it was at home that the two partners came to visit him. They said they needed a lawyer to draw up their contracts and he was just the person they were looking for. Bibiji served glasses of sugared lime water to get a look at them for herself. Later she confided to D that from the start she had doubts about the businessman but that she liked the son of the industrialist. He was not much more than a boy, very well spoken, and with manners learned at one of the best schools in the country.

They came every day, and soon they offered Sahib a partnership in their business venture. All they asked in return was a small investment to help with the initial purchase of gold from certain reliable sources, to be resold at fantastic profits via other reliable sources. He was hesitant, he said he would have to consult his wife. It was then, according to the novel, that they began their secret whispering behind their closed bedroom door. She objected to their total lack of business experience, he mentioned the promised profits, and they argued to and fro, their whispers getting lower and lower as though they were engaged in some criminal activity. And the two partners came every day, and every day Sahib told them he was thinking it over.

Then one morning, when Sahib had left on his usual round, the son of the industrialist came to see Bibiji. She was just enjoying a cup of tea and chatting with Gochi, her old sweeper woman, who squatted nearby with the glass of tea that was part of her wages. On the arrival of the visitor, Gochi gave a last hasty sweep to the floor before taking her bedraggled appearance out of sight, while Bibiji took out another cup to serve the guest. He admired everything – not only the cup but the sofa suite, the carpet and the wall-hanging of *Little Boy Blue* in cross-stitch that she admitted to be the work of her own hands. It was obvious to him, who was himself from a fine home, that she and Sahib came from good families. He admitted that this could not be said of his partner – but then went on to describe a deal this partner had successfully concluded, with astonishing profits. The same result could confidently be expected of their own project. One day, he promised, there would be an even costlier carpet on this floor, even bigger, heavier bangles on Bibiji's wrists. And maybe she wouldn't be in this house at all but in one of the new mansions in the diplomatic enclave, with a motor car standing before the door. No, he smiled, no need for her to learn to drive, a chauffeur would be at her disposal day and night.

He had to pay her only two more morning visits before she informed her husband that she was adding her jewellery to their input of capital. At that Sahib cried out in shock and touched the gold that had adorned her since the day of their wedding. She laughed at him: bigger, better bracelets would be bought, rings, and ropes of pearls, and what would he say to a motor car with chauffeur? All this was described in Dinesh's novel – how she persuaded him, brought him around. His account is in no way censorious; it is with affection D describes her joyful little cries and gestures at the prospect ahead. It is in subsequent chapters that D narrates the scenes of the nightly whispering behind their bedroom door, each blaming the other for what eventually happened. 'You were lucky,' Sahib told his wife. 'It was you – you who should have gone, you who were guilty, not

I.' For answer, she only raised her thin arms to show that their sole adornment now was some coloured glass bangles bought from a street hawker.

One day I found Bibiji on her sofa with Gochi squatting near her on the floor, both of them in tears. What had happened? It was explained to me that Gochi had been forbidden to come here any more by her daughter and son-in-law. Another job had been found for her where the salary was higher and also paid regularly. Her son-in-law was adamant, Gochi said, and no one in their house dared stand against him, a hard man who drank. She clutched Bibiji's feet and wet them with her tears, and Bibiji's tears fell on the spot on Gochi's head where the sparse hennaed hair had worn away. Both of them were helpless and hopeless in their different kinds of poverty.

I suggested there could be more income by way of a third tenant for the empty room. So that was how Karuna – or Kay, as she told us to call her – came to us. I had met her in the Tibetan Colony, where impecunious foreigners like myself ate delicious messes that sometimes made us sick. We were joined there by a new kind of young Indian – modern enough to drop out of school, leave home and family to discover (using the same terminology as ours) their own identity. Kay had not exactly run away from home, but she had staked her claim for self-expression – which her father may not have understood but had tolerantly indulged. He was a brigadier in the army, in charge of a hill station cantonment. She often spoke of him and seemed to admire him, though laughing at what she called his dodo ways. He supported her with cheques sent regularly and frequent calls and letters that she only sometimes answered.

When I met her, she was living in a YWCA hostel. She made scornful jokes about this place, and when I told her about

12

our empty room, she was ready to move in at once. I have to say here that the three rooms for rent in the house were no more than cubicles, each furnished with a string cot, a commercial calendar and a water jug on a stand. This spartan interior was what Dinesh was used to – he had never known anything else – and it suited me perfectly, asceticism being what I had come to India for. It suited Kay too, mainly for being different from her home. Anyway, she soon had a rug on the cement floor and had replaced the calendar with a poster of a dead rock star.

Bibiji liked her immediately and admired her, which Kay seemed to find natural. She was used to people wanting to be in her company, and she chattered away to Bibiji and to Sahib, who was also fascinated by her. I don't think she ever told them anything new or interesting – it was she herself who was so for them, in the way she spoke and laughed at nothing in particular, unless it was the YWCA or her hopelessly bourgeois family.

Dinesh got her hired in the English section of All India Radio. She became the disc jockey of a request programme called *Yours, with Love*. She played recent pop songs from England or America, selected by listeners, with fond messages for their loved ones. She read these messages in a very seductive voice – 'This is for Bunny and a million billion thanks, darling, for the fabulous times' – which made Sahib nod and smile in some sort of recognition, and Bibiji look down shyly as if she were the one being addressed.

To get Kay to work on time, Dinesh often had to wake her. He shouted from outside her door and then, too shy to see a girl asleep in bed, he sent me in. She lay on her stomach, one hot flushed cheek pressed into the pillow, moaning for coffee. Sahib had bought a tin of Nescafé specially for her, and it gave him great pleasure to rush into the kitchen, where he otherwise never set foot, and to pour water over the powder and stir it before handing it over to Bibiji or me to deliver. Dinesh stood outside the door, looking up at the ceiling in simulated disgust.

But he too seemed to enjoy Kay's company. He spoke to her in his usual torrent of often disconnected ideas – and although she kept saying 'Fantastic', she wasn't really listening and interrupted him at intervals, usually with something so far removed from what he was saying that he stopped short in astonishment. I suppose her head was full of thoughts of her own that left little room for anything else.

But one evening she asked Dinesh, 'What about them? ... You know.' She gestured in the direction of the Malhotra bedroom where presumably they were already asleep, or talking together in voices so low that no sound could be heard.

The three of us – their 'paying guests', as they called us – were in the little courtyard from which all the rooms opened up. It was like a well with the sun pouring in all day, but at night some cool air descended from the sky, of which we could see only a patch with a star or two. There was no need of further illumination – anyway, there was nothing to see except a bed with the strings broken, and Gochi's broom of twigs leaning against a wall.

'Their case,' she went on.

Dinesh waved his hand impatiently. 'That was twelve years ago.'

'Twelve years! I was only eight.'

'You must have been a very nasty little brat.'

'I looked like an angel and I was one. Everyone said so.' She ignored his exaggerated laughter. She was combing her hair, which fell around her in dark waves with auburn glints.

Dinesh had been watching her. I could see neither of them clearly in that dim starlight, but I was aware of his eyes gleaming – or maybe I was only aware of his stifled excitement. We could hear the comb as she slowly, lovingly drew it through all that silken luxury; at the same time she said, 'Shall I cut it off? It's such a nuisance.'

'If you cut it off, it might get you to work on time and not be fired, which will happen any day now.'

'Nobody is going to fire me. They love me too much. But seriously: were they both in jail?'

'Who's been talking to you?'

'Oh, everyone talks. As soon as anyone hears where I'm living – aren't those the people in the gold-smuggling case? . . . I suppose no one ever forgets.'

'I suppose no one ever learns to mind their own business,' Dinesh said.

'Do you think they're listening?' She lowered her voice. 'The two of them with their ears glued to the door?'

It was easy to imagine – the small couple crouching behind their closed bedroom door, their hearts beating, wondering, what are they saying? Are they talking – about us? What do they know? The thought seemed to make Dinesh angry and ashamed and he turned on Kay: 'So you sit gossiping with your friends – my landlords did this, my landlords did that –'

'Well, did they? *Both* of them?'

Now he didn't trust himself to speak but turned away and left us, so that Kay wondered, 'But why's he mad at me?'

She was truly puzzled by his attitude. She was used to being admired by men and took it as her due. There was Sahib every morning lingering in wait for the cry for coffee, and in the evenings he came home earlier. Already part of a lively social set, Kay was often on the point of going out – curses could be heard from her room, where she kept discarding one outfit for another. Sahib hovered smiling around the door, clutching a book, and as soon as she emerged, he held it up for her. 'Are you acquainted with this book? What is your opinion of the writing?' Mostly she had no time to answer; she would brush past him on a wave of energy and fresh perfume that drowned his disappointment in sheer pleasure.

When she was home, she wandered all over the house, talking to anyone who was around. If she had to write a letter home – with much underlining and many exclamation points – she preferred to do it in the living room where we could keep her company. This was Sahib's opportunity. He had found a tattered old copy of a novel by Françoise Sagan and it fascinated him. He questioned Kay: 'Is it true? Is this how modern girls behave, so free and knowing so much about sex?' The word sex – enticing, expectant – sat on his lips, waiting for her to take it up. Her laugh hinted at kingdoms hidden from him. He lowered the book. 'And you? Do you have someone for your friend? A cavalier?' He shut one eye. 'A *boy*friend?' More laughter from her and he laughed too, enjoying the conversation, enjoying being teased by her, enjoying her. At such moments his true nature – spry, humorous – seemed to shine out from under its eclipse of disgrace and humiliation. When Dinesh heard Sahib question Kay about books, he would say, 'What makes you think she's ever read one?'

'That's all you know!' she cried, adding, 'Dinesh hates me,' but with a smile that showed she suspected this was not quite true.

In his novel (in the character of D), he admitted that he had never met anyone like her, any kind of emancipated girl from her class. The only women he had ever been close to were his mother and his sisters. There was a constant exchange of letters between them, and it was easy to tell when there was bad news. Paradoxically, he became even more cheerful, except that his teeth seemed set in a grimace rather than his usual smile. Later in the day he announced he had taken leave from the radio station and would be departing on the evening train. When he returned after a few days, he appeared to have settled whatever trouble he had found at home, or at least to have accepted it.

When Dinesh was away, Bibiji did not sing to her harmonium. But the day he came back, she took it out again and accompanied herself to one of her ambiguous songs of love, human or divine. Sometimes Sahib stood behind her, with his fingers in his ears and playfully grimacing at us. But Dinesh, who was a great lover of Indian music and could tell each raga from the first few notes played, listened respectfully. If she made a mistake, he played or hummed the right notes for her. He hated the pop songs Kay presented on her programme; and if he saw the Malhotras listening to it, he made a disgusted face. 'Why are you listening to that stuff? It's for idiots by idiots.'

Once Sahib answered him: 'I love it. It's the music for young people. Don't you like young people?' He became coy, the way he did when he was on the brink of something he called spicy. 'I know one young person you like.'

Perhaps we should have guessed Bibiji's feelings from her explosion of anger at that moment. But how could we, how could anyone? In the novel, D blames himself for his ignorance – but that was years after the events described in it. There is a scene where D talks to Elisabeth about Indian women. 'What do you know about that – how our women have to live? No, how can you – you who are free to run around the world like wild cats.' He continued, more bitter, more angry: 'We won't even talk about the widow – but the wife: when the husband drinks, gambles, goes to women, beats her for the insufficient dowry she brought ... Fortunately,' D says, 'my sisters have a brother – not much of a brother but at least someone to write to so that he can sit on a train and be there.' From his earliest years, Dinesh's attitude towards women had always been a protective one; and that was how he felt towards Bibiji.

He accepted her description of him as her brother. It was the only relationship he knew.

With Kay, he thought of himself as a detached observer, analysing her as a type. Probably he made notes about her, as did D in the novel. She had far less time to think about him than he about her. Often she didn't come home from the radio station but went with her friends to fashionable places he had never seen. Some of her girlfriends were fugitives from arranged marriages, or like Kay herself had simply raised the flag of independence and made their families salute it. For the first time away from their mothers and their ayahs, they were untidy and scatterbrained and gave parties at night, with music and dancing and drinks. Dinesh of course was not invited to these parties, but Kay told him, 'They all want to meet you.'

'Who wants to meet me?'

'My friends.'

'What an honour,' he said. He knew some of these girls from the radio station; they ignored him, as they did all the others who worked there for a living. But now Kay had told them he was a writer, and this raised his status with them, for writers had articles written about them in the magazines, with photographs of their foreign girlfriends who had followed them to India. Dinesh quite fiercely denied being a writer – he said he hadn't published anything yet and maybe never would.

'Then what is it you're scribbling all night?' I heard her challenge him, for however late she returned from her outings, the light was on in his room.

She was standing looking into his room where he sat cross-legged on his bed, writing in a notebook. She had let her hair fall loose – this too was in the novel – and, winding a strand around her finger: 'Are you writing a novel? Am I in it?' It didn't bother her that he ignored her. 'What are you writing about me? ... Let me see – or is it too horrible and mean?'

Then he did look up – only to drop his eyes again immediately, for she hadn't noticed, or just didn't care, that the upper part of her sari had dropped down, revealing her breasts in their inadequate little blouse. He said, 'Kindly shut the door and don't ever open it again.'

'Listen to Mr Grumpy ... What's wrong with you? Did a monkey bite you?'

That night D wrote in his notebook: 'If she weren't stupid and a fool, she'd be a whore.' But elsewhere in the novel it was himself he called stupid and a fool.

It was not long before she left us. This happened the day after her father, the Brigadier, had come to visit us – or rather, to look us over. His army jeep, standing outside, seemed as large as the house; and he himself overflowed the chair he occupied, with one stout leg laid across the thigh of the other. Sahib could not stop making conversation. He spoke of golf, the latest cricket test matches, other topics that should have been of interest to his visitor. But the Brigadier kept studying the watch on his hairy wrist, while asking when Kay was expected back. No one liked to tell him that her hours were as unpredictable as she was.

He had plenty of time to sum us up and evidently we did not pass his scrutiny. I was the sort of foreigner he had no respect for (a 'hippie type'); and the way he looked at Dinesh, in his much-laundered shirt and his glasses mended with tape, made Sahib quickly explain, 'Mr Dinesh is a writer.' When the Brigadier just went on grimly tapping his boot with his army baton, Bibiji added, 'He is writing a novel.'

'Where is she?' was the Brigadier's only reaction; and when we told him that she was out with friends: 'What friends? Who are they?'

But actually he knew very well where a girl like his daughter on the sort of allowance he sent her (out of his love for her) could be found amusing herself with friends. He had no objection to these friends – the children of other army officers, or of high-ranking bureaucrats. What he did object to was her living in the house with us.

When he returned next day, he stayed outside in the jeep with his batman driver while Kay was packing up her belongings. Silent in shock, we stood and watched her. She was in tears but not disconsolate. It seemed her father had wasted no time finding a more suitable place for her: a room in the house of a colonel's widow. 'Those are the only sort of people Daddy knows. Dodos like himself and boring bourgeois.' But it was close to where some of her other friends lived and gave parties. 'I'll come to see you,' she consoled us. 'We had so much fun.' But she said it a bit absently, while shutting her suitcase and biting her lip the way people do when they are just leaving and hoping they haven't forgotten anything.

The days after Kay left were intensely hot – it was the middle of June – and as always at such times the atmosphere in the city was exceptionally charged. That was also the atmosphere in the Malhotra house. There seemed to be a change in the relationship between husband and wife – or perhaps this was the way they always were once their bedroom door was shut and they were alone. Now they didn't wait to be alone, they were bitter and angry with each other and didn't care who heard them. They fought about Kay's departure, for which they did not blame her father but themselves, for letting him receive a wrong impression.

Bibiji said, 'You should have told him you're a lawyer who has studied abroad instead of all that nonsense about golf. And I didn't like the way he was looking at Dineshji.'

Sahib explained, 'You can be a famous writer, an MA from Oxford University, but if you can't talk about whisky and golf, then you're not fit to lick their boots. But with me, he knew he was dealing with a person like himself. A gentleman.'

'Yes and what else do you think he knew?'

'Nothing! He knew nothing!'

'And when you walk in the street, no one knows anything?' She lowered her voice to the whisper she used behind the bedroom door: 'No one says, "He's been inside."'

He came up closer, in threat: 'You put me there.'

She didn't retreat one inch. 'It's my fault. Everything is my fault. This is my fault –' and here she shook her arms with the thin glass bangles on them – 'like a sweeper woman. That's what he thought: "My poor daughter, to live in the house of a sweeper woman."'

He stepped back, lowered his voice: 'No one thinks that. They wouldn't dare.'

'When you're poor, they all dare. They push you in the street.' She had begun to shed little tears. 'The milkman who hasn't been paid calls you bad names.'

He whispered: 'I'll pay him tomorrow. They'll all be paid. Don't. You're still my princess.'

I was not there to witness the beginning of their next fight, and neither was Dinesh. This fight was actually about him, and he reconstructed it in his novel. The scene, in my translation, goes like this:

'What he didn't like was D living in the same house with his daughter. *Looking* at her.'

'He never looks at her,' Bibiji said.

'Is it my fault you have no eyes to see?'

'He has never in his life looked at her!'

'Not even when she is combing her hair?' Smiling, he made the slow sensual gesture of a woman drawing a comb through her hair, each strand alive, tumbling over her shoulders, down her back. 'I wouldn't like you to know what happens to him then.' He came closer to whisper in her ear: 'Like a dog. You've seen a dog?'

It was at this moment that D in the novel – and perhaps also Dinesh in real life – came home. Full of fun, Sahib turned to him: 'Don't you miss her?' repeating the motion of the comb through waves of hair. D couldn't even pretend not to understand, and without looking at him, Bibiji fled into the kitchen. Her hands trembling, she began to peel potatoes.

Sahib was glad to be alone with D. He chuckled, man-to-man: 'These girls, they're sent by the devil to drive us poor devils mad. But isn't it a nice way to become a raving lunatic?'

'She's gone now,' D said, 'so you can relax.'

'Who wants to relax? That's for dead men. Who do you think she liked – you or me?'

D went to his room. His landlord eagerly followed him. He sat on D's bed and watched him change the shirt he wore at work for the one that was too frayed for outside. D's shoulders, now revealed by his undershirt, were not broad or manly, but Sahib said, 'At least you're young, you have a chance. Perhaps she liked you. Perhaps she is saying to her daddy at this moment, "Take me back to him!" ... Don't you think I have a good imagination? I should be writing the books, not you.' He laughed loud enough for Bibiji to hear so that she came out of the kitchen with the potato she was peeling. 'Did you hear that?' Sahib asked her. 'He thinks I should write books and become a famous author.'

'Why are you sitting on his bed? Get up.'

'And when I'm a famous author all the girls will run after me, and it is for me she will say, "Daddy, why did you take me away from him?"'

'Oh my friend,' D said, 'you're talking such nonsense.'

Sahib winked at his wife. 'Did you hear that? What sort of books can a person write who thinks love and romance are nonsense?'

D was struggling into his shirt, for he was both shy and ashamed of his undervest, which was torn. 'Yes, put on your clothes, man,' Sahib urged him. 'Don't show yourself before my wife. She imagines things.'

'It's he,' she desperately told D. 'He's been imagining things – about you and her. All lies. You're a liar –' she turned on Sahib – 'and come out of his room. You shouldn't be here with your *thoughts*.'

'And what about *your* thoughts?' Sahib said, enjoying the mischief rising in him. 'Don't I know you have them? Haven't I been married to you for twenty years, lying next to you in bed while you had your thoughts? . . . Oh, not about me, what am I, a ruined wreck, but others – like your guest, your paying guest, a guest who pays you, what luck . . .'

Was there, as described in the novel, a dust storm blowing that day? It was the season of such storms – day after day of furnace heat, and then, suddenly, wildly, winds laden with the dust of the desert whirling through the city. I seem to remember returning from my teacher's house in such a storm, but it may have been that Dinesh's novel suggested it to me, and he in turn may have invented it as a pathetic fallacy (for he was getting skilled at such effects). Wherever it came from, my memory of that scene in the Malhotra house is set within swirling columns of dust that lashed the tree outside, bending its sickly trunk and stripping it down to the last of its dying leaves. Dust thick in my mouth, dust stinging my eyes, I groped my way inside. The first thing I noticed was that the windows had not been shut, so that the storm whistled and shrieked around the room as freely as it did outside. It was only when I had managed to shut each window in the house that I became aware of the people in it.

They were a group in the living room: Bibiji on the floor, on her carpet, not as she usually sat there, singing to her harmonium, but with her knees drawn up and her face hidden in her hands. Dinesh was bending over the sofa, and he turned to me and said, 'Get a doctor.' I heard Sahib groan, 'Let me die,' before I actually saw him laid out on the sofa.

Dinesh asked Bibiji, 'Where is there a doctor nearby?' Sahib's groans of pain instantly changed into a moan of panic: 'No doctor.'

'Should we let you bleed to death?' Dinesh said. Blood was seeping through Sahib's shirt and slowly spreading over his chest. His eyes were shut, his face had the pallor of a dead man; but he was energetic enough to insist again, 'No doctor.'

I went to find a sheet to tear up for a bandage. Crossing the courtyard, I saw a half-peeled potato lying there and, a little way apart, as though it had been flung there, the knife with which it had been peeled. I picked it up and found that, besides potato peel, it also had blood on it. Dinesh was calling 'Hurry!' so instead of a sheet, I quickly tore the top part of my sari. I helped Dinesh raise our landlord to a sitting position to bandage him. Sahib groaned and cried between us, but when we asked if we were hurting him too much, he denied it and said for the third time, 'No doctor,' and now Bibiji echoed him.

Her voice roused him, he became animated: 'She wants me to die ... Why else did she murder me?'

Dinesh said to me, 'What's that knife?' I had completely forgotten about it. I picked it up from where I had dropped it. Sahib, now bandaged and prone on the sofa, said, 'Get rid of the murder weapon.'

Bibiji got up and took it from me. She regarded it front and back; she told Sahib, 'You can say you did it yourself.' She demonstrated, raising the knife towards her heart.

'Why should I wish to kill myself and not you?'

'People often kill themselves. You yourself, at that time, and if I hadn't found it—'

'I bought it for the rats!'

'You wrote a note.' She whispered, 'A suicide note. The police took it. It is in their hands.'

He too was whispering now – out of weakness and pain, but also that was the way they spoke to each other when they had bad things to say. 'I wanted to die. This is the second time you've killed me.' To Dinesh and me he said, 'Yes, call the doctor. Let him get the police. Let them take *her* away this time.'

'So, all right – I'll go,' she said indifferently.

'You! As if you could stand it there ... Wipe the handle.' She did so on a cushion but not thoroughly, so that he said, 'More, more ... Now give it to me – don't touch it! What a fool. Hold it with your sari.'

That was the way she handed it to him. He pressed his fingers around it but was too weak to hold on, and it fell to the floor. We all looked at it; the blade still had potato peel and blood on it. No one wanted to pick it up.

At last Dinesh said, 'Suicide is also considered a criminal offence.'

Bibiji cried, 'He didn't do anything!'

He opened his eyes; he murmured, 'I tried to kill myself. I stabbed myself with a knife.'

'It was I!' She turned to Dinesh. 'You saw me. And you heard what he said. The lies he told about you. That's why I did it. I couldn't stand his lies.' She sank to the floor. Her shoulders shook with sobs – completely silent ones, but they were more than her husband could bear.

He told her, 'It was a joke. You know how I love to make jokes.' To Dinesh he said, 'Tell her the girl was nothing to you. Tell her.'

Dinesh had lowered his eyes. When he spoke, he did so in the strangled voice of a very truthful person making up a lie.

But Sahib appeared satisfied. He said, 'My poor wife. She doesn't understand that when there is a girl, it's human nature to make jokes. Everyone does it. But really there's only one person, and when she sings and plays her harmonium – oh! oh!'

'I think he's fainted,' I said, for his face was drained and he had shut his eyes again.

'No.' With an effort he motioned for Dinesh to come closer. 'Tell her it's true about her singing: how you love it – because it is very good and because it is she who sings.' When Dinesh confirmed this in the same strangled voice as before, the husband appeared satisfied and said nothing more.

In the novel, the husband dies in the night and the wife goes mad with grief and remorse. But Sahib didn't die and Bibiji didn't go mad. Instead she showed herself very practical, and it was she who nursed him and dressed his wound every day. I tore up the rest of my saris and Dinesh and I rolled them into bandages. We never needed to call a doctor. The only person to help us was Gochi, the old sweeper, who brought a herbal ointment that helped to heal the wound. She asked no questions at all; she was probably familiar with difficult, even violent family situations and was more knowing than the rest of us.

But we too had learned to be less innocent. Since it was necessary to find a new tenant for Kay's room, we took care that it should be not a young but a middle-aged lady who moved in with us. Shortly afterwards, Dinesh asked for a transfer to his home town (he said his family needed him); and to replace him, I found another, and even older lady, whom I had met in my teacher's house. Bibiji began to cook for her paying guests, which increased her income; now Gochi could be employed on a daily basis. The Malhotras no longer ate alone behind the closed door but sat together with their boarders on the living-room carpet to eat in the traditional way with their fingers from little bowls. Sometimes Bibiji took out her harmonium, though more rarely now, and her songs were no longer ambiguous but definitely spiritual.

The visits to my teacher's house became less satisfying to me. Also, I missed Dinesh – anyway, soon after he left for Kanpur, I too decided to go home. Here is my farewell letter to him, describing the new set-up in our household:

'. . . Sometimes the three ladies are all sad together, so I guess they are telling one another their troubles. Gochi squats nearby, drinking tea and contributing her own comments on life's vicissitudes. I can't always understand what they are saying, and I'm beginning to think you're right and that instead of struggling with the Upanishads etc, I'd have done better to learn more Hindi. I can just see your face, you're thinking, ah-ha, she's had enough at last of our ancient wisdom. But it's only that it's difficult for me to think of everything in the world, including ourselves, as nothing but illusion. I don't think human misery is an illusion, and rather than go into total denial about it, I'd like to learn of some ways to overcome it. I'd planned to go to Thailand for a while, but now I've found out that there's a Buddhist teaching centre in Connecticut, not far from my parents' house. So now, if you like, you can think of me with my head shaved and wearing a Buddhist robe instead of my saris. Anyway, as you know, I don't have any left, they've all been rolled into bandages. But I'm definitely going to learn Hindi, so that I can translate your novel. As Kay would say, "Am I in it?" And the Malhotras? And Kay herself, so fatefully combing her hair?'

A Lovesong for India

Although his family had been Westernised for two generations, Trilok Chand – always known as TC – was the first to bring home an English wife. She had been his fellow student at Oxford, the university both his father and hers had attended before them. Altogether there were similarities in their background. Like so many British families in the years before Independence, hers had served in India as judges, district commissioners, medical officers; and as soon as these posts were opened to Indians, members of TC's family, including his father, had been appointed to fill them. Shortly after his marriage, TC himself had joined the civil service and had begun the ascent from rank to rank that their fathers had taken before him.

In his first years, he was posted in the districts, far from New Delhi and from what he considered civilisation. At this time his wife – her name was Diana – was especially dear to him. She was as mild and pastel as the English landscape he had learned to love. She was also fair-minded in the English way, careful to make no judgements and entertain no prejudices. When he returned home to her, often angry and defeated from his day's work, she tried to speak up for the corrupt police chief or the moneylender who so disgusted him. She told him he was applying foreign values to a society that had worked out its own arrangements, with which no one had the right to interfere. When he answered that it was his job to interfere, she had her arguments ready – after all, she had from her schooldays been taught to evaluate and debate all sides of a question. He didn't want to debate anything; he only wanted to be with her and kiss her rosy lips and run his fingers through her silky light brown hair.

The advantage of being posted to an outlying district was the allotment of spacious living quarters. Their house dated from the 1920s, when it had been occupied by the British holder of TC's present position. Although it was called a bungalow, it was very large with many rooms, each with a bathroom that had its own back door for the use of the sweeper. The kitchen was at a distance from the main house but that didn't matter since Diana rarely had to enter it. The cook came to her sitting room for orders; and the bearer who served their meals knew how to keep the dishes hot while transporting them across the passage to the dining room. In winter they had a fire lit by which they sat with their books – he read mostly history, she poetry and novels; in the hot weather they enjoyed evenings on the verandah, though when storms blew in from the desert, they retreated inside with all the doors and windows shut against the dust. This nevertheless entered through every crevice and seeped deep into their books and their carpets and their curtains, insinuating itself forever into the texture of their lives.

For the rest of her days, Diana yearned for the districts of their early years. To her, it had been a recognisable India. The

English bungalow was like those her ancestors had occupied as members of the Indian civil service; it was they who had planted the grounds with seeds brought from Kent and Surrey, and they who lay in the neglected cemeteries of the small Christian churches surviving among temples, mosques and brand-new shrines. Diana never felt foreign here: although she lived in the bungalow with the English garden as in an oasis, the surrounding fields of sugar cane or yellow mustard were known and familiar to her, as were the women with loads on their heads and silver jewellery round their ankles, the wells and the bullocks circling them, and the holy man under a tree with offerings of sweets and marigolds at his feet.

TC had joined the service a few years after Independence, when all the higher ranks had been vacated by the British. Consequently, he and his colleagues were promoted much faster than earlier or later generations, and it was not too many years before he reached the higher ranks of the bureaucracy. TC was by no means a typical bureaucrat. He was ready to bend rules when necessary; he was also decisive and quick to act in accordance with his own independent thinking. There was nothing ponderous about him – even physically he remained flexible, supple, and always looked younger than his age. This was in part due to his heritage: before serving the British, his ancestors had served the Moghul court. There may have been some admixture of blood for they mostly had the fine limbs and features of Muslim aristocrats instead of the heavy build of their own Hindu caste. He and Diana made a not dissimilar impression, both of them slender and fair, she like an Anglo-Saxon and he with what was known as the wheat complexion of an upper-class North Indian.

Their son Romesh was born in 1959, ten years into their marriage. He was completely different from either of them. Much darker and heavier than his father, he appeared to be a throwback to the original strains of Hindu ancestry. He was their only child, but he grew away from them very quickly. He was uncontrollable as a schoolboy, and for a while showed some criminal tendencies – he stole cars and freely took money from his mother's purse when he needed it. But this turned out to be only an assertion of his independence, which later showed itself in other ways. He refused to go to England to study but enrolled in business school in the US. He stayed abroad for several years, and when he returned, he had already established himself as a businessman operating on an international scale, travelling widely in the Middle East as well as in Thailand and Singapore. When he was at home in New Delhi, he fitted in completely, an integral member of young society, enjoying the clubs, the parties and the girls.

At the peak of his career, TC became the Principal Secretary of his ministry and was transferred to the central government in New Delhi. Diana never felt comfortable in New Delhi. They had been allotted a large official Lutyens residence from the 1930s, but they didn't do much entertaining in it. There was something puritanical in Diana, which made her uncomfortable at the lavish dinner parties given with such relish by the other wives of their circle. All of these were Indian and had kept their looks, and from beautiful girls had flourished into magnificent women. Their skin glowed, their eyes shone, their hair had become an even deeper black than in their youth. They loved shawls and jewellery and complimented one another on each new acquisition. But when they said something nice about whatever Diana was wearing, it was in the sweet voice in which people tell polite lies. Diana never wore saris, she didn't have the hips or bosom to carry them. Her frocks were very simple, sewn by a tailor in the bazaar; she avoided bright colours, knowing they didn't suit her complexion, which by now had the sallow tint of someone who for many years had had to shield herself from the Indian sun.

She also felt uncomfortable with her New Delhi servants. These were very different from the cooks and bearers and ayahs with whom she had had such friendly relations in the districts. Her new staff were far more sophisticated and she was rather afraid of them. Although they called her Memsahib, she felt that they didn't regard her as a real memsahib, not like the other wives who knew how to give orders with authority. Reluctant to give any trouble, Diana sometimes surreptitiously dusted a sideboard or polished a piece of silver herself. If they caught her at it, her servants would take it away from her – 'No, Memsahib, this is our work.' She suspected that they commiserated with one another for being employed by such an inadequate person.

For TC, New Delhi came up entirely to his expectations. He loved being near the seat of power, to influence and even to formulate the decisions of his Minister. In the course of his tenure, the government changed several times, and while the Minister lost his position, TC kept his and was able to put his experience at the disposal of his new chief. Of course there were difficulties – the intrigues and manoeuvres he had already encountered in the districts, now on a magnified scale – but these were compensated for by the satisfaction he derived from his New Delhi social life. He had known many of his colleagues from their earliest days in the service, and now at the height of their careers, they had remained in a bond of friendship which included their wives and families.

One of the most energetic hostesses in their set was Pushpa, whom TC had known from their college days. He had even dated her for a while, and it amused her to refer to that early aborted romance. By now she was married to Bobby, who was TC's colleague and the Principal Secretary in another ministry;

33

husband and wife were both fat and jolly and could always be relied on to give what they called a rousing good party. Pushpa's buffet table was loaded with succulent dishes, which were mostly too spicy for Diana. Pushpa scolded her for being so thin – Diana was almost gaunt now – and Pushpa accused TC, 'You're starving the poor girl.' Then she added, 'I know what it is – you don't want her to become fat like me.' She loved to call herself the girl he dumped: 'You think I'm only good enough for someone like Bobby who is as fat and ugly as I am!' Everyone, including Bobby, laughed heartily.

But there was also serious talk – relations with Pakistan, proposals for a new dam – and here too the wives joined in. Diana mostly remained silent. She didn't feel she had the right to enter into their discussions, and especially not into their perennial jokes about politics and corruption. Whereas they could say anything they wanted, she as a foreigner would have caused offence.

The one person Diana liked to visit in New Delhi was her friend Margaret, an Englishwoman in charge of a lay mission devoted to charitable work in India. It was far away from their official residence, and Diana drove herself there in TC's car (neither of them would ever have taken his official driver or any other member of their staff for their personal use). When he was small, Diana would take Romesh with her on these visits, but he soon revolted. He disliked the sombre old mission house with its high ceilings and stone floors impregnated by the smell of disinfectant and stale curries. It was made worse for him by Margaret herself, a large-boned woman with a loud voice who ruled over a bevy of silent humble helpers, most of them girls whom she had rescued from orphanages or bad homes. When he grew up, his antipathy became even stronger. It puzzled Diana; she asked him, 'But why, darling? Give me one reason.' He was never good at explaining his feelings, but at last

34

he came up with, 'If you must know, I can't stand all that holiness and prayer, it gives me the creeps. Thank God you don't go in for all that stuff.' It was true, Diana had laid aside her Christian prayers, as well as the gold cross inset with rubies, a gift from her godmother on her twelfth birthday.

Margaret never spoke to Diana about religion. Instead they liked to remind each other of favourite poems or long-ago Latin lessons, gaily correcting each other's syntax. Although both of them had spent most of their adult lives in India, their original accents had not only remained but had become even more precise and English. Margaret always wore Punjabi dress, including the modesty veil, though she only used it to wipe away the perspiration caused by her long hours of trudging the streets and slums of the inner city. She was mostly cheerful and undaunted, whether it was a day of triumph when she had procured an artificial leg for a client, or a setback with a convert relapsing into alcoholism and wife-beating. Diana never could understand why Romesh said, 'Let her go and do good somewhere else.' But quite often he wrote a cheque for her, always for a substantial amount, which Margaret received with the measured gratitude of one used to accepting whatever was given, fully aware that it would never be enough.

Neither of his parents understood much about Romesh's business activities. 'Something to do with export,' Diana explained to herself and anyone who asked. 'Import-export.' She couldn't really appreciate her son's lavish lifestyle – the big car he drove around in, his constant trips abroad – but she felt proud of his enterprise. He had never for a moment considered following his father into the civil service. 'Thanks but no thanks,' he said. 'You don't catch me spending my life trapped in a job with a measly salary and ending up with a piddly provident fund.'

Although TC's only answer was a wry 'Good luck to you', Diana knew he was hurt. 'It's just that he's a different personality,' she assured him about their son. 'He really respects you enormously.' She knew this to be true for she had heard Romesh boast on the telephone: 'Do you have any idea who my dad is?'

TC had a new Minister – his name was RK Googal, known to everyone as Googa. They had met before, many years earlier, when TC was a district commissioner and Googa sold eggs and butter in the bazaar while making a more serious living as a local politician with power to dispense municipal contracts. At that time TC had thwarted one of Googa's business operations, and in revenge Googa had tried to get him transferred. He failed, but he never forgot this transaction between them. In the meantime TC had had dealings with many more men like Googa and had learned to steer his way around them. But Googa had the character of a potentate and, unable to get rid of his Principal Secretary, he did everything he could to obstruct him, so that TC felt more frustrated than in the many crises he had suffered in the course of his career.

Romesh admired his father's new boss. He said he was a firecracker: 'Googa they call him – or Gunda.' He laughed. 'I guess he is a gunda – a rascal – but he sure gets things done. The country needs chaps like that,' he informed his father.

TC never brought his office worries home, and the only person with whom he shared them was his friend Bobby. Bobby was well aware of the troubles a Principal Secretary could have with his Minister. His wife Pushpa also knew about such situations and listened with sympathy while her husband gave his friend the only advice he could – which was to be patient and subtle in his dealings with such dangerous animals. TC felt soothed in their company and by the domestic ambience of Pushpa's household – the glasses of home-made sherbet that appeared on a silver tray, the smell of spices being fried in onions. After a while they passed from the unfortunate office affairs to more personal matters – gossip about their colleagues, plans for summer travel in the hills.

Once Pushpa said, 'What about your Romesh-Baba?' and to TC's inquiring look: 'Isn't it about time he settled down? These young people have no sense. They think they can run around any way they please for the rest of their lives.'

Bobby humorously shut one eye. 'And hasn't your Romesh been running around with our Sheila-Baby?'

'Why shouldn't they!' Pushpa cried. 'We're not that ante-diluvian. Even in our day – if you remember,' she told TC in a favourite allusion to their past college romance. 'But all the same, someone has to give them a bit of a push now and again.'

'We leave all that to you girls,' Bobby said.

TC was used to discussing everything except office affairs with Diana, and when he mentioned Pushpa's proposal to her, her blue eyes stretched wide and she said, 'That's entirely between the boy and the girl. We have no right to interfere.'

TC was amused by her reaction, which he had expected – Diana questioned everything she considered a denial of the individual's right to free choice. He teased her: 'Sheila's a very pretty girl.'

'That has nothing to do with it. Nothing at all. We shouldn't even be talking about it.' She looked righteous and pale, the way she always did in defence of her principles.

But the next time she was alone with Romesh, she asked him, trying to sound casual, 'Do you meet Sheila quite often?'

He looked up at her from his breakfast. It was usually the only meal he ate at home, and she herself cooked the bacon for him since their Muslim cook wouldn't touch it. 'Has Pushpa auntie been gabbing to you?' Romesh asked. She blushed, but he went on to assure her: 'Don't worry, I'm not there yet.'

37

'No no, I'm not worrying, of course not. I'm not suggesting anything at all, darling, it's entirely up to you.' She watched him eat for a while, which he did as he did everything, with enormous appetite and appreciation. At last she shyly asked, 'Do you like her a lot?'

He had to suppress his laughter at this innocent question. What could his mother know about someone like Sheila – a wild, wild girl, far surpassing any he had been with in America. And not only she but other Indian girls he knew; it was as though in throwing off all restraints, they were compensating for those suffered by past generations of their mothers and grandmothers.

It was Bobby who first alerted TC to the probe that was being initiated against certain government departments, including their own. So far it was being kept secret, but TC soon found that files began to go missing. His visits to Bobby became more frequent; they exchanged news and views about the situation and kept each other informed about its development. As usual, Pushpa passed in and out, though now only to bring them refreshments.

At the end of one meeting, she told TC: 'I hear your Romesh-Baba is going off again on some of his murky business.'

'Who tells you it's murky?' TC answered her in the light tone they had established between them.

'All business is murky,' she said in the same tone. Then she said, 'I wish he and Sheila-Baby would make up their minds. It'd be a big load off *my* mind, I tell you. I'm sure they like each other; whenever I ask her where she's been, she says with Romesh of course, as if that makes it all right. And it would be all right, if they'd only ... ' She appealed to TC, her plump face full of a mother's anxiety.

When Romesh came home that night, TC was as usual

awake and working. He looked at his son: the thin muslin kurta Romesh wore for his social evenings was crumpled and somewhat soiled. His eyes were reddened, maybe from fatigue and certainly from an excess of alcohol. Pretending to notice none of this, TC said, 'I hear you're pushing off again.'

Romesh swiftly glanced at him. Next moment he relaxed. 'I guess I have to. To fill this,' and he patted his stomach, which looked very full already. 'This sinful belly.'

'We'll miss you,' his father said. 'Will you be gone long? ... Sorry to pry into what doesn't concern me, but there's something – well, I might as well mention it,' TC decided, remembering Pushpa's anxious face.

And again Romesh looked at him suspiciously, while he answered with caution: 'I don't know yet how long I'll be gone. It depends. These things always take time. It's something to do with shares, stocks and shares – I won't bother you with details.'

'No, don't. There's no chance I'd understand them. This is about Sheila.'

'Yes. Sheila. A grand girl.'

'Her mother is hoping that perhaps, before you go? But it's entirely up to you; and to her of course. We'd all like it.'

'I'd like it too, but it's not the right time. I'm not ready to get married. Not with all this on my head.' And then he got angry: 'What do they all think! Everything is left to me, I have to run from here to Timbuktu – I told you there's no point in going into detail!' he shouted, though TC hadn't asked anything.

His raised voice brought Diana into the room. She had been awake, as she was every night, waiting for her two men to be home and in bed. Now she stood there in her white floor-length nightgown, looking from one to the other.

'Romesh is tired from his night's activities,' TC explained drily.

Romesh tried to speak more quietly: 'No, I'm not tired

from a little partying but from –' he paused, then rushed on – 'the harassment. The harassment from every side – everyone is sick of it, I tell you that! Foreign investors take one look at your famous rules and regulations and run for their lives. Can you blame them? No one wants to be treated like a thief and a criminal for trying to get a decent business going.' He swallowed, maybe to stop himself from saying anything imprudent. 'Now do you mind if I go to bed? I'm just about done for.'

Diana watched him go to his room. He was shuffling a bit, and she appealed to TC: 'Do you think he's working too hard?' But later, alone with TC in their bedroom, she said, 'I believe people tend to drink more when they're under strain.' And when TC was silent: 'Do you think he is? Upset about anything?'

TC tried to laugh. 'When you're young, every little thing is enough to set you off. You remember how it was.'

'Yes, I remember – but that's not how it was.'

This time he laughed genuinely, with pleasure at the memories they shared of a youth that, whatever their present age and appearance, was not lost for them at all.

It was only a day or two later that Bobby called TC to come to his house in the evening. They sat as usual in Bobby's study, but this time Pushpa did not walk in and out. To explain her absence, Bobby said, 'Gone shopping somewhere, spending all my money.' But soon he was more grave.

He told TC that the inquiry had now reached further into TC's department, and higher – as high as the Minister himself. 'Of course he's taking steps to make sure he's home and dry.'

'We'll see about that,' TC promised his friend, and himself too.

In the following pause Bobby looked like someone who had

something difficult to say. TC waited. 'But there are others,' Bobby said at last. 'He wouldn't be so eager to protect those others.'

'You mean those who've been taking bribes with him?'

'Not only those who have taken. Also those who have given.'

'I see.' TC did his best to speak even more calmly than usual. 'Are there names?'

'There are two very big names – big Bombay tycoons – and there are smaller names. The size of the – of the "contribution" doesn't signify. All will be considered equally guilty.'

'Of course.' TC made his long thin fingers into a steeple; this was his habit when considering official matters. But now he had to clear his throat twice before speaking: 'I believe the boy's name appears only in connection with one of the issues?'

A fat and excitable man, Bobby waved his hands in the air. 'One issue, two issues, or a hundred – this time no one's going to get away. We're not letting one scrap of proof out of our hands. No file is going to disappear, I promise you.' He looked at TC across from him. Their two pairs of glasses gleamed so that it wasn't possible to see each other's eyes behind them. But Bobby could say with confidence, 'I know you want it as much as I do, whatever the consequences.'

And TC answered with the same confidence, 'Yes. Yes, of course.' And after a pause, 'Absolutely.'

That evening Diana told him, 'Pushpa was here today. Imagine! They're sending Sheila-Baby to Australia to study political science – Sheila's a wonderful girl but I never thought of her as being very academic, did you? ... And why Australia?' Into her husband's silence, she said, 'Do you think Pushpa came to tell me something else?'

TC said, 'I think she was trying to tell you that the marriage is off.'

'You mean that's why they're sending her away? But Romesh would have said something. He'd have told us.'

'Does he ever tell us anything?' This required no answer, so TC went on to ask: 'When is he leaving?'

'I think soon. He's already packed – or what he calls packed. But of course, as usual, I'll have to pull it all out and start again.' She smiled, and TC tried to smile too.

Next morning, while serving his breakfast, she asked Romesh about his plans for departure. He was vague in his answer – something about waiting for some papers to be cleared, which she didn't understand. She changed the subject: 'And now Sheila's going to Australia.' He said nothing, so she continued, 'Pushpa seemed pleased, though I thought she had other plans for Sheila ... And for you,' she added with a shy smile.

He shrugged. 'Sheila's a lot of fun, but marriage is not on the cards – not to me anyway. Wait,' he said. The phone in his bedroom was ringing, and he got up to answer it. Through the closed door, she heard his voice raised in excitement; he had only half finished his breakfast, but when he returned, he was in no mood to eat. He asked, 'Where's Dad now?'

'He's in his office, probably in a meeting ... Is there anything I can do?' she pleaded. But he said no, it was just something he had to ask TC. Like his father, Romesh avoided letting her into his difficulties, though with him it was not so much to shield her as himself, against her intrusion.

A message reached TC from his minister, which he had been half expecting. It came in a roundabout way – this too was expected – from a clerk who said he happened to be Googa's nephew by marriage and that he had a message for TC from his uncle. Although the message was clouded, it was clear enough to TC: that there were certain papers in which Googa's name figured along with some other persons; and that it would be convenient if these papers were to be privately dealt with. Fortunately it would not be difficult to obtain them since the relevant file was located in the ministry where the Principal Secretary was not only TC's opposite number but his friend. TC received this message and thanked the messenger in a calm, non-committal manner, which gave no indication of the shame that filled him like a rush of blood to the heart.

A few days later, Googa sent festive boxes of sweetmeats to all his staff. TC's was the biggest, and it was again delivered personally by a relative of Googa's, this time a brother-in-law who explained that these sweets were to celebrate the shaving of the first hair to grow on a grandson's head. 'His *grand*son! Googaji said to remind you that it is now twenty-five years since he sent you sweets for his *son's* first hair-shaving. So many years you have been his father and his mother.'

'Yes,' TC agreed drily. 'We've known each other many years – certainly long enough for him to know that I don't eat sweets.' And he pushed the box aside.

The brother-in-law pushed it back again. He joined his hands in supplication. 'If not you, then for your children who are also our children. Googaji says you have a son who likes sweets very much. Let him eat and enjoy.'

That evening there was a banquet in honour of a visiting foreign dignitary, attended by cabinet ministers, ambassadors and top bureaucrats. It was held in the formal hall of a royal palace taken over by the government; under the chandeliers, the long table was laid as it had been in the Maharaja's time and barefoot bearers in turbans and cummerbunds moved silently around it to serve the guests. Googa, his enormous bulk swathed in yards of white muslin, sat in his rightful place near the head of the table. He was in a fine mood and joshed the other Ministers with bad puns in Hindi – he looked only up the table to where the important guests sat. There was no need for him to look down towards TC at the lower end, or to give any sign of being aware of his existence, let alone of any business between them.

Bobby sat as always near TC at the end of the table. To relieve their boredom, they were in the habit of exchanging cryptic remarks or glances to express their feelings about the guests at the superior end. But today Bobby did not notice TC any more than Googa did, engaging himself in conversation with his neighbours at the table. Once TC called across to him with their own kind of banter and, while not completely ignoring him, Bobby gave the puzzled half-smile of one who failed to understand the reference. Then TC looked down at his golden plate and again a wave of shame welled up in him.

One evening Diana surprised her husband and her son in the middle of a talk that appeared to be difficult for both of them. But they were united in their determination that she should know nothing, and it was not until she was alone with TC in their bedroom that she could ask anything. Brushing her hair, she could see him in the mirror, and the expression on his face made her turn around quickly before he could change it. Then she did challenge him, though only with: 'Romesh still hasn't packed properly – I think he's just waiting for me to do it for him.'

A flippant white lie on his lips, TC looked into her eyes. It made him say quietly, 'He's not leaving.'

They sat side by side on the edge of their bed. Even when she put her arms around him, his back remained stiff and straight. He said, 'They've impounded his passport. He can't leave because he's wanted here for questioning.'

She tried to speak lightly: 'What's he supposed to have done? They can't just hold him for nothing. If he's done nothing.'

'He says he hasn't. Or only what everyone else does.' He

almost lost his patience. 'That's what they all say: "Everyone does it – what's wrong with it when everyone does it?" That's supposed to be the excuse; not the shameful admission but the excuse.'

She had never seen him like this, so bitter and hurt. 'Let's lie down,' she whispered. It did seem a relief to him to lie with her in their bed, the same they had had in all the years of their marriage. The way they lay entwined was the same too, so that for a few hours they could sleep as if there were only the two of them – two lovers alone with each other and safe from all the world.

Next morning, when she went into Romesh's room, she found him asleep with his face pressed deep in the pillow, not wanting to see or hear. His suitcases stood open, the clothes tumbling out of them. She unpacked and put everything back in the closet. When he opened his eyes, there was the momentary look of relief of one waking from a nightmare and realising it was not real. Then he realised it *was* real; also, from the way his mother was looking at him, that she knew what it was.

At once he rushed to his own defence. 'Dad doesn't understand that it's the way business is done. If you want your motor to run, you have to oil it. Grease it. Grease their goddamn palms. Dad has his job, his little salary, no hassle – you two have no idea what's going on, what I have to do. My God, if only you knew!'

'I don't know anything because you never tell me anything. If you did, I'd try and understand.'

'I wouldn't even want you to. You're so English, you've stayed English though you've been here donkey's years. You even think that the English don't do it – that they're all like you and Dad. That's just baloney! They do exactly what we do. Exactly . . . Let me get up now. I can't stay in bed all day.' But

45

she kept on sitting there, waiting for him to say more, take advantage of her presence.

He said, 'I guess that's why they've sent Sheila away. Isn't it? . . . So she wouldn't be in a dirty country like this with a dirty person like me. God, they're all so innocent, such babies. Bobby – what a dumb name, but it suits him. Sheila-Baby. Pushpa-Baby. Baba Bobby.' Suddenly he collapsed; his face was puffed, tears ran down it. 'Dad could help me. Ask him. He's not listening to me. If you tell him, he'll listen.'

She put her arms around him; he laid his head in her lap, his face hidden against her. She stroked his hair – already it was thinning – she didn't know what she could promise though he was begging her, the same sentence several times: 'He'll listen to you.'

Whenever she couldn't talk freely to anyone, Diana felt a need to confide in Margaret; but when it came to the point, she never could. It happened again that day. At the mission, she found Margaret out on the verandah, surrounded by her usual crowd of petitioners and upbraiding a milkman for watering the milk he sold her. She overrode his protests until he had to admit his fault, while bystanders murmured approval of the scolding he received.

Margaret's anger was assumed. She told Diana that she had already dismissed this milkman once before, but what to do? He had a family to support, four children of his own and two of his dead brother's. Anyway, she still had to find a milkman who did not water his milk; when finally caught, their excuse was always the same – '"Everyone does it, so why not I?"' Her big shoulders shook with laughter. 'I've heard it a thousand times: "Everyone does it" – it's not an excuse but a perfectly valid explanation.'

Diana smiled with her. Today she refused the mug of tea she usually drank with Margaret, she said she had to drive back, that TC was waiting for the car.

Margaret dealt all day with people in need, and it was easy for her to sense anyone's trouble. Walking with Diana to her car, Margaret asked her, 'Can I do anything for you?' Diana shook her head; she thanked her friend and drove away.

The only person Diana had ever asked for help or ever would was TC, and she did so that night. She knew he was awake beside her and in distress; his back was turned to her and at last she clung to it, whispering, 'Won't you try – for him?' He turned and held her against his chest. She said it again, but when he was silent, she said nothing more, and neither did he, though he could feel her tears seeping through his nightshirt.

The arraignment for Romesh came at the same time as the one for Googa. While TC resigned his post immediately, Googa showed no inclination to relinquish his. He had many supporters who accompanied him to court, loudly shouting slogans in his favour. He made the most of the presence of journalists and TV cameras to declare his innocence, his forgiveness of his enemies and his determination to continue serving his country, to the last drop of his blood if this should be required of him. His well-wishers followed him inside, so that the small courtroom was soon overcrowded and fetid with their sweat and eructations. Romesh, accompanied only by his father and his lawyers, took care to appear in court newly shaved and in a suit and tie; he listened intently to the proceedings and passed notes of instruction to his lawyers. His fortunes appeared linked to Googa's, and both of them were usually granted bail. Once they were remanded in jail, and even there Romesh extracted special privileges from the wardens and the convicts he knew had the power to grant them. When he was released, he showed no signs of depression but was very busy consulting with his lawyers, whom he changed twice. His energy and pluck reminded Diana of the time when he was a schoolboy, always in trouble, up to all sorts of mischief and defiant when caught at it.

For the first time in their married life, TC and Diana discussed money. It had never been an important subject for either of them. They had not invested anything, nor built a house. Now, with his resignation, they had six months to give up their official residence. They assured each other that they would manage. Since TC no longer had to attend an office, they could sell their car. They had also stopped going out socially. Diana continued to visit the mission and Margaret had arranged for her to be transported by one of her protégés on his bicycle rickshaw. Diana felt ashamed to be sitting behind his emaciated back while he pushed the pedals down with all his feeble strength; but Margaret, aware of her feelings, said, 'You can hardly ask this boy to stop making a living because you feel bad about it.' She was also impatient with TC and Diana when she found that they hadn't yet tried to find another house. To discuss their problems, she often came to see them. She sat in their largest chair with her legs apart and her voice cheerfully booming; her only comment on the situation was once to TC when he saw her out. Seating herself voluminously on her protégé's frail rickshaw, 'It's a mess,' she said, 'but anyway, you did the right thing.'

Romesh did not think that his father had done the right thing. In resigning his office, TC was giving up the chance of exerting pressure on behalf of his son. It might also be taken as an admission of guilt, which Romesh himself was far from making. Instead he worked energetically to extricate himself. With the help of his lawyers, he discovered the weak links obstructing his case – a chain stretching from the lower ranks up to the occupants of some top positions. He knew whom to avoid – Bobby for instance, whom he shrugged off as useless; so were most of his father's former colleagues, though with some surprising exceptions. Romesh found himself frequently on the same track as Googa, whom he learned to respect for his ruthless energy and ability to make things work for him. 'Not a bad chap,' he said. And it was Googa who finally resolved matters for both of them. This was during a parliamentary crisis when Googa, with his command over a substantial block of votes, could make himself very helpful; and after that it was not long before it was decided that the charges against him and his co-defendants were completely baseless.

Romesh's passport was returned to him, and he was left free to continue his business. He now shifted his base of operations to Bombay, which he said was a much livelier city, geared to modern business practices, and also with even wilder girls in it. He wanted to move his parents with him, but they were now well settled in the little flat Margaret had found for them. It was far from official New Delhi, in a bazaar area that Diana soon came to know well. Over the years she witnessed many changes in their new neighbourhood. An alley that had once been occupied by vegetable stalls and cooked-meat shops was now given over to motor parts. The site of a rotted old textile mill had become a propane-gas plant; and there was a brand-new charitable eye hospital under the patronage of a cabinet minister whose face – it happened to be Googa's – loomed on a poster encircled by little coloured bulbs. Margaret's mission was nearby, and here everything remained unchanged. Her helpers were still orphan girls in cotton saris, and shoes and socks to save their feet from ringworm. Out on the verandah the petitioners still stood waiting for Margaret to help solve their problems, which never seemed to grow different or less.

Diana tremendously admired Margaret's selfless devotion to India, which she couldn't help contrasting with her own selfish devotion to only two Indians, her husband and her son. But her sense of guilt left her as soon as she got home to where TC was

49

writing his memoirs and waiting to read his day's work to her. His style had been honed for official reports: 'In November we moved to Sitapur where we encountered a variety of incidents, some of them of a humorous nature, others rather more serious.' She knew all the incidents and was able to flood his spare prose with her memories. Often, while he read, it was not the city noises outside that she heard but the jackals and peacocks surrounding the bungalow of their early districts. She didn't need to look out of the window of their cramped little flat to know that the sun setting over the city streets was the same that she had watched over the unbroken plains of their first postings. The moon too would be the same, spreading a net of silver over the people asleep outside the shuttered shops.

Romesh came to Delhi to visit his parents. Stout, middle-aged, shining in a silk jacket and some gold jewellery, he burst in on them: 'So what's new!' Of course he knew there never could be anything new for them, washed up in all their innocence, their total ignorance of life in the world. What he couldn't account for was their happiness, though he was aware that it included him, all the years of his existence as their son.

Bombay (pre-Mumbai)

If it hadn't been for her grace and beauty, Munni might have become like any other unhappy Indian woman whose arranged marriage had turned out badly. As it was, her family – from a provincial town in the Punjab, her father a small subcontractor – urged her to adjust to her circumstances and the brutal husband they had found for her. But she knew, had known since puberty, that there were many people out in the world willing to help her, and she had learned to take advantage of their good intentions without indulging their bad ones. So it was that a friend in Air India arranged for a ticket to New York, and another friend for a place to stay there, and yet another to find her a hostess job in an upscale Indian restaurant. This place was as luxuriantly oriental as she herself was. It was decorated with erotic Rajasthani miniatures and niches holding plaster-cast statues of burgeoning Hindu goddesses. Munni might herself have been one of those goddesses, stepped out of a niche to welcome the guests. She had to use all her charm and tact to put off the many men – including the proprietor and his several sons – who wanted to establish some relationship with her beyond her professional duties. Some of them persisted and kept coming again and again and followed her with their eyes as she glided in her sari and smiled and greeted everyone in the low sweet murmur of a highly cultivated courtesan.

At first Davy, who became her husband, was part of a group of loud, rich and confident Americans and Americanised Indians. She noticed him even then, if only because he was different from the others. He was neither loud nor confident and probably not as rich, for it was never he who picked up the cheque. He seemed apart from his companions – there was a sort of melancholy abstraction about him, as if he were not really present with them but elsewhere. She was soon aware that he *was* elsewhere, was in fact with her. Even when she wasn't looking in his direction, she felt his attention following her; and when she did look – which she couldn't help doing more often than she wanted – his eyes lit up and he smiled. His smile was charming but, even with her, aloof. Soon he was coming on his own; he simply showed up, knowing a place would be found for him. If he suspected that she had kept it waiting for him – perhaps that she herself was waiting for him – he took it for granted as his due.

One day he turned up at her apartment. He may have followed her – she could imagine him doing that, in his shy persistent way – or he could have simply inquired about her within their compact Indo-American Manhattan circuit. She shared a small East Side flat in a jerry-built, whitewashed block with two other Indian girls who had more or less the same stories as her own. She had never mentioned Davy to her room-mates, but the girl who let him in gasped and ran to Munni: 'It's Davy! He's asking for you!' It turned out she was the only one ignorant of his identity. 'Where have you *been*? You mean you didn't know who his father is?'

'Oh my God!' Munni said when they told her, holding her hand in front of her mouth in shock, delight, amazement. His father was Abhinav, the legendary film star, the king, the emperor of Bombay talkies, even now when he was in his sixties and hadn't made a film in years.

Davy – his real name was Dev Kumar – was made so welcome in her apartment that he soon became part of the household. He stopped going to the restaurant and instead waited for Munni to come home. When he followed her into the bedroom, she made him turn around while she changed her clothes, though after some time he was allowed to unhook her bra, and after some more time to catch hold of the two magnificent breasts that came tumbling out. But when he asked her to marry him, she laughed in his face: 'No way!' She treasured her job, her girlfriends, her wonderful freedom; and she had had enough of marriage – more, more than enough – it was the last thing, she assured him, she wanted, now and forever.

Nevertheless, she married him. It was not his proposal she accepted but his father's, who had come to New York for the purpose of making it. She learned at once that it was not possible to say no to Abhinav – how could anyone? He was a huge and hugely powerful man, physically and in his renown. When Munni got to Bombay, she found that even now, years after his retirement, a permanent cluster of spectators stood outside his mansion in the hope of catching a glimpse of him. As the tall gilt gates were thrown open, the porter – a dragoman in his scarlet and gold uniform – ordered the crowd surging forward to retreat before the advent of the automobile, a silver Mercedes of royal size. And Abhinav, royally seated behind his chauffeur, raised his hand in acknowledgement of the reverence paid to him – children were held up – and inclined his head in stately humility before the acclaim of the millions who had adored him for generations, not only in India but over vast areas of the world. He was always in Indian dress, always in white, the cloth as sparkling as the diamond buttons in his high-collared coat.

Inside the palace too he was a king – even a god, in the loose muslin robes he wore at home; these wafted around his frame and gave him the appearance of the mythological figures descending from clouds he had famously portrayed on the screen. Many people were waiting for him in a special room set aside for them: producers still begging for a comeback appearance, financiers with underworld ties in the Middle East. Then there was an inner ring of associates – ageing actors and playback singers, the new big stars eager to inherit his mantle (none ever did), even a few quite humble people who had helped him in his own humble days. Often feasts and entertainments were laid on for his guests – music, poetry and food, and always a showing of his famous old films in the soundproof screening room installed in the basement. Munni moved among his guests with the same sinuous grace as in the New York restaurant. Only now no one dared raise their eyes to her, for she was no longer an employee in a commercial establishment but the hostess in the great house of her great father-in-law.

Yet there was Shirin – his wife, his consort, who should have been the hostess. It was a role she had abdicated long ago, maybe right from the start of her marriage to Abhinav. Her part of the house was completely separate, and she did not allow her husband or any of his friends to enter it. She herself sometimes wandered into the main halls – it amused her to appear at one of his sumptuous parties, to make her way among his guests. She was like a ghost among them, for they glittered, men and women alike, in brocades and gold and precious gems whereas she wore only her rope of pearls and her pale pastel chiffons imported from Paris. And whereas they were dusky and shiny and plump, she was frail, bird-like, with the sallow complexion of her Parsi ancestors. Everyone drew aside to let her pass, their hands joined in respectful greeting, which she did not return. Her silent contempt took in not only the guests but the ambience in which they moved – in which her husband moved – the over-ornate furnishing and the excessive banquet set out in silver and gold dishes and the bottles of black-market liquor (it was the 1950s, the years of Prohibition). Her only words were of complaint addressed to her husband, always in an angry undertone; then she turned and tripped back on her high heels to her own quarters to collapse there in relief. There was the same relief among the party she had left – they gave each other significant nods and spiralled their forefingers against their temples. Abhinav pretended not to notice; probably he had long since known that she was referred to as the Madwoman, which was maybe the best interpretation of his unfortunate marriage.

Davy and Munni had their own quarters set aside for them in his father's part of the mansion, a bridal suite prepared for them before she had consented to be the bride. Under the rose-coloured canopy of a four-poster with carved foliage, Davy took possession of Munni's body, as splendid as those of the famous stars his father had wooed on the screen. Davy quoted poetry to her – in his adolescence, he had written poetry himself but now he only quoted from the old poets. Sometimes it was a love song in praise of her beauty, but just as often it expressed another part of his nature: the melancholy that lay behind his smile – 'Give not thy heart to the flirting hag of the world, she is the bride of too many grooms already' – and so on, all of it nothing to do with them and the good times they had together.

He took her up on the roof to show her the panorama of

Bombay and the Arabian Sea like a private body of water flowing at the foot of the flowering hill on which the mansion was perched. He explained to her that this site, the most desirable in the whole city, was his by a double inheritance. It had once belonged to Shirin's father's father, who had inherited it from his father. After the family's bankruptcy, the property had had to be sold, and Abhinav had bought it. Razing the original European Palladian-style house, he built his own imitation of fifteenth-century desert palaces, which were familiar to him from historical and mythological film sets; but although his turrets and balconies and battlements were built of concrete, they had somehow retained the same flat quality, of cardboard and make-believe, as their screen counterpart.

At that time, that is at the beginning of their marriage, Davy often took his wife to visit his mother in her quarters. These had been furnished entirely from her parents' household, much of it derived from their parents and grandparents – the heavy Edwardian interiors of wealthy Parsis who had travelled abroad and brought back what was sold to them as valuable antiques. It was usually late afternoon when Davy took Munni to visit here. 'Mummy gets up late,' he said, and in the evenings she preferred to be alone with her cocktail and her gramophone records. But in the beginning she sometimes said, 'Oh no, don't go yet, Bébé, leave this lovely girl with me a moment longer,' and she smiled at Munni to show her how much she liked her. Then Munni had to sit and listen to the gramophone records and pretend that it was music she cared for (Moonlight Sonata and Chopin Preludes). 'Isn't it delicious!' Shirin exclaimed, adding: '*Délicieux*,' for she had gone to finishing school in Switzerland and had retained some French.

Shirin went out once every day, always at the same time and to the same place, tea at the Taj Mahal hotel. At first Munni was expected to accompany her, and they both sat at a little round table specially reserved for them at the top of the crimson-carpeted staircase. At this table her aunts had sat in their time, two skeletal spinsters in French chiffon and high-heeled court shoes. From here they had observed the guests ascending and descending the stairs, and just as Shirin did now, they had deplored the lack of refinement they observed in this tide of newly rich humanity.

For some time Shirin continued to seem fond of her new daughter-in-law. She caressed Munni's hand in her own very small and delicate one, which was adorned with some costly rings. One by one she slipped them off to try them on Munni's fingers but none of them fitted, they were much too small, which made her laugh. 'You're a big big girl and I'm a little little one,' she said. She wrinkled her nose at Munni's name – a lower-class pet name – 'What's your real name?' and when Munni told her, she commented, 'That's not much better ... Let's call you something else.' She came up with various alternatives and finally fixed on Muriel. She called her Muriel for a while, but then she dropped it and didn't call her anything.

Abhinav liked his daughter-in-law's name – he said he remembered several little cousins affectionately nicknamed Munni. Altogether his memory matched hers in various ways, for he too came from a modest Punjabi family. He still loved the food he had eaten in the winter sun of his family's courtyard, the millet bread and bitter spinach leaves; and although the language he mostly used was the Hindustani of film dialogue, he enjoyed speaking the earthy dialect of his boyhood. It had been Munni's first language too, superseded by now, along with other family memories she had deliberately erased; but when he spoke to her in it, she answered with all those homely phrases that made them both smile. It began to happen that, when they were alone, they used it with each other; but never when Davy was there, for he didn't understand their spicy dialect.

Munni's greatest satisfaction was being in charge of Abhinav's grand parties. She loved these occasions and her own role in them. Her pleasure made her beauty glow, she illumined the room more than the shining marble and the crystal chandeliers (condemned by Shirin as second-hand imitations of the real ones that had hung in her grandfather's house). Munni was indifferent to the admiration she aroused in the guests, and the only person she glanced at for approval was her father-in-law. Often he expressed his satisfaction with her by a splendid gift, and then she fell at his feet: not only in the traditional gesture of respect for an elder but in admiration for him, his generosity, his greatness.

She was shocked to discover the way some of his servants plundered him. He said, 'What to do?' Then suddenly he flew into a rage – roaring and threatening, so that the servants cowered as under a storm at sea. Next day he regretted his outburst and reinstated the offenders he had dismissed. But Munni couldn't bear to see the waste; and when she again mentioned it to him, he said, 'You see to it, *bitya* (little daughter).' Now she wore a big bunch of keys at her waist and walked around like any Hindu housewife on bare feet and in a cotton sari. Her careful control of expenses offended some of the servants, so that she had to dismiss them. But most of them adapted themselves to the new regime; and Munni herself was a considerate employer, and they even admired her strict management skills.

Abhinav hardly kept track of his enormous expenses. Often his grand exits through the gilded gates ended up at the races, where he accumulated large losses. He opened a safe full of cash and, thrusting in his hand, took out bundles of notes without counting them. Other debts were made at cards played in the house with friends. Their games carried on for many hours, during which bottles of contraband Scotch were called for. Sometimes Munni came in to watch the game. She didn't understand its rules, but it did seem to her that these were not adhered to by everyone.

Once she followed her father-in-law when he got up from the game to go to his safe. She said, 'How is it, sir, that they're always winning and you're always losing?'

'They're lucky and I'm not – except of course in my daughter-in-law.'

'Perhaps you're honest and they're not.'

He smiled when she tried to stop him extracting his usual bundle of notes. 'You don't trust me?'

'I trust you, sir, but not others.'

'Yes, those horses, they're very untrustworthy – they keep losing.'

'And your card-playing friends who keep winning?'

With a simple grand gesture characteristic of him, he handed her the bundle of notes he had taken out. She counted them and put most of them back. She didn't know what happened after that between him and his friends – the games continued, but he always allowed her to pay out his losses. And after a while he also asked her to take care of the ones at the race track and other places such as the wrestling matches he frequented. And then it was easiest to hand over the key of the safe to her; and instead of adding it to the bunch of store keys she already wore at her waist, she hung it on a string around her neck to nestle there and come to rest between her breasts.

It was there that Davy discovered it. He stopped in his caresses to ask, 'What's this?'

'Your father's key.'

'Key to what? To his heart?'

'To the safe, you idiot.' He asked nothing further. Making

59

love to her seemed more important to him than any key, even if it was to his father's safe.

A few days later Davy asked her to take some money out of the safe for him. It was a substantial amount, but he asked for it casually. Then he added, 'Mummy needs it. She has tremendous expenses, you have no idea.' And then, 'You don't understand about Mummy. Of course Daddy is very famous and all that, but Mummy comes from a very noble family, even if they did go bankrupt and left her with nothing.'

She asked Davy about his parents: 'How did it happen? How did they get married?' Then he showed her magazines of thirty years before, featuring them in their youth. It was the time when Abhinav had been the leading hero, dashing and daring and not only on the screen. It was only later, in his maturity, that he began to take on the roles of the divinities and emperors that had become the expression of his entire personality.

He had first seen Shirin at a dance in the exclusive Willingdon Club when he and his entourage were on a round of New Year parties. The rest of them, soon moving on to more rowdily festive places, couldn't understand his decision to stay on. But Shirin understood very well, and it made her foxtrot more prettily and even to induce her staid partner to twirl her around once or twice in a more fashionable dance.

'Wedding Bells???' Munni read in the old magazines. She and Davy were lying across their bed in their usual way. 'Haven't you read enough yet?' he asked. 'Old stuff like that. Come on, Munni.'

She gave in and they kissed, lying face to face. She said, 'You don't look like him, not a bit.'

'Of course not. That's why I'm not a national hero, but just an ordinary guy.'

She waited for him to fall asleep – kissed him once more, brushed a lock of hair from his forehead – then returned to the magazines. She found many articles about the wedding. Most of these gave some details of Shirin's family, mentioning the bankruptcy along with hints, and more than hints, about their mental balance. There were pictures of their mansion in its heyday, built in 1912, cream-yellow with white trim; in front of the pillared portico stood a carriage full of Parsi gentlemen in their round hats setting out on a picnic. But even at that time, Munni read, there had been one room in that mansion where a family member was kept locked up, with a servant to look after him (or, as often, her) and bars at the window through which to peer at a lost world.

In the past, Munni's girlfriends had often called her from New York, with eager questions about her marriage and her life in her father-in-law's palace. As time went on, she became reluctant to answer them, so that they made haughty faces at one another to show what sort of a person she had become. But it wasn't that – it was that she needed to keep this new life she loved to herself, not to be touched by any outsider's curiosity. And more than her friends, it was her family she wanted to keep at a distance. She was not on good terms with them; she had not forgiven their attitude at the time of her divorce when they wouldn't let her back into their house. After her elevation to be Abhinav's daughter-in-law, they were eager to travel to Bombay and participate in her new splendour; and when she wouldn't allow them to visit, they condemned her as her friends did, only more bitterly.

Later, when the rumours began and were taken up by all the gossip magazines, they spread so far and so rapidly that they reached her family in their small town in the Punjab, six hundred miles away. Her father wrote her a letter in terms as virulent as those he had used about her divorce. She read a few lines, then tore the letter across and threw it away. More letters came and those she destroyed without opening them. She didn't have to read them, she knew what was in them, and worse, she could see and hear her father, unshaven in a creased and stained shirt, banging his stick on the ground in fury as he denounced her for having blackened his name.

The rumours may actually have started within the house, in Shirin's domain. A cook whom Munni had had to dismiss came pleading to Shirin for reinstatement. After throwing himself at her feet, he squatted close by her chair to tell her things that evidently could not be said aloud. He stayed a long time, and next day he came again, and soon he was employed in Shirin's kitchen, to learn her bland European dishes in place of Abhinav's fiery curries.

Not long afterwards, there was another big party, and Shirin made one of her entrances. This time she linked her arm in Munni's in order to parade the room with her. But suddenly she let go of her and, surveying her from head to foot, she flicked at Munni's splendid brocade sari: 'Did you get that piece of cloth from one of the "temple dancers"?' she said loud enough for surrounding guests to hear. 'I'm told they're fetching a good price nowadays – the saris, not the "dancers", as the poor old things call themselves ... And this?' She fingered Munni's antique necklace, another of Abhinav's gifts. 'It must weigh a ton – luckily you can wear it. With your thick neck.' Then, plaintively, she called for Davy to take her away from this place that was stifling her with its smell of over-spiced food and all the people drenched in cheap bazaar perfume (she alleged unfairly about her husband's high-profile guests).

By the time Munni's hostess duties were concluded, Davy was already asleep in their bedroom. She woke him by first flinging her necklace and then, unwinding herself from her sari, flinging that at him as well. 'She's seen them so many times before – what got into her today? What have I done to her?'

Rousing himself from sleep, Davy tried to make excuses for his mother: 'She wasn't well tonight. She must have had one of her attacks of indigestion.' And at Munni's indignant cry, he retracted: 'Well, maybe not indigestion – but what if it's her heart? You must understand about Mummy, how much she's been through.'

'But that's not my fault. I've always tried—'

'I know you have. You've been very sweet with her.' He kissed her gratefully, then he picked up the necklace where it had fallen on the floor. He ran his fingers over the stones and mused, 'It really is worth a fortune.'

'She can have it. I'll give it to her gladly. It doesn't mean a thing to me.'

'No no, of course she wants you to have it. And it wouldn't suit her the way it suits you.'

'Because of my thick neck?' Munni said, half laughing though still angry.

'Your beautiful neck.' He ran his fingers over it the way he had over the jewels.

While suspicions and innuendos swirled around the house, inside it no one seemed to be aware of them. The guests at Abhinav's parties acted as though nothing were further from their minds than the scandal that had attached itself to their host and his daughter-in-law. And he made it easy for them. He ignored or simply overrode everything that was written, with no change at all in his expansive manner, no diminishment of his majestic personality.

It was more difficult for Munni. She read the same thoughts in everyone who looked at her, and it made her want to put her hand over the fine pieces of jewellery her father-in-law had given her. While she continued to dress up for her role as his hostess, now it was with a feeling of discomfort and even shame. But she decided that she would not accept any more gifts from him, however difficult it might be to decline them.

He especially enjoyed bestowing some munificent present on her at the end of one of his grand parties, to thank her for making it a success. He was very proud of the occasions when famous classical musicians came to perform at his house. His tastes had been formed by the musical numbers of Bombay films in which he himself had sung and danced; but with classical music, he took his cue from others when to sway his head and give out sounds of ecstasy – principally from his son. Davy truly loved Indian classical music. When he was younger, his mother had tried to make him learn the piano, but instead he engaged a maestro to teach him the sitar. At first these lessons were a success, but after a while, disappointed with his progress, he gave up on them.

It was at the end of a music recital that Abhinav tried to present another gift to his daughter-in-law. He proudly opened the velvet case delivered by his jeweller that morning. 'These diamonds belonged to the Turkish bride of a Hyderabad prince. They have been specially set for you – please wear them,' he said, lifting the heavy necklace from its velvet bed. She stepped back, but just then Davy joined them. He was still humming the raga they had just heard and didn't stop humming while taking the necklace from his father. 'Your husband will help you,' Abhinav smiled. Davy had stepped between him and Munni, so that his father didn't see her putting her hand on her throat in refusal. 'No no,' she mouthed at Davy, pleading to him. He turned to his father. 'She wants to try it in front of a mirror, to be the first to admire herself. Women are so vain,' he told Abhinav, who gallantly denied the accusation. Taking the case from him, Davy replaced the necklace in it; he began to hum again and did not stop till he and Munni were back in their own rooms.

There he threw the velvet case on the bed. 'Refusing his gifts! You hurt my father's feelings.'

'I can't do it, Davy. I can't keep taking things.'

'Why not? When he loves to give them to you.'

'And your mother?'

'I've told you about Mummy. She has her moods and there are things she just doesn't like.'

'She doesn't like me.' She spoke simply, in a matter-of-fact way.

He too spoke simply: 'How can she? With everything that's written in the papers.' This was the first time anyone in the house had mentioned the gossip surrounding them. But now he went on: 'You see how careful we have to be.'

She snatched up the case he had flung on the bed. She thrust it at him. 'Here, it's yours! You're his son, they can't very well write filthy scandal about a son taking a gift from his father!' Next moment she sank against him. 'Please take it, Davy. I don't want it. Please keep it.'

'All right,' he conceded. 'I'll ask Mummy to keep it locked up in her safe ... You know what would be nice? If you gave it to her yourself. She'd be pleased.'

'She wouldn't be pleased to see me.'

He frowned. 'You're being very selfish. You've even been letting her go alone to her tea at the Taj.'

'But she said she didn't want me to come with her ever again!'

'That's because you weren't good company for her. She said that instead of talking to you, she might as well be talking to herself. That's what she's been doing – she's been sitting at her table talking to herself. She doesn't harm anyone, she just says out loud what's on her mind, but the manager called to say not to let her come any more. Now all she can do is stay home talking to the servants. It isn't even that they've been with her forever, like Daddy's people; they're always new ones and she doesn't really trust them.'

Munni was aware that there was only one servant Shirin trusted, and this was the cook whom Munni herself had had to dismiss. Whenever she visited her mother-in-law's quarters, he was there to welcome her – obsequiously, but making his favoured position clear. He was there now when Munni entered with the latest velvet jewellery box. 'Oh look who's come to honour us!' Shirin cried. When Munni extended the gift to her, she waved her towards the cook. 'Give it to him.'

He held out his hands for the box, and when Munni hesitated, Shirin said, 'You see, she doesn't trust you. She thinks you're a thief. She thinks everyone is a thief, but we know who has stolen what.'

Munni was still standing, still with the jewel box. The cook offered her a chair, settled a cushion on it, dusted it. Shirin ordered her to sit on it – but next moment she told the cook, 'Open the piano so she can play for me. And take that wretched box from her, she's sitting there like a box-wallah come to sell me some trash.'

The servant obeyed. He lifted the lid of the piano and the box from Munni's lap. Shirin didn't allow him to keep it. 'Over there,' she said. 'On that table. My son will know what to do with it, he knows where I keep my things ... Why aren't you playing? Do you know Chopin? No? *No?*' In despair, she laid her delicate hands over her eyes; when she uncovered them again: 'Look at my eyes – yes, those are my tears.' She leaned forward for Munni to see them but there were none, and only the cook made pitying sounds. 'Why are they there? Because in all our family only I have a daughter-in-law who can't play the piano. A daughter-in-law who smells of oil in her hair and the spicy

66

peasant food she eats with her father-in-law. Now look – look at her face! What's in her mind when I mention her father-in-law?'

What was in Munni's mind was Shirin herself and what was written about her family history in the gossip magazines. When she spoke her fears to Davy, he shrugged, sadly, then changed the subject. 'Ask Daddy not to get you any more of that antique jewellery,' he said. 'People don't like it much nowadays so it's not worth what it used to be ... Yes, I know you don't wear it but still, it's property. We have to think of that. A rainy day and so on.'

'But, Davy, aren't we terribly rich?'

'Daddy is. You and I aren't. And Mummy's family money – whoosh! Gone with the wind. That's how things happen and suddenly everything's changed.'

*

'Once there was a palace whose turrets reached the sky
And on its portals kings rubbed their foreheads . . .'

As with music, Abhinav respected classical poetry more than he loved or understood it. But there were frequent symposia at his house, arranged by Davy, who invited famous poets to perform. Like her father-in-law, Munni was better versed in popular film lyrics; and what she enjoyed at these symposia was to watch Davy deeply immersed in the recital. When he drew in his breath at the beauty of a sentiment and the apt rhyme in which it was expressed, she too breathed in ecstasy, though hers was not for the poetry but for him.

Nevertheless, that day, she was the first to see her mother-in-law enter in the middle of a recital. Shirin came not with her usual imperious sweep but slyly sidling like one with a secret to impart. As she made her way towards Davy, Munni started up – her first thought was not to have his enjoyment interrupted –

and respectfully she tried to detain her mother-in-law. Shirin shook her off and continued to stumble over the audience to reach the front row.

At this disturbance, the poet faltered, and Davy, in quick reaction, jumped up to take charge of his mother. She clung to him, she whispered to him, loudly in her agitation so that some of her words could be made out. He led her to the door, and when they passed Munni, Shirin clung more tightly to him; her whisper became louder. 'It's her, I'm telling you. They're in it together.' But Abhinav had already given the signal for the recital to continue, and the poet's voice drowned her:

> 'Now I see nothing there save a crow sitting on a cornice
> And in my ears I hear its mournful caw:
> "Where has it all gone? O where? Where?
> Kahan? Kahan?"'

It was very late, almost dawn, when Davy at last joined Munni. She was sitting up in their bed, waiting for him. 'Tell me,' she said. 'Whatever it is, I have to know.'

He sighed, drawing his finger along her cheek in his usual tender way. At last he said, 'Mummy says she's being poisoned – yes yes, but it's what she thinks. At first she suspected only the servant –'

'And now?' Munni held her breath.

Davy paused, continued reluctantly: 'He says when he came home from the bazaar, he found someone in his kitchen stirring something into the soup he had left to simmer. But what could he do? How could he, a poor man, accuse a person so close to her, a member of her own family?'

'And she *believes* him? She actually believes him?'

'Yes, she believes him.'

'And you? . . . Davy! You? You think I did that?'

68

'Of course I don't! Of course not!' He gathered her ample form in his arms. They lay down together, and he buried his face in her. 'She's sick,' he pleaded. 'Mummy is so terribly sick. I'm so afraid for her.'

'We'll care for her,' Munni promised. 'We'll do everything for her. She can say and think about me whatever she wants, I know it's not her really who's thinking it.'

'Yes *we* know, but others don't. Others don't understand, they'd want to lock her up in a hospital with people far more sick than she is. Or in a room – never let her out of a room with bars on the window. You've seen them, haven't you? In the old houses? The faces looking out and the kids in the street laughing at them. I used to laugh too when I was a kid.'

Again she comforted him, promising how they would care for her, he and she together, and Abhinav of course.

He sat up. He didn't smoke often, but now he lit a cigarette. 'We'll have to speak to Daddy,' he said. 'About taking her away ... You know the only time she's been truly happy? When she was a girl at school, in Switzerland, she loved it, the mountains and the lakes.'

Munni was silent. Her heart was heavy. She cared nothing for mountains and lakes, she had never seen them, but she cared deeply for this house and their life in it that Abhinav had made for them. Nevertheless, she said, 'If that's what you want – what you think would be best for her – we'll go.'

'And there are doctors there and good places where she can rest and be cared for ... It'll be expensive of course, and Mummy and I have nothing, and the jewellery Daddy gave you didn't fetch the price I had hoped.'

'And that's all the money we have?'

'But you have the cheque books and the key to the safe. Daddy trusts you absolutely. And he'll give you more things, every time you and he have a party. He's so pleased with the

69

way you manage everything. He couldn't ever be without you.'

She snatched the cigarette from his lips and flung it on the carpet. He went after it and stamped it out with her slipper. 'You'll set the house on fire,' he said. 'Besides poisoning Mummy – that's a joke!' But she had already cried out, 'You're crazy! You're completely nuts!'

'I know it,' he said humbly. He lit another cigarette, lightly blew smoke. 'But there's nothing like that in Daddy's family. You're best off with him. He and you. Careful!' he said, shielding his cigarette.

But she made no move to snatch it. Instead she sank down on the bed, sitting on the side of it, her hands clasped in her lap. 'What is it?' she said. 'What are you planning?'

'I'm planning your future. I want you to be happy, and Daddy to be happy. It's what everyone says. They even say it in print! "Is she his daughter-in-law or is she his ...?" Hey! That's a quote, why are you mad at me?' He put up his hands to shield his face and her blow landed on his arm. He rubbed it. 'Let's be reasonable,' he said. And he spoke in a reasonable way. 'No, listen – really, what am I? Remember, in New York, when I asked you over and over to marry me? And you refused, till he came: then at once – *yes!* See, you *knew*, as soon as you saw him. And of course, why not? Look at the two of you. Both of you so healthy ... You've read what they've been writing – "And the little crown prince? What's wrong with him? Why no little stranger? *She* looks strong enough and so does the father-in-law ..."' Now she covered her ears so as not to hear him quote what she knew only too well. But he shrugged. 'It's the sort of thing people like to read. I think I might like it too if it wasn't about me. And it's true; you *are* strong.' Smiling, he rubbed his arm where her blow had landed.

She clasped her arms around his neck. He felt her tears

coursing down his face; he whispered, 'You'll see. Everything will be much better when we've gone.' She held him more tightly, she moaned no no, she didn't believe him; but it turned out to be true.

After a while, even the gossip magazines stopped writing about them. And when a year or two had passed, it seemed to have been forgotten that Munni was the daughter-in-law and not the consort of Abhinav. As Davy had said: 'Look at the two of you' – they were indeed like a king and his consort, or a god and his goddess. It was the way they lived too, royally in their domain. The festivities were even more lavish than before. A favourite pastime now was to watch Abhinav's old films in the screening room, and then come upstairs into the marble halls to enjoy the same numbers performed by live girls, half spangled and half nude, waving their veils at the audience. The mood was heightened – it was the end of Prohibition – and the guests, sprawled among cushions, were raucous in their appreciation.

Moving among their inebriated guests, Abhinav and Munni seemed to be floating slightly above them – just as, in the films viewed in the screening room, a god and goddess presided over their subjects from clouds in the empyrean. It would have been blasphemous to speculate about the relationship of such a pair. There were never any signs of pregnancy, but as the years passed, Munni burgeoned into new magnificence. Her jewellery and brocades matched the splendour of her figure. She wore them openly now: as the reigning mistress of the palace, she was entitled to her adornments and had no need to lock them away like a guilty secret.

She did keep one secret – the letters she received from Switzerland. They were as private and personal to her as her own thoughts. Davy often asked her to send money, admitting

that his father's allowance had run short again. There was the
time he needed to buy a piano, he thought learning to play
again might be good for Mummy when she came for weekends
from the sanatorium. After scanning quickly over the business
part of his letters, Munni came to what was for her their true
gist. Usually he ended with a quote, and sometimes she could
take it as addressed to herself ('O cypress of lovely stature'); or,
more often, it was an expression of a melancholy sense of loss,
the crow's cry echoing through the ruined palace. And both –
the romantic and the melancholy – were characteristic of Davy
as she never ceased to think of him. It was how she had first
seen him, in the restaurant in New York. Now she imagined
him in another country at another café table. And here too,
though surrounded by a group of friends, he would be silent and
aloof, smiling to himself while sad old verses murmured in his
mind.

Where? O where?
Kahan? Kahan?

School of Oriental Studies

The first time Professor Maria von R saw and heard the poetess Anuradha was on a public stage. Anuradha, huge and stout, glittered like a star – she *was* a star, in her achievement and in her person. She was wearing a bright orange sari and her hair too was turning orange, with henna; she was hung around with gifts of gold and jewels from her admirers. The hall was over-full, extra chairs had to be brought in, more carpets spread in front, more intimates allowed to sit on the stage. They breathed in her words of poetry, not silently but with little cries almost of pain; she roused them to a pitch, and when they had reached it, she smiled and let them subside – till she was ready to let them strive once more to reach those heights that she alone seemed to attain without effort.

Oriental studies were a family tradition for Maria. Her Prussian father had for ten years been a professor of Sanskrit in Göttingen until, in disgust with the German regime of the 1930s, he had accepted a position at an American university. Born in America, Maria had followed in the same field and at the same university, and had become a prominent scholar in her own right.

She was also in a modest way a poet. In coming to New Delhi to meet Anuradha, it had been her dream to be allowed to translate her poetry into English. She had no idea how to begin to suggest this, but on her first visit Anuradha herself said, 'So, where would you start?' as though the two of them had already had a long discussion on the subject. Lighting a cigarette – raw tobacco folded in a brown leaf – Anuradha said, 'Of course it's all a mess. *I'm* a mess, always have been, from birth.'

Maria was perched on a stool near the poetess who was sprawled on her floor-height divan. She tried to explain herself, why she had come, attracted by the magnet of just that mixture in Anuradha's poetry and in Anuradha herself, whose father had been a Hindu and her mother a Muslim. It was also there in the room where they sat, in the house that Anuradha had inherited from her father. She had turned the front room into the place where she worked, ate, slept, received, entertained and bullied. All the good pieces from her father's time, like his bookcases crammed with Western and Indian classics, had gravitated here. The walls of this salon-bedroom held another kind of mixture – the abstract paintings by one of Anuradha's lovers from her years in Paris, Moghul miniatures of princes in their garden palaces, bazaar oleographs of prostitutes in pearls.

Maria hardly remembered how it had happened that, only three days after her arrival, she had moved in with Anuradha, right into her home. It must have been at Anuradha's instigation, or rather her insistence. Maria herself was shy and always afraid of imposing, a hesitant personality whom Anuradha could easily override. But Maria was glad – she had been in a hotel and was not used to being on her own. On her previous travels she had always been accompanied by her mother, a forceful German lady who made all the arrangements. Maria had been very close to her parents, who had referred to her as 'the Child' – 'das Kind' – even after she was forty. Now both her parents were dead, and Maria was left floundering on her own.

On their first day of work together, Anuradha challenged her: 'How do you think you can translate even one part of me, let alone the rest?'

Maria fully understood the difficulty. She knew Sanskrit very well but not its present-day derivatives; the Hindi she spoke was so stylised and archaic that no living person was able to understand her. (This both amused and irritated Anuradha.) During her father's lifetime, Maria had deeply immersed herself in the Hindu scriptures; it was only later, when she was left alone, that she realised she needed something more personal than the Absolute of Vedanta philosophy. That was when she had begun her studies in Persian and its derivative Urdu, with their much greater emphasis on an approachable, caring Presence; and it was also how she had been drawn to Anuradha's poetry with its combination, in language and feeling, of both the Hindu and the Muslim areas of Maria's studies.

Maria was struggling for words – it was all so difficult to express, and to express in English! Fortunately for her, Anuradha never really listened to others. She cut across Maria in mid-sentence. 'So he's asked you to get him a fellowship in America. Very good. He should be doing something more than get stuck in a lecturer's job here – so ridiculous! My son!'

Her son Som was an economist – a field far from Maria's, but she had many contacts in the academic world where she was greatly admired for her scholarly achievements. Her inquiries on his behalf had been positive: there were several openings, and Maria discussed them with him, while Anuradha listened.

Her only questions were about the location of the various universities they mentioned. One was on the East Coast, another on the West Coast. 'Let him go to the one farther away,' Anuradha said. Afterwards Som explained that what his mother wanted was to get him as far away as possible from his current girlfriend.

Anuradha complained to Maria about the girlfriends. It seemed they were all the same type – all academics, all doing their Ph.D. on subjects no one had ever heard of, all skeletons with nothing up in front – not that they needed it, for what was it that they and Som could possibly do together except discuss each other's thesis? Yes, she concluded gloomily, it was right for him to go abroad, perhaps there he might at last find a proper daughter-in-law to bring home to his mother, who would welcome anyone, even a dance hostess. At that she laughed out loud and coquetted with her veil in a way she considered characteristic of a dance hostess. Maria was used to these changes of mood – they were there in the poetry she was struggling to translate, where Anuradha was now imperious like a Hindu god flinging his thunderbolt and next moment a young girl sick with longing for a lover.

Although the front of the house was imposing with Doric pillars and a verandah leading into Anuradha's spacious salon, the back of it comprised only two cramped rooms, one of them occupied by Maria, the other by Som. Maria often had to shut the door of hers so as not to overhear the terrible rows between mother and son; but even through the closed door, Maria couldn't help hearing how Anuradha cursed her son and her own womb that had borne him. The whole house heard her – in fact, the whole neighbourhood, for when he ran out she followed him down the street with her curses. She had rented out the property she owned at the back of her house, and if she saw the tenants leaning out to listen, she turned her fury on them. They accepted it all from her – everyone did, however outrageous her behaviour. Maria too very soon got used to it. Whenever Anuradha was displeased with Maria's translation, she scrawled her pencil across it, impressing down so hard that she tore through the paper; sometimes she also broke the pencil and flung away the pieces.

Since all the furniture had gravitated to the salon, Maria's room had only a rope bed and a rickety cane table and stool with the cane unwinding. This spare whitewashed space suited her; her home in Boston, now that she lived alone, was a small apartment sparsely furnished. But asceticism was not the whole of her. She may have looked spinsterish with her glasses slipping on her nose and her thin hair turning grey; but she liked dressing in silks and also wore some jewellery, modest but gold, and even her glasses were gold-rimmed. Behind these, her eyes were pale blue pools, enlarged by the correction for her extreme near-sight; they were slightly protruding, which gave her a perpetually eager look as one leaning forwards in order not to miss anything.

This was exactly her attitude from the moment she woke and feared missing the summons to the salon. Anuradha slept late into the day, while everyone walked around on tiptoe. Usually it was well past noon when the awaited cry came from the salon. Then the household flurry began, with the old man who tended the boiler carrying buckets of hot water to her bathroom, then another old man fanning up the fire in her kitchen (or cook-house, as it was called), the maid, also old, laying out her towel and the day's freshly washed clothes. Anuradha sang as she poured water over herself from the bucket of her bath, and this morning hymn was as joyful as the sunrise.

When at last Maria was sent for, she came trembling with

anticipation for their work to begin. But sometimes she found Anuradha in a very bad mood. Once she was having her feet massaged by her old maid when, in an access of temper, she kicked out one foot so that the maid fell over backwards. That made Anuradha angrier; she shouted, 'Did you go to the eye doctor? No? Good, go blind then, you stubborn fool.' The maid muttered what time did she have for eye doctor, running here and there for Anuradha day and night; and when Anuradha stuck out her foot again, she refused to resume her work on it, instead gathering up her paraphernalia, her oils and balms.

'This is what I have to put up with,' Anuradha complained to Maria. 'No respect anywhere; the least little wish of mine ignored and trodden underfoot. Even my own son! I tell him, "You're thirty-five years old and what is your work? What are you? Who esteems you in the very same university where your grandfather was the vice-chancellor?"'

At mention of her father, her mood improved. His portrait hung above her divan. He was in formal European dress with some sort of order on a crimson ribbon around his neck. She spoke of his nobility and courage: a high-caste Hindu, he had married a Muslim girl at a time when this was dangerous enough to cause a riot. After she died, he had devoted himself to their daughter Anuradha, educating her like a son, even sending her abroad to study in London and Paris.

'And when I came back, I married his secretary – can you imagine?' She laughed at herself for doing that. She had loved her late husband, who had been, like their son Som, small and slight, gentle in manner. But he had never come to anything, and it was his lack of ambition that she now saw reflected in their son Som and led to more quarrels with him.

While her father hung splendidly portrayed above her divan, she kept small snapshots of her husband in a nearby drawer.

This she opened frequently, taking out a sandalwood box to show to Maria. Besides the snapshots, it contained a rosary, a bundle of yellowed papers tied with a red thread, some dried and dusty margosa leaves, and her husband's spectacles with a crack across one lens. She handed the box to Maria. 'Open it, smell it.' Mingled with the sandalwood, Maria discovered a delicate scent as of evaporated incense or long-dead blossoms. The photographs had all been snapped outdoors and were so faded that Anuradha's husband, frail in his white shirt and Gandhi cap, appeared insubstantial, ghost-like, a saintly spirit. He may have been further reduced by Anuradha's kisses – she never shut the box without pressing his image to her lips. She described how he was the only person in the world who had ever been able to still the turmoil within her – yes, even when it was turned against himself as, God forgive her, it often was. He would put his arms around her, which was not easy since she was so stout; he murmured her name into her ear, soothingly, sweetly. How she missed that loving restraint; now there was no one to whisper 'Anuradha, Anuradha' and bring her back to herself, quietening the demons that made her rage against even those, especially those, whom she loved. Here she squeezed Maria's hand, and then how willingly and gladly Maria forgave all Anuradha's harsh words whenever she was dissatisfied with Maria's translations.

There were times when the two of them had very intimate conversations together. Anuradha was completely outspoken about her life, including the two abortions she had had in Paris. Remembering those, and especially what had led up to them, she flung her hands before her face and rocked to and fro with laughter. 'And you?' she asked Maria. 'No husband, no lovers?' Maria smiled shyly, regretfully. Then Anuradha thought of helping her by changing her appearance. Unlike herself, whose mouth was painted a bright moist red and her eyes black with kohl, Maria only wore a very pale pink lipstick. 'That's not the way to make anyone fall in love with you,' Anuradha advised her; but although she presented Maria with some potent dyes, Maria continued to use her own, applying it so sparingly that it was almost invisible. It was a part of her, along with the thin gold jewellery and the silk dresses – adornments worn not to enhance herself but to pay homage to an ideal of beauty.

One day Anuradha said, 'You've done so much for me. I would like to give you something. What can I give you?' She looked at her critically, from head to toe. 'When I first saw you, I thought – her dress is pretty, she has fine taste – but see here, the hem is uneven, the waist is dragging where the hip should be.'

She decided that she would have new dresses made for her and that they would go together to the bazaar to order them. At once she told her tenants to send around their car and driver, and at their mild reminder that these were needed to bring their children from school, she advised them to hire a motor rickshaw.

Although Anuradha's poetry was full of imagery taken from nature, nowadays she rarely left her house. She said everything was inside her, the earth, the oceans and rivers, the heavens above, and the hell below trying to push up through every available rift. But when she did go out, as now with Maria in the tenants' car, she was excited by all the sights on the way. Impatiently pushing aside the satin curtains shielding the passengers from view, she pointed out well-known landmarks of this city that was hers. Here was where the Emperor Humayun had fallen to his death from the steps of his library (some said after an overdose of opium); here the 'Gate of Blood' where the Persian invader Nadir Shah had ordered the massacre of the citizens of Delhi; there the convent school Anuradha had attended, just like the girls they passed now in oiled pigtails and white socks; and there the lane where in 1938 a Hindu-Muslim riot had had to be suppressed when her father married her mother.

On arrival at their destination in the cloth market, Maria discovered that Anuradha was herself a popular landmark. Although she was a classical and highly sophisticated poet, some of her lyrics had reached a much wider audience through being sung in popular Bombay films. Anuradha was recognised the moment they left their car and walked the few steps to the shop she patronised. People sang out lines of hers that everyone knew by heart: 'How many petals has the lotus – are they One, are they Four, or are they Seven?' She sang back: 'What fool would count the Stars of Heaven?' before entering the open front of the shop. Here, welcomed as the empress, the star she was, she was enthroned on a special chair brought for her, while Maria perched on the narrow bench meant for ordinary customers. Anuradha made the shopkeeper and his assistants bring down bolt after bolt of silk cloth. Nothing pleased her, she kept pointing to new ones further up, beyond reach so that a ladder had to be brought. Maria was embarrassed, she hated giving trouble to anyone and usually bought the first thing she was shown. Now, with the sea of silk spread on the platform before them, she was too bewildered to make a choice; but finally and without hesitation, Anuradha extracted from those billowing waves the exact pattern she had had in mind for her friend. This was not the dazzling colours she favoured for herself but tiny buds ingrained in the silk and entwined with the delicate glitter of gold thread. Maria engrossed herself in admiring and stroking the soft texture and tried not to hear Anuradha's robust bargaining with the shopkeeper. But she blushed again when the tailor, summoned from a nearby shop, had to take her measurements, which were so pitifully inadequate that the tailor shook his head in disbelief and Anuradha stifled a smile.

It was the tailor's fault that Maria had to postpone her departure. Her six-month sabbatical was coming to an end, and she was to leave at the end of July. Although Som's fellowship wasn't due to start until a few months later, he had been planning to go on the same plane; and until he got settled, she had invited him to stay with her in her apartment in Boston. But when the tailor came to fit the first of Maria's new dresses, Anuradha was so dissatisfied that she ordered him to take it back. The same happened at the next fitting; and when Maria, always reluctant to give trouble, was ready to accept them, Anuradha turned on her: 'Just see! You're ready to take the first clumsy piece of bad work, whereas I – I aim only for Perfection.' Then Maria too had to reject the dresses. After several more tries, she informed Som that they would have to change their date of departure; she could not leave without his mother's gift.

He at once recognised his mother's stratagem. Although at first Anuradha had welcomed and encouraged the fellowship, once she found that his current girlfriend was no longer a danger, she changed her mind. 'To leave your mother's house,' she accused him, 'for some stupid Ph.D. that's no use to anyone. This is all Maria's doing.'

At the sound of her name, Maria had emerged from her room. She did something of which she would not have thought herself capable: she crept to the door of the salon to hear what was said between mother and son.

'I should never have let her into the house,' Anuradha was telling Som. 'These foreign women are very wily.'

'She only wants to be helpful to you, and to me. She's said I can stay in her place in Boston till I get settled.'

'*Stay* with her? *Live* with her?'

Maria heard Som shout, 'Now what's on your mind!' and then a deep sigh from Anuradha: 'She's stealing you from me.'

'Everyone's always stealing me – if it's not my girlfriend, it's Maria. She's your age, for God's sake. She's like my mother; like you.'

'That's how it is with these women who have never lived. When their age is past, they no longer want lovers, they want sons. Other women's sons. Call her! Call her in here, talk to her in my presence!'

Maria had sunk to her knees to look through the keyhole. She saw Anuradha point to the space in front of her where Som and Maria were to stand and speak. Maria quickly got up and scuttled off to her room. She thought of her parents, who had lived up to a strict code of moral dignity; she herself too had followed the same code. Yet now she had eavesdropped on others, peered at them through a keyhole. A shudder passed through her – not of shame but of fear and helplessness against these new feelings, which were so hard for her nature to bear that they seemed to her to be unnatural.

But next day, when she came to work with Anuradha, she found her in a very good mood. That was a happy day for Maria. Anuradha was at her best: stern and passionate, she laid bare every nuance of meaning while Maria stumbled after her, labouring to come up with a not entirely inadequate parallel. Again and again she failed and was rejected, but she liked it, being made to reach for perfection. After a few hours they were both exhausted – Maria tried to hold out but Anuradha fell on to her divan with a great exhalation of breath. She was pleased with herself and with Maria, and she patted the place beside her for Maria to join her. At first Maria was shy, also afraid of discomfiting Anuradha who was taking up most of the divan, with no indication of yielding an inch of it; but finally Maria, making herself as small as possible, squeezed in sideways to lie beside her. She heard her own heart beating – or was it two hearts beating, though she didn't dare think that Anuradha was as deeply affected as she was. The poetess, a huge mound rising, pressed against her with her fat hot flesh, suffusing her with the by now so familiar, so beloved smell of rose-scented oil, garlic and perspiration. Just as in that day's work, Maria had never felt herself so ecstatically close to her. One of Anuradha's hands with its many rings pressed Maria even closer, may even have groped a little under her dress, though by that time Maria had shut her eyes and was no longer sure of what was happening.

She woke, feeling Anuradha's breath in her ear, whispering, 'Promise me something'; then, more insistently, 'You mustn't say no. You must promise to say yes.'

'Yes,' Maria murmured drowsily.

'All right, you've promised. Sit up.'

They both sat up. Anuradha said, 'You must tell him the fellowship is cancelled. Or given to someone else. You can think of *something*. I leave it to you, and surely you'd be happy to do this for me. For a mother. And remember,' she ended up in irritated warning, 'you said yes.'

Telling a lie was a sin Maria's parents had taught her to be unforgivable, so she had had no practice at it. She had also been brought up never to break a promise – and especially, she felt now, one that had been given under such intimate circumstances. Som, on the other hand, had lived all his life with his mother and had quickly learned how to detect a lie – and moreover, whose lie it was. His reply to Maria was, '*She* told you to say that.'

Maria was incapable of a second lie. She lowered her eyes and said, 'I couldn't refuse her.'

'Please come with me.'

He took her to the salon where Anuradha was already waiting and ready for a confrontation. With a face of surpassing innocence, she said, 'I don't tell her what to say and what not to say, so how would I know what she's told you?'

Som was a gentle, peace-loving person in all his relations except with his mother. He shouted, 'You don't know, you never know anything! You don't even know who it was that told my girlfriends all those lies about me.'

'Your girlfriends.' Anuradha made a sound with her lips as contemptuous as spitting. 'You should be thanking me on your knees that I got rid of them for you.'

'Oh yes, thank you! Thank you thank you!' He was beside himself. 'But this is the last time, I tell you – the last time you interfere with me.' She turned away her face and he grasped it and turned it back again: 'Do you hear me? The last time!'

'Oh my God, help me!' She put up her arm to shield herself. 'My son is striking me!'

Maria also cried out, but Som said in disgust, 'As if I would.'

'Now you see with your own eyes,' the stricken mother told Maria.

'See what?' Som demanded. 'What's she to see with her own eyes?'

'The kind of son I have who would strike his mother, may God forgive him!'

She burst into a storm of sobs and Maria tried to comfort her. She would not be comforted; she shook her head, she flung her hands before her face – though with one eye kept free, she saw Som leaving the salon. She told Maria: 'Call him back.' When Maria didn't move quickly enough, she reproached her: 'You're not helping me.'

Som had left the house and Maria had to pursue him down the street. Unlike his mother, she gave no entertainment to the neighbourhood by making a scene but remained her usual sedate self. When she caught up with him, she said quietly, 'You mustn't hurt her.'

'Of course. Everything I want to do for myself hurts her.'

Maria would have liked to say something like 'Because she loves you so much'. But although she had lately learned to know such feelings, using words for them did not yet come easily to her. Instead she said, 'Please come back. She's there alone waiting for you. She just wants to see you.'

She was pleading as though for herself. Som was amused; he said, 'How she makes everyone dance to her tune.' He was still amused when he returned to the salon with her, so Anuradha felt relieved and glad. 'Come here,' she said. When he joined her on the divan, she kissed him and ruffled his hair, which was thinning. She said she would rub it with an ayurvedic ointment to make it grow again, and when he joked that this might make his scalp fall off, she said in loving reproach, 'As if a mother could do anything to harm her son.' She kissed him again, at the same time glancing towards Maria in some sort of triumph that said 'You see how my son loves me'.

Maria found herself experiencing another new sensation for which she had no name. Vaguely she realised that it was something to do with Som and his mother – the way they were together, excluding everyone. Yet, in their collaboration, Anuradha had begun to draw Maria more and more intimately to herself. In order not to interrupt the work, she even insisted that they should spend their nights together in the salon. Then she opened up for her each of her words, subtly extracting, as from the seeds of an exotic fruit, its most piquant scent and flavour. If Maria was slow to follow, as she often was, Anuradha checked her anger and became patient and loving, as though only the most delicate touch could be brought to the work in hand. Maria no longer thought of her departure, and neither apparently did Anuradha.

It was Som who reminded them both.

Anuradha sighed deeply. 'Yes, we shall miss her very much,' she said, fondling Maria's face.

Som smiled. 'And me? You won't miss me?'

Anuradha stopped fondling Maria and Som stopped smiling. 'You knew it,' he said. 'You knew I was leaving.' Anuradha said nothing.

Afterwards Som told Maria, 'This is her way. She pretends that something she doesn't want to happen is not happening.'

Maria said, 'If we both go, she would be left alone.'

Next day Maria came to Som with a new suggestion. She prefaced it with, 'No, of course you have to go, you can't give up your fellowship. Absolutely not.'

Then she said that, while it wouldn't be possible for him to postpone his fellowship, she might be able to extend her leave again. He accepted this proposal gratefully, and on the same day Maria cancelled her ticket and confirmed his. Although this new arrangement was made for Anuradha's sake, each failed to mention it to her. When Som was uneasy at leaving her to face his mother alone, Maria assured him it was all right, that she would manage. She was herself astonished at the way she *was* managing, to the extent of packing her suitcase to convince Anuradha of her departure. She also helped Som to make his preparations in secret, and to deposit his luggage with a friend.

The end of August was very hot, and since the only air conditioning was in the salon, Som spent the last few nights before his departure sleeping on the roof. Too stout and breathless to be able to follow him, Anuradha stood at the foot of the stairs to call up to him. When there was no answer, she sent Maria with some message invented on the spur of the moment; this Maria recognised to be only an unnecessary pretext to assure him that his mother loved him. Maria went to the foot of the stairs, stood there for a while and returned to say that Som was asleep. Anuradha smiled at the thought of her son sweetly asleep on the roof of her house; but mixed in with her smile there was something sad, a nostalgia for her own nights on that same roof, years ago when she could still get up there.

Those nights continued to exist in a cycle of poems she had written about them, and it was these she was now inspiring Maria to translate. They spoke of the sky above the roof veiled in night and pierced by stars, and the new moon, frail as jasmine, set above a nearby minaret. But mostly they were about the lovers who had rolled around up there with Anuradha, one hand on her mouth to stifle her screams for fear of arousing her father asleep downstairs. And in later years it was not the father but the husband in bed downstairs, and one night Anuradha discovered that he was not asleep. From beneath her lover (a minor poet), she opened her eyes and met those of her husband gazing at her from the entrance to the roof. By the time she had freed herself from the embrace, her husband had gone, so that she might have taken her vision to be imaginary. Yet she knew he had been there and that he had seen. Next day, apart from a slight contraction of his lips, he was his usual tender self with her, as silently understanding as no one, no other human being had ever been with her. And for that she loved him the way she had never loved anyone – no, not even those lovers up there under the stars who had aroused her to an ecstasy that made her completely forget the husband she so loved.

This stanza about the husband was the end of the cycle that Maria translated. It was also the end of her sabbatical, and Anuradha arranged a farewell party for her last evening. Maria knew very well that it was not her last evening but Som's. Fortunately, with his own farewell parties given for him by his colleagues, Som was rarely at home; and when he did return, he crept straight up to the roof. Anuradha several times sent Maria to inform him about the party – 'And the time! Make sure he knows the time!' for, like herself, Som was habitually late. Maria again went to the foot of the stairs and stood there for a while before returning to reassure Anuradha.

The evening party was attended by poets and musicians, some of them famous, others half starved. Leaving their shoes on the threshold, they crowded into the salon and sat on the carpet with their naked feet tucked under them. The air was suffused with the heavy perfumes worn by the wealthier artistes and the cheap bazaar ones by the others; also, mixed in with the spiced delicacies brought in from the cook-house, there was the smell of the fierce little brown cigarettes, many of them chain-smoked along with Anuradha. A lot of teasing went on, mainly of one famous old poet who was half paralysed and sat in a wheelchair. The fun revolved around the coquetry of his manner and of his dress – the finest Lucknow kurtas, bracelet and earrings to attract the young girls he still so ardently desired. He didn't deny it, and contentedly chewing his betel, he quoted famous verses in Persian and Urdu from dead old poets renowned for their undiminished libido.

Anuradha, shining in purple silk, reclined on the divan; at her feet, Maria was perched on a stool, clutching the pages of her translation from which she was to read. Anuradha hissed at her, 'Are you sure you told him?', for Som had not yet appeared. And again, 'Are you sure you told him the right time?' Maria couldn't answer, her mind was confused by the fear about the secret departure, as well as the fear of reading her translations before this assembly of experts.

At last Anuradha decided she could delay no longer. She intoned the original of one of her stanzas and, waiting for the ecstasy of her audience to subside, she signalled to Maria to read out her translation.

Maria was so nervous that she dropped some of her papers and had to be helped by the nearest poet to retrieve them. Then she discovered the pages had got mixed up, so that she was no longer sure her translation was of the stanza Anuradha had recited. It made no difference – she knew that whatever she read couldn't in any way come up to the sonorous sounds of the original that still reverberated in the salon. She saw Anuradha frown, her dissatisfaction with Maria exacerbated by Som's failure to appear. 'You forgot to tell him,' she accused Maria – and then she launched into another grand and glorious recitation, eliciting more cries of pain and joy from her admirers.

Maria tried to read her translation; but aware of her inadequacy, she trembled so much that she could hardly go on. The paralysed poet took pity on her and began to declaim one of his own compositions. This swept over the audience with the same effect as Anuradha's, though his way was more delicate, more feminine, and – quite unlike Anuradha – submissive and accepting. But passionate too, and with a force that made Maria tremble with excitement. Far from being cast down by her own failure, she felt exalted to be in the company of these poets. Behind her gold-rimmed spectacles, her pale eyes shone with new resolve – to dedicate herself completely to Anuradha, to be guided and moulded by her, to become worthy of her.

And when everyone, deeply satisfied with the evening's entertainment, had taken their leave, Maria wanted to *declare* herself to Anuradha. But even if she had been able to find the right, or any, words for this, Anuradha didn't give her a chance. She indicated the papers in Maria's hand: 'Tonight you heard the difference: the waters flowing from a living heart and this – this – a stagnant pond; a wooden tongue.' Snatching the pages, she threw them to the floor, and then she poured out the kind of invective she usually reserved for her servants, her tenants and for Som; and maybe some of it was meant for him, for not being there.

It was at this moment that he arrived home from his own farewell party. Hearing his mother's furious voice from the salon, he opened the door – Anuradha saw him at once. She shouted, 'Where were you? Everyone was asking, "Where is your son?" And I had to say, "No, I have no son!"'

Bewildered, Som looked at Maria – at once Anuradha pounced on her. 'You didn't tell him!' Before Maria could protest – 'You're lying!' Anuradha cried.

Maria hid her guilty face by bending down for her scattered papers. Som tried to help her, but his mother commanded, 'Give them here!' She took the pages from him, then tore them across, first one, then another, then all the rest, flashing bolts of fury out of her kohl-rimmed eyes.

It was a relief to Maria to take refuge in her own room. But that night she was entirely sleepless, and finally she tiptoed back to the salon. She put her ear to the door and heard Anuradha sighing and muttering to herself. She called timidly for permission to enter, but Anuradha wouldn't let her. 'I'm displeased!' she called back. The word 'displeased' pleased Maria – it was mild, it could easily be overcome. Probably soon Anuradha herself would call for her. Maria sat waiting for this call in her little room. Her spuriously packed suitcase stood open, and she decided to unpack it the next day, after she and Anuradha had got up and Som would have left.

Suddenly she remembered that she hadn't given him the key to her apartment in Boston. Very quietly, though alert in case this was the time Anuradha decided to call for her, she made her way up the stairs to the roof. How different it was here from the nights of Anuradha's poetry. There were no stars or moon visible in a sky overhung with pollution; and instead of the scent of flowering bushes, the air was thick with some smell acrid enough to be burning rubber tyres.

Som was awake, slapping at the mosquitoes that whined around him. As soon as he saw Maria, he said, 'When she finds out that I've gone and we've lied to her – no, I can't leave.'

But he *had* to leave! 'Don't worry,' she said. 'I'm here to care for her. Don't worry at all. You mustn't.' A mosquito sat quite blatantly on her cheek; she let it, alert to not missing a call from downstairs.

He said, 'I can't run off to Boston and leave you alone with her. After all, she's *my* responsibility, not yours.'

'No, *mine*,' Maria almost exclaimed – too passionately, she felt at once, so she continued in a different tone, in her scholar's voice: 'You know the Sanskrit word *Sraddha*? No, it's not your field.' She smiled, remembering what Anuradha said about his studies, which she compared to a donkey being made to pull a load of useless books up a mountain. '*Sraddha*,' she explained. 'The attitude of the aspirant to the guide. This attitude is of devotion; of faith and reverence; of obedience.'

'Yes. Everything she's always wanted from me and everyone else in the world ... She's trying to come up,' he said with alarm at the sound of a step on the stairs.

'She's trying to come to me,' Maria said. 'That's there too in our word: not only the desire of the student for the master but that of the master for the student. Sanskrit has so many levels of meaning. For instance, besides everything else, *Sraddha* means pregnancy.' Caught up in her favourite subject, she was about to tell him that pregnancy here carried the sense of yearning – the way a pregnant woman yearns for something that alone will satisfy her deepest appetite. But she stopped herself, considering him not ready for such esoteric knowledge. Instead she said, 'Your taxi is coming at six a.m. I'll be with her all night, and by morning she'll be fast asleep. She won't hear a thing.'

More clumping footsteps could be heard on the stairs, and Som became desperate: 'She'll fall, she'll twist her ankle, sprain her wrist – it's happened before; and then of course I have to stay – what good son wouldn't be there for his mother?'

'Here's the key,' Maria said. 'One is for the upper lock – you'll have to work it out, which is which.'

She hurried to the top of the stairs. She saw that Anuradha had reached the third step and there she had to sit and rest. She looked up at Maria, and there was something so piteous in her look that, without a backward glance at Som, Maria ran down to her. She squeezed herself beside her on the third step; she twined her long thin arms around the massive poetess, she whispered in her ear, 'Anuradha, Anuradha.'

Whatever had been Anuradha's intention of calling for her – whether it was to curse, insult or to beg for her forgiveness – now, as that whisper of her name dropped down into her fiery soul, Anuradha, like Maria, thought only of the work that lay ahead of them, the hours and days and months and years of their nights of poetry, their wild nights together.

MOSTLY ARTS AND ENTERTAINMENT

Talent

Although highly organised in her office – she was a talent agent – at home Magda was terribly untidy. 'How can you live like that,' her mother said, whenever she came to visit her. But she wasn't encouraged to come often. No one was: Magda liked to keep her place to herself. She didn't have many personal friends. All her time was taken up by business, her lunches, her dinners, even breakfasts were turned into conferences. Only weekends were free; and by the time they came around, she didn't feel like seeing any more people, and anyway there was no one to see once the offices were closed and everyone left for their weekend places or plans. Magda stayed mostly in bed, reading the newspapers; if the telephone rang, it was always her mother asking if she was coming to see her. Magda said yes, she would come, although by Sunday afternoon she usually decided she wouldn't but would just stay where she was until everything began again on Monday morning. She dug herself deeper into her crumpled bedclothes, only getting up to heap plates of left-overs for herself from the refrigerator. Often Sunday nights she couldn't sleep, from indigestion caused by excessive amounts of stale food eaten too quickly. Her sheets were stained with grease and with the tears she shed, usually without cause, or any that she knew of.

All this changed after she met Ellie. For one thing, she cleaned up her apartment. She threw out long-discarded papers, wiped her grimy windows – she stood on a ladder, whistling as she reached up high to rub and shine. It was like a new beginning; it *was* a new beginning. Yet her first meeting with Ellie had not been auspicious. She hadn't cared for the way Ellie had dawdled into her office, with no idea what a big favour had been extended to her, a completely unknown young English girl. Magda was doing this favour for one of her colleagues, who had asked her to give a few minutes of her time to what might turn out to be a new talent. Five minutes was all Magda did give – she had a string of other appointments and was certainly not going to put herself out for this ungracious girl. When Ellie sauntered out, as casually as she had sauntered in, she left a tape on the desk, which Magda failed to see and might very well have thrown in the trash if she had; but her secretary conscientiously put it in Magda's briefcase, where she discovered it in searching for something more important. This happened at the end of one of those long empty weekends, so that Magda played it out of boredom, with no expectation at all. But the voice that emerged from the player startled her; she played the tape again, and then again. Next day she sent for Ellie – not to the office but to the French Pavilion where she gave her a big expense-account lunch.

Whenever Magda took on a new client, she worked out a strategy on how to advance that particular talent's career. She considered each one individually, meticulously and with cunning – it was what made her such a fabulous agent – so that it could not be said that she gave Ellie more consideration than anyone else. What was different was that she introduced her to her cousin Robert, for the first time mixing her family and her business – although Robert, besides being her cousin, could also come under the category of business, for he was a highly successful composer of musical comedies. Magda's reluctance to make use of the relationship could be traced back to various causes, mostly to do with their childhood, and with his mother, and with her mother, and so on into the tangled web of a family's wariness with each other. She *was* wary of Robert; she couldn't exactly say that she didn't like him or trust him – though sometimes, it was true, she did neither. Yet she trusted him with Ellie, calling him in as part of her game plan for her.

'Must I?' he said when she asked him to see Ellie. This was on the phone, but she could exactly picture his expression of weary distaste (he had had it as a boy, for practically all suggestions coming from his cousin Magda). But when he did meet Ellie and had her sing for him, he at once agreed about her talent. That was the beginning of Ellie's career, though it was a few more years before it became spectacular.

Meanwhile, she lost her place to live. One day she arrived in Magda's office – this was becoming a daily event, for Magda had ordered her to report to her personally on her auditions and to discuss other prospects; and just generally to report. Unfortunately, Magda was too busy to give as much time to Ellie as she would have liked; and on that particular day she had looked at her watch twice and said, 'Oh God.' Usually Ellie was complaisant about being shunted out, but that day she just sat on; as though waiting, or as though having nowhere else to go. This latter turned out to be the case: for when Magda looked at her watch again and said, 'I really must *run* – come in tomorrow, OK?', Ellie remained where she was. She looked up at Magda, who was poised to depart; she said, 'I lost my place.'

Magda looked back at her in surprise. 'I thought you didn't have a place.'

'I don't. They've turned me out of theirs; their place.' Ellie usually assumed that everyone was as familiar with her circumstances as she herself was and needed no explanation. However, she now gave one more clue: 'Because of her boyfriend moving back in.'

Magda suspected rather than knew Ellie's living arrangements. They did not bear looking into very carefully, consisting of shifting from one hole to another in a part of the city that was common ground for criminals and young middle-class bohemians.

'Don't you have anywhere to go? No other friends?'

Ellie became uncharacteristically voluble. She explained how she had parked her stuff with some people she knew and that some other people she knew had allowed her to sleep on their floor, but since they were expecting a sanitary inspection due to an infestation of cockroaches, she could only stay there for a couple of nights. 'And then?' Magda asked. 'Then I don't know,' Ellie said, and again she raised her eyes to Magda, in candid submission this time.

Magda was not the first person to whom Ellie had appealed for help. She had only gone to her after Robert had turned her down. She had gone straight to his studio; she thought he lived there. He didn't, but then she knew very little about him except that he was Magda's cousin; and of course this famous composer. She had only met him that one time when she had sung for him. He hadn't said much to her about her voice but she was aware that he liked it – and there was something in the quality of his appreciation that *she* liked. Maybe because she herself tended to be monosyllabic, she felt the full weight of the one syllable he had uttered. 'Yes,' he had said – the sort of yes she said in her own mind when something came out right.

His studio was the top floor of a brownstone. On her first visit she had asked for him by name, but this second time she only said, 'He sent for me,' tilting her head towards the top of the house from where piano music sounded. 'You know where to go?' asked the young man who had opened the door the first as well as the second time – was he the butler? He was very good-looking. She went straight up and didn't even knock, knowing she might not be heard above the piano. As soon as she entered, he stopped playing. 'What do you want?' he said, his voice suggesting even to her, who was too needy to be sensitive, that maybe her visit was a mistake.

'I told you I'd send for you when I had something,' he said.

'I know.' She hovered within the door so miserably that she was sure he would relent and be nice to her.

'Then why do you come slinking in here?' he said, not nice at all.

'You said you liked the way I sing.'

Robert, still sitting at the piano, looked towards her with narrowed eyes. 'Did she tell you to come? What's-her-name – Magda?'

After a split second, in which she tried to decide whether it would be better to lie or not, she shook her head. 'I lost my place,' she explained but was met by an icy stare that forced her to continue: 'So if you wanted to send for me, you wouldn't know where to find me.'

'What's that accent you have? It's appalling.'

'That's what they say: my mum and dad. They've got lovely accents, like actors. They *are* actors. Shakespeare and Noel Coward and all the other classics.'

He waggled the fingers of one hand for her to come over to the piano. He pointed to some notes he had scribbled and told her to sing them. After frowning at them for a moment, she did so, evidently to his satisfaction for he said 'Yes' again. Then he told her to leave, which she did, slowly and in the hope of being called back, but he had resumed playing his piano before she even reached the door.

When Ellie moved in, Magda expected that everything would soon be covered with a young girl's disorder, discarded panties and lipsticks that had lost their tops. But this did not happen. Ellie left nothing lying about, as if she had nothing. After every meal she ate, she washed and wiped her plate and cup and stowed them away. When Magda marvelled at her neatness, she said it was because of always living in a very small space. From her earliest childhood, she was used to occupying a single room with her parents on their tours, when they were lucky enough to be hired by a repertory company; and when they weren't, they waited out the time in lodgings in some far-out London suburb, usually the upstairs part of a semi-detached house, with a gas-ring to cook on and the lavatory on the landing.

In the mornings, dressed up for her meetings in her business suit and blouse with matching bow, Magda would tiptoe into the spare bedroom, careful not to wake Ellie. But she was always awake, sitting up in bed and brushing her hair. Magda reminded her of auditions she might have fixed for her that day, and also asked, trying to sound casual but sounding shy instead, what time she thought she might be calling in at the office? She longed to but refrained from inquiring about Ellie's plans for the evening. She herself came home earlier than she had ever done before; sometimes Ellie wasn't there, and if she came in very late, Magda would leave supper for her and go to bed, so that Ellie shouldn't feel she had been waited up for. Next morning she said, 'Where did you go yesterday?'

Ellie yawned. 'Oh, the usual.'

'In SoHo?'

'And around there. Thanks for the quiche last night.'

'Did you like it?'

'Yum-yum.'

Ellie went mostly to the same place: the house in the Village where Robert had his studio. Usually the same person let her in – he *was* the butler, and his name was Fred. She went straight upstairs. The first couple of times Robert had fussed again, but after that he let her stay. She was no trouble at all, sitting very quietly against the wall with her arms around her knees; sometimes she was useful, when he asked her to sing something he was trying out. She stayed till he sent her away – which was later every day, for as his work progressed he worked longer hours. She had assumed that he lived in the studio, but one day he left off early and said he had to go home. She said, 'You *are* home.' He didn't bother to answer but opened the door to let her precede him down the stairs. When they got to the street, he said, 'I go this way'; she tried to follow but he said, 'No, you go that way.'

As it happened, Magda too got home early that day and was delighted to find Ellie already there. At once Magda suggested all sorts of outings – dinner in an Italian restaurant, a movie, whatever Ellie wanted; but it turned out all Ellie wanted was to stay home and talk to Magda. 'No, really?' said Magda, laughing and pushing back her hair fallen into her flushed face. She went into her bedroom to change into something more relaxed, care- ful to put away her clothes as neatly as Ellie did hers; in this respect, Magda had become a reformed character. She was just slipping into her kaftan – her best one, gorgeous in black and gold – when Ellie came in without knocking. Magda quickly tugged the robe down over her hips and thighs – had Ellie seen them? 'Oh sorry,' Ellie said, so maybe she had. Magda flushed scarlet; she really must go on that diet, or eat less, or both, or something. But Ellie had other things on her mind than Magda's figure.

'When's he calling people? Robert? For his new piece?'

'How do you know he's writing one?'

'Oh, you hear things. At the auditions. Like who's doing what when. Everyone talks at auditions.'

'How did you get on today? Are they calling you back?'

'Maybe.' Ellie tried to remember to what audition she was supposed to have gone; she had forgotten to attend, as she did most days. 'Funny, isn't it: he's your cousin and you don't know what he's doing ... Don't you like him, or what? Then why do you never see him? I mean, your *cousin*.'

'Well, actually I was supposed to see him today. But I got out of it, and thank God I did because now you and I can have the evening together. What do you want to eat? I'll call Callcuisine, their menu's right here –'

'Where?'

'It's in the drawer behind you.'

'Where were you going to see him today?'

Magda was puzzled for a moment, then she laughed. 'Oh you're still on Robert? His mother's having her birthday party today: Aunt Hannah. Big deal. Of course Mother's there – *my* mother, Lottie –'

'But shouldn't you go? If it's her birthday and she's having a party and all. You haven't said you're *not* going?'

'I called to say I have this ghastly throat. Hannah's scared to death of germs. Just hand me that menu, would you – in the drawer, just behind you? Thank you, darling.'

'You could say you're better. Then we could go. We could both go.'

'You must be joking.'

Ellie's lips trembled so that she could hardly speak, but she managed it somehow: 'You're ashamed of me.' Magda quickly laid her hand over Ellie's mouth to silence her, but Ellie removed it. 'That's why you don't want me to go to your aunt's party or meet her or anyone. I *know* you don't want me to meet your mum – you speak to her every day and you've never even told her about me. You're ashamed of me, that's the reason. I'm not grand enough.'

Magda gave a dry laugh. 'It's me who's not grand enough. Oh, she's proud of me in a way, that I'm this agent with this big deal agency everyone knows about. But it's not what she wants; not for *her* daughter. "You're more like Hannah," she tells me, and believe me, coming from her that's *not* a compliment. Hannah? I told you: Robert's mother.'

'Are you?'

'Like her? Certainly not! She's the Teutonic side of the family. I used to dread going to her place as a kid. "Don't tread on the carpet with those *shoes!*"'

'What about Robert?'

'I never did fathom how he can bear living with her, but he must like it all right because he's still there. His studio is strictly for business, for his work. For everything else he runs home to Mother. He's a classic case, if ever there was one.'

'Where do they live?'

'On Park, in one of those stodgy old apartment houses full of bankers and real-estate developers. People like my parents preferred to live on Fifth—'

'Where on Park?'

'No, on Fifth – oh, you mean Hannah? Park and 85th, as if it matters. I cannot believe, Ellie, that you and I are having this one evening together and we're sitting here talking about *my family*.'

Ellie was perched very meekly on one of the throne-like velvet chairs that decorated the stately lobby. When Robert stood in front of her and said, 'What are you doing here?' she silently stared up at him. 'What do you want?' he said, tapping a foot impatiently.

'To see you,' she answered and got up, still staring at him. She followed him through the main doors held open for them by a doorman. As soon as they were outside, he told her, 'You must not, ever, come here.'

'But if I have to see you very badly?'

It had begun to get dark, also to rain. The road glistened with the reflections of headlights swimming down the Avenue and a swarm of lit-up windows glimmered through the wet dusk. Rain appeared to be Ellie's natural element: the way it washed her pale face and made her hair cling to her cheeks recalled centuries of English waifs growing like tall weeds out of their gutters.

'And I don't want you coming to the studio either.'

'Oh but I *have* to.'

'Why? Why do you have to?'

'To see you.'

He had no time or inclination to be kind to a crazy girl. 'I'm going to tell everyone not to let you in so you'd better not try.' When she was silent, he said, 'When I'm ready, I'll send for you. Till then, stay away from me. You understand?'

She shivered with awe and pleasure. 'You're so cruel.'

'Yes, and I'm getting wet too, so I'm going in and you're going home, wherever that may be.'

'I'm staying with your cousin but I want to stay with you. I want to sleep with you. I mean, only to sleep near you. In the same room and hear you breathe.'

He put his hand in his pocket and took out some notes to give her for her cab fare. She held them carelessly in her hand, where they got wet. He tried to wave down a cab, but they had all turned on their Off Duty signs and swiftly slithered past, one of them so close that it splashed him.

'Your suit's getting spoiled,' Ellie said. She touched it admiringly – Ellie knew nothing of men's clothes, or any clothes, but she recognised quality when she saw it.

'I don't have to stand here with you,' he said. 'You can get your own cab.'

'I can walk.'

'Or walk, or whatever you want.'

'I'll see you tomorrow then.'

'What did I just tell you?' Already half turned towards home, he stood still to look down at her sternly. She was so wet by now that she looked stringy, half drowned, pitiful, but the way she looked back at him, smiling slightly in a superior way, it was as if she pitied him – for being unaware of the situation that had arisen between them.

All day Magda had been looking forward to an evening alone with Ellie. She took care to get home first, which gave her time to dress up – she chose the black and gold kaftan again – and lay the table very nicely with candles and silver and cloth napkins. She heard a key in the lock and called out: 'Is that you?'

'Yes it's me, darling.' It was Lottie, her mother, the only other person with a key to the apartment.

'Oh, you look gorgeous! Stunning!' exclaimed Lottie at the sight of Magda dressed up. Next moment she was thrown into even greater astonishment, for not only Magda but the apartment was transformed. Instead of the former mess, it was as clean and fragrant as a bower where two virgins lived. Lottie's eyes fell on the table laid for two. 'I see I've come on the wrong day,' she said coyly and seemed completely prepared to depart immediately.

Magda muttered, 'You can sit down for a bit.' It *was* the wrong day, but her mother came rarely. She was very discreet about spacing her visits, though she must have had many lonely hours by herself at home.

'Are you sure, darling?' Absolutely delighted, Lottie unpinned her little hat from her golden coiffure. Lottie was always turned out perfectly and could be viewed any hour of the day, or even night except for her hairnet. 'I haven't seen you for such ages – and you haven't been calling, darling, but now I see you're otherwise engaged.' Her eyes twinkled at the laid table again, and from there at Magda, who remained expressionless. 'And you didn't get to Hannah's party – lucky you! It was the usual disaster. What I find disgusting is the way she trumpets her age around. So all right – you are whatever you are – but you don't have to write it in pink icing all over your birthday cake. Next she'll have that many candles – if there are that many candles to be had ... Is it someone you just met?' she could no longer refrain from asking about the table laid for two.

'It's a client.'

'Oh. A client.' Lottie was pleased, excited. 'Anyone very famous? Would I have heard of him?'

Magda hesitated for only a moment. 'It's a she.'

If it hadn't been so irritating, she might have been amused by the way her mother's face fell. Since Ellie would be home any moment – and why wasn't she already? – Magda thought it best to continue: 'She's living here. Only for now. She's got nowhere to stay.'

'Why not?'

'What do you mean, why not? Not everyone has a ten-room duplex on Fifth Avenue, you might be surprised to hear.'

'But she's your client. I thought they were all rich and famous. That's what Robert says,' she defended herself against Magda's response. 'He said it again the other day – he told Hannah, "Don't worry about Magda, she has all these rich and famous clients."'

'And why should Hannah be worrying about me?'

'Oh you know, her usual.' Lottie squirmed, partly embarrassed, partly indignant. '"What's wrong with your Magda? I don't hear any mention of a boyfriend and why isn't she getting married?" *She* should talk,' said Lottie, indignation winning out. 'But of course she has her line about Robert: "He'll never get married and it's no one's fault but my own for making it too cosy for him at home." As if she didn't know, along with the rest of the world.'

Ellie had slipped in so quietly that Lottie had a shock when she was suddenly in the room with them. Magda was used to Ellie's stealthy movements, and anyway had been waiting for her. 'This is Ellie,' she said to Lottie, who acknowledged her with a gracious inclination of her coiffure. She mistook Ellie for the maid and was about to congratulate her on the unwonted neatness of the apartment when Magda said, 'She's my client I've been telling you about.'

'*She's* your client!' exclaimed Lottie with an amazement that bordered on scorn, and it took her a moment before she could come up with an apology. 'I was expecting an older person.'

'I'm nearly twenty,' Ellie said.

Lottie measured her up and down, not in appreciation: 'You look younger.'

'I could go on the bus half-fare till I was eighteen,' Ellie said.

'I'm not surprised. You're English, aren't you. I love the English accent, I could listen to it all day. Sid and I had some very memorable vacations in London. We always stayed at the Savoy; it's so central and you can get to all the theatres. We saw some great shows. Sid was interested because he had money on Broadway.'

'You never told me your father was in the theatre,' Ellie said to Magda.

'No, dear,' Lottie said. 'My husband was in the refrigeration business but he had money in Broadway shows – what they call an angel and that's exactly what he was: an angel. He was a wonderful human being and Magda takes after him completely, bless her.'

Ellie said, 'I can see she doesn't take after you.' That made Lottie laugh, though as usual at the mention of her late husband she had become tearful. 'I mean like she doesn't look like you,' Ellie went on, not because she felt she had been tactless but to be more explicit. It was true that mother and daughter, though both large, could not have been more different. Magda was dark and chunky, muscular, whereas Lottie was soft, fat, pastel.

'No, she's dark like her daddy. I'm the only blonde in the family. The one thing Magda has from me, unfortunately, is a weight problem. We should both go to that place in Florida again, darling, I'll treat you for Christmas and we can get rid of some of this,' she said, playfully poking herself in both hips. But aware of her daughter's mounting impatience, she said, 'Well, I guess I should be going and leave you two girls to talk about your business.'

'Why don't you eat with us?'

This invitation came from Ellie, and after waiting a fraction too long for Magda to second it, Lottie gathered herself for departure. 'Thank you, dears, but I'd better go see my sister Hannah or she'll start feeling sorry for herself. I tell her, we all have to face it, being on our own, it comes to all of us in the end.'

'But she's got Robert living with her,' Ellie said.

'Oh, you know Robert? She knows Robert?' Lottie asked Magda and continued: 'These days he's working very late at the studio and anyway he has his own life to lead – young people do, they should.' She finished pinning on her little hat and said to Ellie, 'I hope you'll come visit with me, if you can spare a little time. I know you have a very busy schedule.'

'I've got lots of time. When should I come?'

*

Ellie spent most of her days at Robert's house. She drifted there slowly, stopped on the way to look into boutique windows – there were several selling funky antique clothing, with fringes and trailing skirts and pointed satin shoes, the kind she might have liked to own if she thought about clothes or had money to buy them (later, when she did have money, that was what she bought, not second-hand but made specially for her by designers). She hopped over the sidewalk on one leg and in the same way up the stoop to the restored Federal entrance of Robert's house.

It was always Fred who let her in, and one day he said, 'He's been asking for you.'

'Oh my God,' said Ellie.

'Says he needs you upstairs.'

'Oh my God. How do I look?'

'Same,' Fred said.

Nervously smoothing her cotton frock, she went upstairs. Robert was working at the piano, but he nodded for her to stay and finally he told her to sing something he pointed out to her. She got it wrong a couple of times. 'Oh shit,' she said, but he was patient and told her to try again, and then again. When she did get it right, it was like nothing on this earth.

He took his hands off the piano keys and shut his eyes, indicating fatigue. When he opened them again and saw her still standing there, he said, 'Thanks, that's all.' She didn't move, so he said 'Thank you' again, more sharply.

'She's thrown me out,' Ellie said. He didn't react, so she continued: 'Because of you. She said I wasn't to come and see you and I said I'll come and see you till I'm dead.' She corrected herself: 'Even after I'm dead.'

That made him laugh, if not quite in amusement. But next moment he drew in his breath and then blew it out again, as if trying to blow something away. She continued undeterred: 'I've got nowhere to stay.'

'So what am I supposed to do?'

'I could stay here.' He exclaimed in a way that made her urge: 'You're not here at night so it wouldn't be all that horrible for you. I could sleep on that thing there – look,' she said, nimbly getting on his chaise longue. 'It's quite OK for me, I can almost stretch out.'

'For heaven's sakes! And with shoes on! Have you any idea what I paid for that fabric?'

She got up. 'I could stay with Fred,' she offered. 'Not in his room but in the kitchen. Why *not*? I'm very clean.'

'Don't you have any friends?'

'Only you and her. If you are my friend. And she's thrown me out, so where am I?'

'I could give you money for a hotel.'

'All right.'

She sat with her hands patiently folded, while he got his chequebook out. 'What's your name?' he asked.

'Ellie.'

'I think I knew that – your other name?'

'Ellie Sprigge.' He was about to write it when she asked him to make the cheque out to 'Cash' because she didn't have an account. 'Do you think I ought to change my name? For the stage? So they don't make up rhymes like Ellie Sprigge is a pig, or worse, like they did at school.'

'Sprigge is perfect. Part spring, part sprig.'

'Is that how you think of me?'

'What makes you think I think of you at all?'

He gave her the cheque, which was for a large amount; money was the one thing Robert was generous with. She hid it in her knickers, and when he told her to leave, she did, not wanting to push her luck any further that day. Usually she walked everywhere, always having plenty of time on her hands, but now she treated herself to a bus-ride uptown. She felt it was time to follow up on the invitation Magda's mother had extended to her.

Lottie's apartment was on a high floor, with plenty of light and air, and the rugs were white and the furniture white and gold. Lottie loved company and nowadays didn't have anywhere near enough. And it was a special treat for her to have a friend of Magda's interested in seeing all her photos. She brought out albums that started from the day of Magda's birth: Ellie peered in eagerly, but all she saw was Magda and Lottie and Sid and their friends, and just once – 'There's Robert, my nephew.'

'Where?'

'That skinny boy behind Magda – looking as usual like no one's good enough for him.'

Ellie had seen enough; she leaned back and asked, 'Is that what he's like?'

'From day one. He'd come to Magda's birthday parties, too grand to play any of the games, just went off by himself to try out our piano and tell us it was out of tune. I'm not saying it wasn't, but imagine – the chutzpah, from a boy of six. But it was his mother's fault, and even today she's still treating him like he's God. You should see her apartment, it's a regular shrine for him –'

'I'd like to. See her apartment.'

'You'd hate it. She's got no taste at all.'

'I want to get to know all Magda's family. I think it's very nice to have a family.'

'Now isn't that sweet: from a young girl like you. That's really touching. I'm touched.'

When Robert came home, he found Ellie sitting between his aunt Lottie and his mother, who had taken out her albums of photographs of himself. Ellie looked up from her study of four-year-old Robert on the beach with bucket and spade; she locked eyes with the adult Robert, whose expression was as knowing and alert as the child's. But anything could be read into *her* eyes: were they amused, triumphant, submissive, rueful, or really just blank?

Robert's mother Hannah was very particular whom she received in her home, but she continued to allow Ellie's visits. Ellie was no trouble at all. She asked for nothing and received nothing – Hannah did not serve between meals – and she seemed perfectly happy being allowed to sit there and look at Hannah's photograph albums. Hannah was no conversationalist, and Ellie's visits mostly passed in silence between them, except for questions and answers about Robert's age in one of the photographs, or its location. The ambience of the apartment was as sombre as Hannah herself – in this as in all else a contrast to Lottie's apartment, where Ellie visited immediately afterwards. Lottie was lavish with refreshments, and Ellie made up for her abstinence in the other home. Lottie was also lavish with her conversation, but here Ellie drew less sustenance than from the few crumbs of information she received from the other sister.

When her husband Sid was still alive, he and Lottie used to laugh about Hannah and her massive furniture and silver bowls and ugly paintings that she presided over so meticulously. They also mocked the dull parties she and her banker husband held in there for their banker friends, with stolid food prepared by their German cook – so different from their own entertainments, to which actresses came. But now the memory of those parties made her apartment seem all the emptier to Lottie, and she was glad to have her sister only two blocks away. Sometimes she stuck it out alone till almost ten o'clock; but however late she came, Hannah never said, as she would have done not so long ago, 'What a time to visit people – I was just going to bed.'

'What, Robert's not home yet?' Lottie asked on one such evening, arriving past everyone's bedtime.

'He's working very late these days. And it's going to be even later once they go into rehearsal. The price of fame,' she smugly sighed.

'Same with Magda. I worry myself sick about her working so hard and not looking after herself. In a way, I'm glad that girl's with her – at least she's someone around the place and she's very devoted to Magda, so that's something.'

'She's very devoted to Robert too. He's her idol – she's said it to me not once but every day.'

'She comes to see you every day?'

'I don't mind it. She doesn't say much, poor thing.'

'No, she's not very interesting. It's really kind of Magda to let her stay. She's not her type of person at all, when you think of the sort of fascinating people Magda knows. I think that's your phone. Who's calling you so late?'

'It must be Robert.'

It was; and when she returned from answering, Hannah reported, 'He said not to wait up for him. He always calls when he's working late. He's so thoughtful. Sometimes he can't get away till three or four in the morning – but he always comes home; he doesn't like to stay in the studio. Naturally, this is his home; all his things are here.'

'Well, you're lucky he's not married,' Lottie said, but with a sigh.

'Oh, a man like Robert could never marry,' Hannah assured her. Lottie stared at her in surprise, but Hannah went on calmly: 'Look at him – home at all hours, who would stand for that? His work is who he's married to.'

'I guess it's the same with Magda. It's a shame ... No, not for them, what do they care – for you and me! I'd kill for it,' she said. 'A little grandchild, just like Magda, a little girl with bangs and fat legs, running up and down.'

'You could always adopt one.' Hannah defended herself

against Lottie's angry cry: 'There are so many orphans looking for good homes, it would be an act of charity.'

'I want my own. Mine and Sid's.' She began to cry. Hannah stared into space, betraying no feelings, one way or another.

When Magda discovered that Ellie had failed to show up for most of her auditions, Ellie said it was because of him: Robert. She explained how he didn't want her to audition for anyone else because he needed her. When Magda challenged the truth of this, she clamped up. Her face became like a little fist and she said in a dead voice, 'Aren't we going to eat?'

Magda knew she would have to confront Robert. She phoned him and said grimly that she wished to speak to him about her client, Ellie Sprigge.

Robert was surprised. 'But you threw her out.'

'*I* threw her out?'

She said she was coming to talk to him in his studio. There was nowhere else private enough for what she had to say to him. She didn't like going there; too many things went on in the house that she wanted to know nothing about. For instance, this Fred who opened the door, besides being the butler, whose lover was he – the architect on the first floor, the two antique-dealers on the second, or Robert's? But it was none of her business, she told herself, when Fred had taken her upstairs and shut the door to leave her alone with Robert; her business was Ellie. To show how uninhibited she was by Robert and his surroundings – his Steinway grand stood on a Persian carpet woven with flowers and yellow tigers – she took off her coat and flung it on his chaise longue (Robert hung it up). She sat down opposite him, square, aggressive, with her legs apart in a posture she knew to be distasteful to him.

She didn't care – it was in reaction to her childhood, when

she had cared too much. Every time she had been taken to play with Robert, her mother had adorned her beautifully, in taffeta and bows; but as soon as they got there, Magda knew she was dressed all wrong, especially compared with Robert, who looked elegant, debonair, even then in his boy's shirt and shorts. Sometimes his mother Hannah would point out to her sister Lottie that a particular frock was too short for someone with Magda's legs, and wasn't it time the dentist did something about the child's teeth? Although these suggestions may have been well meant, they infuriated Lottie, and often it ended with Magda being snatched by the hand and marched away in the middle of her game with Robert. Aware of the cause of their retreat, Magda was overcome with shame at her own ugliness; and while they were still going down in the elevator, she tore the ribbon out of her hair, stamped it under her ankle-strap shoe and burst into tears. These tears made her mother kneel down and put her arms around Magda; and they stayed like that even after the elevator doors opened and people in the lobby stared in at the two of them entwined in this embrace.

Now, in his studio, it wasn't long before Robert believed Magda's passionate assertion that she had not told Ellie to leave. But when he proved that Ellie had also lied about the auditions, Magda accused him: 'You raised her hopes. You promised her things.'

'I said I might call for you if I need you; I never said don't go to other auditions.'

'That's what she said you said. Why would she make up such a thing, just like that, out of the air?'

'Because she's a little liar,' smiled Robert.

He stopped smiling at the flash of fire that emanated from his cousin. He knew passion when he saw it, and respected it. But Magda herself felt she had given away too much. She pulled herself together – literally: she closed her legs and also adjusted the neckline of her two-piece. She said, 'There's no need for you to communicate with any client of mine except through me.'

'Exactly,' said Robert. 'That's why I told her she mustn't come here any more. I've given orders not to let her in.'

'You have *what!*' Her legs opened again, showing her under-clothes. 'I can't believe this – that anyone would be so hurtful to her. So all right,' she overrode anything he might try to say, 'she cut her auditions, she made a fool of me. And she fooled you that I'd thrown her out and she had nowhere to stay. But why did she do it? Because she trusted you; she thought you'd do everything for her.'

'Well, maybe I could do something,' said Robert. 'She's good, you know.'

'You think you're the only one who can recognise talent when they see it? Don't forget it's I who found her and sent her to you in the first place. Only to have you kick her out of the house –'

'I wouldn't worry too much about her. She'll find her way back in very quickly.'

In fact, while they were talking in the studio upstairs, Ellie was in the basement kitchen with Fred, eating a piece of his lemon-chocolate cake. She and Fred had become friends – fellow-conspirators, really, after she had persuaded him to disregard orders and let her into the house. 'I'm not going upstairs,' she assured him. 'I just want to be with you.'

He had begun to enjoy her company. They spoke of all sorts of personal matters. Fred was only a few years older than Ellie, but he had been in the city since he was fifteen, so he knew a lot more than she did. He had arrived with just a few dollars in his pocket after paying his fare on the Greyhound bus. That money was still on his conscience for he had stolen it out of his mother's welfare cheque: for her own good, he told Ellie, so she could be rid of him, for she had enough problems without a teenage son who was beginning to get into police trouble.

Ellie was very understanding, and she also told him more about herself than she had told Magda, or Robert, or anyone. Ellie hadn't stolen money from her parents, they had freely given it to her, as much as they could scrape together. To pay for the ticket to New York, her mother had sold a little brooch with a ruby in it. It was very hard for them to send her away, but they had to, because of her singing teacher. 'I was in love with him,' she told Fred, who was very interested and asked what was he like.

'He was old,' she said. 'And he was homo and he wore a toupee.' They both giggled. Then she said, 'I'd have died for him. I nearly did. I took pills and had to be pumped out in the hospital, it was horrible.'

Fred gave her another piece of his cake. She ate it, leaning with one elbow on the kitchen table. 'It's funny. I don't even think of him now, and if I do, it's only to laugh.'

They both laughed again, then were silent, thinking of very serious subjects. She said, 'Maybe it's nothing to do with a person really, the way you feel about him.'

'You don't want to start feeling about him,' Fred said, jerking his head towards the studio upstairs.

She laughed again, drily, like a much older person. 'You don't actually get to choose, do you ... What's he like, then?' she said, licking crumbs off her fingers.

'He's very kind,' Fred said. 'Very considerate.'

'And?'

'Cold as ice,' Fred said.

She shut her eyes; her two thin eyelash fringes glistened with one tear each. 'They always are. The other one the same. Maybe it's got something to do with being an artist.'

'Is that so?' Fred said. 'Then give me someone who's not but can truly love and care for me.'

'Don't hit me!' cried Ellie.

'I wasn't going to hit you,' Magda said. But Ellie still didn't trust her – she squinted at her fearfully from behind the elbow she had raised to protect herself, like an orphan child who was used to being beaten.

'Why would I hit you – why would anyone?'

'He did,' said Ellie. 'My teacher in London. Pulled my hair and pinched me ... No, I don't want to eat. I ate at your mum's. Well, why shouldn't I visit her? Getting to know your family isn't a sin, I hope. She's introduced me to your aunt too, she was dying to meet me, Robert told her about me, about my voice.'

'Why did you tell Robert what you told him?'

'I can't stand this,' said Ellie. 'I'm going to bed.'

Magda barred her way. They stood face to face. Of course Magda was much bigger and stronger and could easily have forced her to stay. But it was Magda who moved aside. She said, 'As if I would ever ask you to leave – I wouldn't. I couldn't.'

Ellie nodded briefly, in acceptance of this situation. She went into her room, with Magda following and standing in the door. Ellie undid a button of her frock, then another, then she stopped. 'I want to change.'

'You can change with me here.' Magda stepped into the room. 'I'm not stopping you.'

'... Is this my room or isn't it my room?'

A terrible fury seized Magda, pounding in her veins (fifteen years later, at fifty, she would die of a stroke). But now she managed to control herself, though she couldn't trust herself to speak, or to stay any longer.

Ellie dismissed her from her thoughts as lightly as from her presence. She stepped out of her clothes and, since it was a warm night, she didn't bother about her nightie but lay on the bed, naked and smiling and humming to herself a little bit. A muted sound of traffic came up from the Avenue and fused with Robert's composition, which she was humming. It was filled with the sound not of brooks and nightingales – Robert couldn't stand the country – but of trashcans, garbage trucks, road-drills and the spike heels of office secretaries tripping down the steps to the subway and then running faster and faster as the train was heard arriving at the platform.

Ellie began to go to auditions again and, in spite of her unpromising personality, she got on well and was several times called back. It was not too long before she was offered a part; not a lead of course, but she had a few moments on her own in which to make her mark. It was a big show – Magda and her agency wouldn't have handled anything else, and the money they negotiated for Ellie was good too; so it was an important break for her, which she owed entirely to Magda. The two of them had a little celebration together, not in the sort of place where agents entertained their clients but in a modest neigh-bourhood restaurant. Magda had been coming here for years and was known to the proprietors. She had often eaten here alone and had even celebrated events by herself, ordering champagne by the glass. But now she and Ellie were together, and they had a bottle between them, which brought a little sparkle even into Ellie's pale green eyes.

Magda had a gift for Ellie: a beautiful aquamarine box out of which emerged a little gold heart on a gold chain. 'May I?' She reached forward to fasten it around Ellie's neck. For a moment, she totally enveloped her in her big warm arms, naked except for a silk fringe that formed the sleeves of the elaborate black dress she had chosen to wear. As she drew back, this fringe brushed across Ellie's face like a bat, causing her to give a little cry. Magda interpreted it as one of pleasure for the gold heart she had given her, and she put out her hand to fondle Ellie's face – lightly and only for a moment, withdrawing it to kiss her own fingers that had touched Ellie's cheek.

'What's that?' Robert asked, for as Ellie leaned forward to see the notes he was pointing at – she was slightly near-sighted and he didn't like her to stand too close to him – the heart slipped out from inside her blouse.

'She gave it to me.' Ellie never called Magda by her name when talking to Robert; she didn't have to. 'Because of – you know what I told you.'

She peered into his face for some reaction, but there was even less than when she had first told him of getting an important role. He held the heart for a moment to examine the diamond that glittered in its centre. 'It's like an eye,' he commented. '*Her* eye.' That made Ellie giggle, but he was already back on the phrase he needed her to sing.

'Do you think he's pleased?' Ellie later asked Fred. 'He still hasn't said anything.'

Fred himself had congratulated Ellie cordially when she had brought him the news of her success, which showed up Robert's silence all the more. 'He's busy,' Fred tried to explain. 'He's like that when he's working – nothing gets through to him.'

Ellie said, 'Maybe he doesn't want me to take it. Because he needs me here with him.' Fred tried not to look sceptical. She went on: 'And what if I'm tied up in another show when he starts his rehearsals.'

'He could work for months and then throw it all in the trash. I've seen him do it. And then he starts over. It could take years. Meantime he wouldn't want you to lose your chance with something else.'

'But if he needs me?'

'You could ask him,' Fred said, only to be kind.

She was afraid – both of asking and of not receiving the answer she wanted to hear. But she had now advanced far enough with him to ask for other things: for instance, money. One day she had simply informed him that she needed some, and he said, 'For a hotel?' After that it became a joke between them. 'I need to go to the hotel again,' she would say. If she hadn't asked for a while, he himself said, 'What about the hotel?' And she would say, 'Yes, all right.' It became a regular transaction between them and would have made her as independent of Magda as Robert assumed. But Magda began to ask, 'Don't you need some cash?' and although once or twice Ellie said no, in the end it was easier to say yes. This worked out well, for it enabled her to send money orders to her parents in London. They got very little work nowadays and couldn't always afford their little extras, like their evening gimlets or the flowers her mother liked to buy to put a bit of colour in their room.

Robert said, 'We'll try this again tomorrow.'

'Tomorrow's my rehearsals,' said Ellie. And after a pause, 'You never said not to.' Maybe he failed to understand what she meant, so she made herself clearer: 'If you think I shouldn't, I won't.'

'Come over here a minute. I want to try it another way.'

She went gladly, standing by his shoulder while he scribbled some changes on his score. 'Now,' he said; she lifted her voice and it spread its wings and floated all by itself till she made it come down again. It was so right, he didn't even have to say 'Yes'. Their eyes met and she tried to enter as far into his as she could; they were a deep blue like a woman's eyes and with a woman's thick honey-blond lashes. She lingered, her left foot draped around the ankle of the right so that she stood on one long skinny leg like a stork. When he looked up and saw her still there, he gave a nod of dismissal. 'See you tomorrow then?' she said and tried to catch his eye, but his gaze was too abstracted for any kind of understanding.

Next morning, Magda, riffling through Ellie's closet, moaned, 'What are you going to *wear?*'

Ellie said, 'It's only rehearsals.'

'We'll have to get you some new clothes.'

'OK,' Ellie agreed indifferently. She glanced at Magda, who was ready to leave for a breakfast meeting in a smart polka-dot two-piece. Ellie said, 'You've got lipstick on your teeth.'

'Oh hell.' Magda rushed to the mirror with a Kleenex. After wiping the lipstick off, she surreptitiously blew into her hand to check up on her breath before gathering up Ellie's frail form wrapped in a sheet. 'Just a hug for good luck.'

'I've got nothing on,' Ellie protested, but Magda only embraced her closer.

Later that day Ellie packed everything she had into a suitcase and left. When Fred opened the door to her, she didn't go down in the kitchen but up to the studio. 'Hey!' cried Fred, but she only briefly turned: 'He said I could.' She went straight in and put her suitcase in the corner where she herself usually crouched. Robert let her stay, and when Fred brought up a tray for him at lunchtime, he told him to make some more sandwiches. 'Very well,' said Fred, as though he were a real butler, and when he returned, he offered the tray to Ellie with a frozen face.

In the afternoon he returned to say that Magda was on the phone. He said, 'She's asking for her.'

Ellie said to say she wasn't there, and Robert confirmed: 'She's not here.' When Fred hesitated for a moment, he asked, 'What's wrong with you?'

'Nothing,' said Fred and went out to do as he was told.

Ellie said, 'They must have called her from the rehearsal.'

Seeing Robert frowning over a crucial passage, she kept quiet and banished all thoughts that might disturb him or herself.

So the hours passed, and Ellie saw the day's light change to dusk and then to dark. At last Robert pushed back on his piano stool and stretched; and Ellie stirred a little bit, in case he had forgotten her. He looked not at her but at her suitcase. 'Do you need a hotel? . . . I mean really.' He smiled. 'A room in a hotel.'

'I could stay here,' she suggested, but even if she hadn't seen his frown, she would have realised at once how wrong it would be for anyone – let alone a girl like herself, who might even be having her monthlies – to do anything as physical as sleep in his place of work.

He told her he was going home and would drop her off at a hotel on his way. She picked up her suitcase and followed him. It was only when they were in a cab that she said she didn't want to go to a hotel.

'Then where?' he asked. She said nothing, so he said, 'You can't come with me. You know I live with my mother.'

'She likes me.'

'Not that much,' Robert said.

Several times he told the driver to let Ellie off, but she wouldn't get out, so that Robert had to tell him to keep on driving.

Magda burst in, demanding, 'Is she here?' though one glance told her that her mother was alone.

Lottie had just settled down by the TV for a programme that sometimes made her laugh. She had lit her evening cigarette, and now she quickly had to get rid of it, for she had assured Magda that she had stopped smoking completely.

'You're not hiding her, are you? I know she comes to see you.' Loud laughter came out of the TV set and Magda yelled, 'Shut that thing up!'

Lottie turned the programme off. 'It gets sillier every week,' she said.

'Then why are you watching? And why the hell are you smoking?'

'I know I shouldn't, but sometimes I have to have it. I just can't control myself – you know how I am,' Lottie said humbly.

But it was Magda who lost control. She sank on to the sofa and buried her head in her hands. Lottie looked down at her, at her wild dark hair. Once she had read somewhere of someone – it may even have been an emperor – who had circled his dying son's bed, praying to draw the boy's sickness into himself (and the emperor had died). Whenever as a child Magda had been ill, with mumps or measles, lying in bed with fevered eyes, Lottie had thought of this story, and she thought of it now.

'I don't know where she is,' Magda said, still with her head buried so that it was difficult to hear her.

But Lottie heard. 'She was here yesterday. She said she was starting rehearsals today – she was excited about it. That's where she is.'

'You don't know anything. About rehearsals or anything,' Magda said. 'Anyhow, she didn't go.'

'So what? She'll go tomorrow.'

'They won't have her tomorrow. They'll have cast someone else.'

'That's her funeral then. You've done all you could, and more – my Lord, a girl like that, she should count herself lucky you've taken her on.'

'A girl like what?' Magda had raised her face, swollen like a child's with tears.

'Well, I'm sure she's got a pretty voice but you could hardly call her – I mean, nothing like your other clients, dear.'

'There's no one like her! She's head and shoulders above all of them! Above everyone!'

'OK, I believe you, but why are you yelling at me?' After a moment, she said in a nice bright voice, 'Have you eaten?' and though Magda angrily waved this away, she went right on in the same voice: 'Oh but you should. You have to build yourself up, with all the work you do. Look at me – I don't do a thing all day, but I have to have my three meals.' She laughed. 'And you can see where it all goes.'

Magda began to wipe her eyes. 'Yes, look at you,' she said.

'It's time I booked myself into that place in Florida again. What about you? Just for a week? Of course I like you the way you are. If you're built big, what can you do? Your father hated the skinny ones – he wanted a woman who had something you could talk with, that was his joke ... Oh don't cry again, darling, it's not worth it, nothing is.' She moved closer to Magda on the sofa and she put her arms around her and they sat in silence for a time. Then Lottie began to wipe Magda's face, her eyes, her cheeks, and holding the handkerchief to her mouth, she said, 'Spit for me, darling, there's lipstick on your teeth,' but at once Magda burst again into a storm of tears.

Robert and Ellie rode around in the taxi cab for a long time, till at last he gave up and told the driver to take them to Hannah's building. He strode ahead, leaving Ellie to follow with her suitcase; he didn't even hold the elevator doors for her, so that she was nearly caught between them. Once upstairs, he curtly told his mother that Ellie would be spending the night and then disappeared into his room. Hannah gaped at Ellie, who smiled ingratiatingly; no one had asked her to sit down, so she stood with her suitcase wedged between her legs.

'Carmen's not coming till tomorrow,' Hannah said. 'I haven't got a bedroom ready.'

'I could sleep here. On the floor.' She indicated it, not daring to mention the grand sofa.

Hannah drew a deep breath, as in pain. 'I'll see,' she said. She went into her bedroom and stealthily dialled her sister. 'That girl's here. She wants to stay the night. What shall I do? Did you hear what I said?' for Lottie still hadn't responded.

Lottie said, 'I'll come get her.'

'Really? You don't mind? ... It would be very inconvenient for me to have her here.'

'I'll be there in a minute.'

'I appreciate it.' Hannah remained sitting on the edge of the bed, examining the polish the girl at the nail spa had put on her.

Lottie, having let herself in with her own key, found Ellie still standing patiently with her suitcase. When Lottie told her to come with her where Magda was waiting, Ellie squeezed her legs together, in case anyone should try to take the suitcase out from between them. And when Lottie did try, she began to protest so loudly that it brought Robert from his study and Hannah from her bedroom.

'I'm not going with her,' Ellie told Robert.

'It'll be such a nice surprise for Magda,' Lottie urged. 'You look quite nice too, you've done something different with your hair. And what's that?' She looked closer at the heart with the diamond sparkling on Ellie's chest.

'It's my present from Robert,' Ellie said.

At that, Hannah also came to see, with burning eyes, which she then lifted to her son.

'I'm taking her to a hotel,' Robert said. He even picked up Ellie's suitcase, though when they were outside, she took it back again, not wanting to burden him.

Hannah explained to Lottie, 'He's taking her to a hotel and then he'll come home to eat.'

'I told Magda I was going to Chez Cheese to buy something for her and she said, "It's past nine, they're shut long ago," so I made up some other lie. Just to keep it a surprise who I was bringing ... Well, I'm glad I didn't tell her.'

'What's it all about, Lot, do you suppose?'

'God knows, I don't; and I don't want to know and neither should you.'

Robert didn't take Ellie to a hotel but to his studio. He opened the front door with his key and they both crept up the stairs very quietly. Nevertheless, Fred heard them and appeared in the door of the little room where he slept just under the studio. 'It's all right, Fred,' Robert said, as to a dog who has barked in angry alarm. Ellie, coming behind with her suitcase, smiled at him; Fred didn't smile back but silently watched them go up, and then he shut his door.

She was relieved to put down her suitcase again in a corner of the studio. They both looked at the piano. 'Shall we?' said Robert, opening it with an almost guilty little smile. Ellie watched his hands run over the keys, taking charge of them in the way she loved. He played the composition he had been working on for the last few weeks, and it sounded completely lovely to her. But he wasn't satisfied and changed it here and changed it there and still wasn't satisfied. Ellie, squatting near him on the floor, dropped off to sleep now and again. It was dawn when he asked her to sing a passage for him, so that her voice, rising as usual in perfect purity, might have been the first bird to wake up for the day.

Critic

Theodore Fabrik was a highly respected and well-paid film critic, but it was not the profession he might have chosen for himself. There was a bitter twist to his lips, which were sensuous, rosy and full, as though meant for something romantic rather than cerebral. It may also have been due to his distaste for the kinds of films he had to review. But his comments ranged far beyond them – sometimes they were scarcely mentioned – into thoughts on the current state of society and culture and meditations on the human predicament. His editors allowed him many pages, for he was avidly read as much for his weighty ideas as for the devastating wit with which he expressed them.

Besides being brilliant, Theo was attractive to women. Above his sensuous lips, his features were finely modelled, his brow very high and very white. The women he chose were always of the same type. He hated scruffy girls and what he considered their scruffy ideas; even at college, he had only liked students who were well groomed and well mannered. While this usually meant a moneyed background, it was not the money he valued but the breeding it had bought. Eileen, who became his wife, had all the virtues he esteemed. Shortly after the marriage, he and his mother, Madame Sybille, moved into the large Upper East Side apartment Eileen had inherited from her family. Here he had a leather-furnished, mahogany-panelled study that admitted practically no sounds and gave him everything he needed for his creative work.

At that time, still in his twenties, a married man living in luxury with his wife and mother, he mostly wrote plays. This was due to the influence of his mother. Madame Sybille had been an actress in her native Hungary, but on moving to New York, she had to earn her living as a sales lady in an upscale department store. Her talents were not wasted here – tall and gracious, she exuded distinction and ruled her floor like a queen of the stage. Her head remained held high – literally and otherwise: she was confident that the disappointment in her own career would be more than made up for by her son's success and fame. But when finally recognition came to him, it was not through his plays, nor the novel he was trying to write, but through the critical articles he was publishing. In the end, he became the undisputed reigning critic of a prominent cultural magazine, and there he remained for more than a decade, forming the taste, and distaste, of an entire generation of readers.

In those years he put on quite a bit of weight. His life was sedentary, moving from screening rooms to his study where he sat for hour after conscientious hour polishing up the steel of his fine prose. Some nights he worked late to meet his deadline, and then stayed to sleep in his study so as not to disturb his wife. Other nights he was out – if he gave an explanation, it was always of some professional gathering he had to attend; whatever he said, Eileen accepted it, though not as the truth.

While he grew plump, Eileen, who had always been thin, became gaunt. She couldn't have children; Theo didn't miss them, and she had many nieces, nephews and godchildren. She also kept up with her friends, most of them women dating from her school and college days, with whom she recalled amusing incidents of their past. She joined a fitness club, and the hours Theo spent on his articles and other pursuits, she spent on the treadmill, her ears plugged into a tape, which drowned out her thoughts with music.

Theo and Eileen were never heard to shout at each other – their differences of opinion were conducted with polite words uttered through pinched-in lips and nostrils. Eileen's eyes and the tip of her nose were often red, usually on account of some affair Theo was having. The worst for her was not when this was at its height, but later, when it was winding down and he needed her help to extricate him. Then he would ask her to deal with telephone calls that he didn't want to take, and while she refused at first, in the end she gave in and could be seen trying to be patient with the hysterical caller at the other end. Afterwards she retreated to her bedroom and no sound could be heard from behind her closed door.

They had persuaded Madame Sybille to give up her job as sales lady, so she was idle most of her days and unable to sleep at night. With Eileen's great-grandfather's grandfather clock striking out the midnight hours, she wandered around the huge apartment, back and forth between two closed doors, her son's study at one end and Eileen's bedroom at the other. Sometimes she stepped close to listen at the latter, not out of curiosity but compassion. Only once did she hear what sounded like muffled sobs, and after receiving no reply to her knock, she opened the door. Eileen was lying face down on the bed, but she sat up at once and groped for a tissue. She said she had a cold.

'Oh, my dear,' Madame said and tried to press her close.

Eileen held herself aloof. 'Be careful. I don't want you to catch my cold.' And she smiled. 'Two sick women in the house would be more than Theo could bear.' Next moment, still smiling, she defended him. 'For his work,' she said, wiping her reddened nose. 'He needs to save himself for his work; all of himself.'

Madame thought, what work? For unspoken, secretly, she was disappointed – that he was a critic and not the great artist she had expected. But to Eileen she joked, 'It's my fault. I should have encouraged him to become a doctor, a lawyer – some respectable work.'

Eileen half joked back: 'Oh but then I couldn't have fallen in love with him. Not with an ordinary person.'

Madame knew about and blamed her son for his infidelities. But sometimes, within her heart of hearts, she made excuses for him. She reflected that, if she was disappointed in his work, how could he himself not be? He was her son, his nature as full of storm and stress as her own. With that whole side of him kept unsatisfied, it was no wonder that he should try to find fulfilment in women as romantic and passionate as himself – that is, women who were totally different from Eileen.

If she imagined that he was having affairs with fabulous stars, she was mistaken. His integrity depended on remaining aloof from their world and accepting no favours from it. Some of these favours were crudely offered by production companies, money men, and it was not difficult to reject them. Others came mostly from aspiring actresses, who took him to be a more powerful insider than he was. Sometimes he did take advantage of their misconception, but the truth was he never liked them much: for him their neediness put them in the category of the scruffy college girls he had rejected in his younger days. His preferences had remained for women who had inherited or married the money that gave them the style he admired. And so he took up with rich women at whose dinner parties he could shine. He enjoyed that for a while but never for long, and since there was a choice of ambitious hostesses married to elderly businessmen, he went easily from one to the other. But as the years passed, the twist of his mouth became more bitter, and his prose took on a more virulent edge.

He had invitations to every premiere, film festival and awards ceremony on the calendar, but he didn't often take them up. The popular attraction at these glittering venues was always the stars, the tall and gorgeous men and women who made everyone else appear small, including Theo, though he had spent the week cutting them down to size. Eileen rarely accompanied him, and when she did, she felt herself to be dowdy and out of place. But her presence made him feel better. He knew she was not dowdy but understated with a breeding these people were not qualified to appreciate. Like himself, she was different, more highly evolved. The two of them often skipped the last course of a banquet, relieved to get out of the perfumed precincts, past the limousines and lounging chauffeurs, turning the corner to hail a yellow cab.

It was different when he took his mother. For Madame Sybille it was like reclaiming a past she had not had. Her clothes were old, her jewellery undistinguished, but she herself had the bearing of one who belonged. When Theo wanted to leave early, she begged to stay till the end. It was what had happened at the premiere of a film he had just demolished in his column. He had especially targeted the leading actress – who of course was present at the party as its centrepiece.

Theodore was used to two kinds of reaction from his victims. Actresses usually showed him how little they cared – they turned their backs on him, tossed their beautiful heads while loudly enjoying the company of their circle of admirers. The second reaction was more common with actors, but on this occasion it was the leading actress who came up to him, caressing him with her smiles as though she had not read his review, or cared nothing about it, or even agreed with him. Her name was Patty Pope, she was twenty-eight years old, at the height of her beauty and ready to ascend to the height of her career.

Theo and his mother were seated at a less than distinguished table. Their host was an independent producer, and although he had bought a table for ten at $2,000 a head, he was not important enough for all his guests to show up. So it was easy for Patty to join them – 'May I?' she breathed, slipping into a chair left empty between Theo and Madame Sybille.

She concentrated most of her charm on the mother, hovering over her with her perfumed half-bare breasts. She only occasionally smiled at the son over her shoulder, amusing him by her effort to show herself above all feelings of resentment. 'I knew it!' she suddenly exclaimed, and from the way his mother preened herself a bit, Theo guessed that she had just confessed to being an actress herself. 'Of course,' Patty said to Theo, 'how could she not be.' She was referring to Madame's air as of some great diva, unbowed after the curtain had fallen.

The speeches had begun – producers, actors and financiers stood to thank one another, some with humour, others with sentimental tears. By this time Theo would have long since left, but Patty and his mother could not be parted. They had moved even closer together, and from time to time Patty whispered something that made Madame smile and lay her hand on Patty's. Theo had to let them sit there and he with them right through the speeches, which set his teeth on edge. He heard them exchange addresses and telephone numbers – on the way home he asked his mother, 'What do you want with her?' and was further irritated by Madame's silent, knowing smile.

Patty called two days later. She announced herself for the same afternoon, just giving Madame time to bake some of her flaky confectionery. Then she stood in the doorway to welcome her visitor: she threw her arms wide and Patty entered into them. Patty made herself at home at once, slipping out of her leopard-skin jacket, unwinding her scarves, looking around the apartment: 'It's just the classy sort of place I'd expect him to live in.' His mother apologised for his absence; as usual in the afternoon he was at a screening. 'But I've come to see *you*,' Patty said. 'And what a heavenly smell – are we going to have something lovely to eat?'

She was licking flaky crumbs off her fingers when Eileen came home from the gym. 'Oh please don't get up,' Eileen said. Patty had made no move, but Eileen didn't know what else to say: she was embarrassed, overwhelmed. There was something overwhelming in Patty's presence. Naturally, she was a star, carrying the admiration of millions. She also exuded a sense of money – not the sort that had been expended on this apartment with the inherited furniture but what had been lavished on Patty herself, by daring young designers, even by dentists who had made her teeth sparkle along with the rest of her. But she carried her load of beauty so lightly that she appeared utterly unaware of it. It was Eileen who was aware of herself, of her gym clothes and her face sweaty from her exercise.

In the course of the afternoon Patty made herself more and more at home, kicking off her shoes and tucking her feet under her. There was a lot of conversation, most of it from Patty, though she fell silent whenever Madame spoke, respectfully listening to what the older actress had to say about parts she had played or had wanted to play.

'They really knew what they were doing in those days,' Patty said to Eileen, not leaving her out for a moment. 'That was real acting, not the sort of monkey thing we have to perform for our bread and butter.'

Madame got up and with appropriate gestures she declaimed Schiller in German.

Patty applauded. 'Isn't that marvellous. Brilliant. The worst of it is, there's no one nowadays to appreciate the real thing. Except Theodore Fabrik, of course. That's why I don't care at all when he gives me a bad review. I'm grateful for it. Because I know he's right.' She unwound her feet from under her. 'I'll creep away before he gets home. He'll want to be quiet to write his review.'

His mother and his wife said nothing, not wishing to admit that there may have been no screening, or that he had gone on to some other appointment they didn't really need to know about.

That day there had been such an appointment, and Theo came home long after Patty had left. He found his two women in a state of excitement. Madame Sybille was pacing the passage and declaiming aloud, only interrupting herself to seize her son's lapels and draw him close to kiss him.

Eileen was in bed, wide awake and eager to tell him about their visitor. He was not pleased. 'She admires you so much,' Eileen urged, but this too did not please him. Eileen said, 'It's so good for Mother to meet someone who knows about acting.'

'It's bad for her,' Theo said. 'She's over-excited. You know what her doctor said about her blood pressure.'

A new friendship had developed, and Patty didn't let up on it. She called a day or two later, and Madame Sybille accepted an invitation to visit her. Patty lived across the Park in a building that, rising in one long shaft above the earth, seemed unsupported by anything more material than a feat of theoretical engineering. The interior was completely separate from anything going on outside: self-enclosed, self-generating in columns of glass and lights, and at its centre a fountain that rose and then descended in further arcs of light. Everything was mirrored and multiplied, glass within glass, soaring and spiralling right up to the apex where Patty lived.

Her door was opened by a young man in jeans and polo shirt. 'Hello! I'm Simon.' Was he a guest, a butler, maybe a lover? He gave no clue. 'She's in the butterfly room,' he said, leading the way. There was also no clue why it was called the butterfly room. Evidently it had been done up by an interior decorator and glittered as much as Patty herself, though today she was dressed like Simon, in jeans and polo shirt. The room was untidy, making it clear that the money spent on it – the silk walls and painted panels – was of no consequence. An interior staircase led up to further floors, there may have been two or three, inhabited by Patty's large retinue of employees, guests or hangers-on. The telephone rang constantly, but the only call Patty took was from her agent and it made her angry.

She told Madame that all her agent, a woman called Robyn, ever got for her was rubbish, and Patty was tired of playing rubbish. What she really wanted was to get back to the theatre, but Robyn wouldn't let her because of the money. All she was interested in was the money earned from films, which was a lot, it was true, and Patty needed it because not only did she have an agent, she had a manager too, and a lawyer, and her personal staff, all of whom needed to be paid.

'And of course there's the alimony,' she said, taking it for granted that her visitor read the sort of magazines in which a star's personal life was displayed. But Madame did not, and she was too tactful to ask any questions.

Later she asked Theo, and although he didn't care for personal gossip, he did know that Patty had been married to an actor when they were both very young. She had prospered and he had not, and by the time she realised that they were incompatible, he needed an income and considered himself entitled to a share in hers. He clung on through the years, even after she had married again, this time a rock star; that marriage too broke down, under the weight of two stars, in less than a year.

'She's too intelligent,' Madame concluded.

'Is that what she told you?'

'Too intelligent for the roles she has to play. Did you know that she wants to leave films and go into the theatre?'

'I didn't know but I could have guessed,' Theo said. 'Her last film didn't do well, the big film she was hoping for went to another actress, and that's usually when they decide that their real talent is for the theatre.'

Madame's visits to Patty continued. For Patty, Madame was the inspiration she had not had in any of her relationships. If her parents had guided her, she confided, she wouldn't have married in that stupid way before she had even graduated. But though her parents were professional people, they had cared nothing for Patty's education or her artistic development. Her mother, now living in Santa Fe with a third husband, was only interested in Patty's career for the publicity it generated and to be photographed with her on showy occasions. There was no one in Patty's life with Madame's background, the talent and training she had been able to transmit to her son.

'It's not only that he's fantastically clever and brilliant,' Patty said. 'He also has a sort of European culture that people here just don't have. I long to do something he could at least approve of. If only someone would write a decent part for me! But I guess nowadays that's too much to hope for.'

As usual, Patty wanted to send Madame home in her chauffeured limousine, but Madame loved to walk. She strode across the Park, as upright as any of its trees. It was a windy day, she was bareheaded, her white hair flew around. She felt strong as a prophetess and full of an idea that excited her.

Before she could enter the study alone, she had to wait until both Theo and Eileen were out – he maybe at a screening, she certainly at the gym. She knew the place where he kept his plays and his unfinished novel. There was one play she especially remembered from its production in a small theatre club. It was an interesting subject. The hero was a famous conductor whose affair with a young piano student went further than he had intended. He divorced his wife of twenty years, he married the girl, but from there on everything went downhill, and what he had loved – her naivety, her innocent questioning – became a source of intense irritation. But the author – Theo – saw both sides, as did his hero, who realised that, instead of admiring his fame and brilliance, she was now judging him for his daily shortcomings: his temper, his ageing, his sour breath in the morning. The play had been well received by the club members, mostly elderly subscribers, but had not gone anywhere after its week-long run.

Madame carried the play in her large handbag across the Park. She presented it to Patty as a gift and watched her unwrap it. When she saw what it was, Patty said, 'I don't believe it,' and a moment later, looking up from a page, 'I do believe it.' She said she knew that Theo was not just a critic – was something more than a critic – much more, she said, leafing through the bound script. She wanted to read it right away, but Madame asked her to wait till she was alone, without the author's anxious mother there to watch her. Again Madame walked across the Park, her handbag empty now and lighter, and her heart light too and soaring upwards.

'Give the child time,' she told herself when no word came from Patty for three days. On the fourth day she asked herself how much time was there – she was seventy-five years old and

141

how much longer did she have to wait for the recognition of her son's true talent? At last she picked up the phone and dialled Patty's number – her secret private number that she had entrusted to her. Patty was terribly pleased to hear her: a lovely surprise, she said. She appeared to be in a busy place – in a restaurant, a creative meeting? Madame knew Patty's days to be full of events, of exciting people. Nevertheless, Patty called across the noise, 'We have to talk. About the play.' Madame offered to walk across the Park again, but 'No,' Patty said, 'I'll come to you. When will he be home?' It was with Theo, it appeared, she wished to talk.

She arrived unannounced – on the spur of the moment, of *her* moment – carrying flowers and his play. It was a rainy day and the flowers were wet, and so were her cheeks, dewy like her eyes. At her entrance, waves of excitement displaced the air, and the seismic change penetrated the closed door of Theo's study. He appeared; she held out his play. 'I love it of course,' she said without fervour. 'But there's a lot we need to discuss.'

Taking his play from her, he stood looking puzzled. Madame began to explain; she was embarrassed and too slow for Patty, who took over: 'I've been making Madame's life a misery till she got it for me. I think she had to steal it.' She laughed and Theo twisted his lips into a smile.

'I thought it was so perfect for her,' Madame apologised.

Theo said, 'You mean, as a starring vehicle.' He appeared amused not angry, so that Madame lowered her eyes as one who had been unexpectedly forgiven.

'God, no,' Patty said. '*You're* the star.' He pretended to believe she meant it, he put his hand on his heart and bowed his head.

'But these are for you!' Patty exclaimed, handing over her flowers to Madame, who inhaled them. She said tulips were her favourites; these were particularly gorgeous, tall and upright, scentless, shining like prima donnas.

'All right.' Theo spoke as though something had been settled in his mind, a situation accepted. 'How about some tea,' he ordered Eileen, who went out into the kitchen. By now Patty was ensconced in a corner of their sofa; her legs were crossed, she was wearing knee-high leather boots.

'So you like it,' Theo said. 'It wasn't much of a hit, you know. Rather a damp squib, in fact, though that may have been the audience. The subscribers in these theatre clubs are never less than a hundred years old and the seats much too hard for their ancient buttocks.'

'I'm not thinking of a club,' Patty said. 'But it would have to be a different play. I want it to be different. I want it for *me*. You hate me for saying that.'

Madame, her arms full of flowers, was watching them. Their presence together was thrilling. He was standing, his elbow propped on the mantelpiece; she looking up at him from the sofa. They were a scene, a play, the eternal duel, man and woman.

'Shouldn't you be putting those in water,' Theo suggested, making his mother exclaim, 'Poor thirsty darlings!' She tore herself away and joined Eileen in the kitchen. But once there, she left the flowers lying on the table and herself sank on to a chair, exhausted with hope.

'Eileen, it may happen. They'll work together.'

When Eileen carried in the tea, they were as Madame had left them. Eileen had always admired her husband's personality. Although not very tall, he had the bearing of someone in a position to look down on whatever he chose to notice. However, Patty, looking up at him as he stood above her leaning against the mantelpiece, was not submissive. On the contrary, there was something challenging, even masterful in the way she sat with her legs crossed in leather boots; nor did she seem shy of stating her opinions.

That night, getting into the twin bed next to Eileen's, Theo stated his opinion of Patty's opinions. He wished she did not have any. He said he wished it could be as in the past when actresses were discovered working in a laundromat. It had been easier to deal with them then than it was now when they had all been to college and been given ideas about their own intelligence.

Eileen never disputed with him, but she knew he was always ready to listen to her, so she said what Madame had told her – that his play would benefit if the principal role was performed by a star like Patty. He replied that he preferred success on his own merits, not on the meretricious attractions of an actress. 'You're right, of course,' Eileen said, as though she considered the subject closed. She knew it wasn't – that he would be lying awake for a long time, turning over in his mind whatever had passed between him and Patty. She said goodnight affectionately and lay with her back to him, not wishing to appear to be spying on him in his secret thoughts.

Theo enjoyed his daily routine – the hours spent in the deep plush soothing executive armchairs of a hushed screening room, often alone, sometimes with a producer and his minions seated at a respectful distance behind him. Then afterwards in his study offloading the contents of his mind on to his computer, alone and with the door shut – a door of a solid wood used only in the older apartments, through which no sound could penetrate. He never heard the telephone, and anyway knew that Eileen would be dealing with all his calls, professional ones for invitations he didn't want to accept, personal ones for lovers he no longer wanted to see.

But now, when he emerged from his study, he began for the first time to ask: 'Any calls I ought to know about?'

'None, dear.' She added humorously, 'Unless you're dying to go to the Paramount premiere on Thursday?'

He groaned, she smiled, they sat down to their meal and she chatted to him about her day's doings.

Madame also began to listen for the telephone, and when it rang, she came hurrying to ask, 'Who was it?'

Eileen told her, but it was never what Madame wanted to hear. Until one day Eileen said, 'Just someone selling something. So irritating, but poor things, they're only trying to make a living.' Two red spots had appeared on her cheekbones: Eileen was a very poor liar.

Madame said, 'If it's Patty, he'd want to talk to her.'

'I don't think we should be disturbing him, do you,' Eileen said, the spots on her cheeks a deeper red.

'I'll tell him. It's important.' Madame strode to the study door and raised a knuckle to knock.

Before she could do so, Eileen had come up behind her and seized her hand. 'I told her he's busy. He's doing his work.'

'*That*'s not his work,' Madame said. 'His work is with her. They have to talk.'

Eileen released her, but at the same time she said, 'Please don't disturb him.' She spoke quietly, but herself a very self-controlled person, it was not difficult for her, when necessary, to exert control over others. Madame turned from the door, she went to her room, she lay down on the bed, she felt defeated.

It was past noon by the time she emerged, and Theo and Eileen were together at the end of a companionable lunch. He had a screening at two, and before he left, Eileen said, 'I think I'm in the mood to make my famous blanquette de veau for supper.' And clearing away the dishes, 'Will you be home, do you think?'

He mused, 'Tonight, hmm ... Well, there's the NYU prizegiving but I think I'm entitled to give it a miss. Yes, I believe I'll be home.'

Madame followed him into the entrance hall; she helped him into his fur-collared overcoat; it was one of her privileges. She gazed into his face; she told him, 'Patty called. She wants to see you.'

Eileen came out. 'Oh goody, you're still here ... I wanted to ask you: about the wine? With the veal?'

He decided the question and she returned to her tasks. He left but stopped on the threshold and came back again. He told his mother: 'Would you call her and tell her I'll drop in after my screening? About five? Five thirty?'

She lived as he had suspected – like the messy students he had avoided, though on a different scale. There were many people, none of whom knew who he was or why he had come. Worst of all, she too stared at him. 'What's it about, sweetheart?' But the next moment: 'God yes! I've been thinking about you! We must talk! If you can find somewhere to sit.'

There was actually very little furniture in the room, which seemed to function as a place of exercise or yoga. She herself was crosslegged on the floor, where he refused to join her, though she assured him that it was very good for the back. Instead he removed a teddy bear – did she have a child or was it hers to play with? – and lowered himself on to a seat. Telephones were ringing in the floors above where there was a lot of activity. She called, 'No calls! Except if it's Robyn!'

'Robyn's my agent,' she explained. 'She wanted to meet you but I said no, so it's just you and I. She's a terrific agent though, I'd die without her.' She was snacking out of some little bowls, and now she stretched one up to him, but he held up his hand in refusal so she went on eating by herself.

She said she wanted him to rewrite the part of the girl in his play to suit her, not as she had been but as she was now. She looked up at him from where she sat, not quite at his feet but nearly: without make-up, her hair loose, in jeans and polo shirt, her pearl earrings her only mark of status. She admitted that she may once have been like his little piano student but now she was – well, she said, smiling, snacking some more, while waiting for him to finish the sentence for her.

'A very famous film star,' he said, twisting his mouth into his sardonic smile.

'No. That's not me. I said no calls,' she said to the young man who had entered with a telephone. 'It's Robyn,' he said, and she took it and cried into it: 'Angel! But of course I want to talk to you!'

'I'm Simon,' the young man told Theo. He was dressed exactly like Patty except he wore only one earring. He stood in front of Theo, examining him quite boldly. 'Tea? Coffee?' He shut one eye: 'Something stronger?' It may have been just his style, but his attitude and tone were distasteful to Theo, for whom such familiarity was overfamiliarity.

'I'll tell you all about it,' Patty said into the phone before handing it back to Simon. He lingered – he picked up one of the empty bowls: 'Should I get you some more yum-yum?'

'No, but you should bugger off,' Patty said pleasantly, making him depart with another wink at Theo, who chose not to see it.

'Simon is English. He used to be with the Duke of Something and now he's with me. Not what you think. Everything you think about me is wrong.'

'So tell me what I should think.' He spoke in the slightly flirtatious manner he instinctively adopted towards any woman with whom he expected to commit adultery.

'You confuse me with the idiotic parts that Robyn and everyone gets for me because they think they *are* me. Maybe once upon a time years ago but now ...'

'Now?' he smiled, maybe patronising, but she was serious.

'I'm twenty-eight years old. I've been married twice, both times to bastards. I have to support an entire gang who can't stand each other. All they have in common is me. The same with my parents: my mother has to have very expensive spa treatments, so-called, and my father likes to take his young girlfriends on world cruises, and guess who pays. I'm not complaining – OK, that's my life, but I don't want anyone to think I'm a fourteen-year-old dumb showpiece. I don't want *you* to think that.'

He moved in – not yet physically, but speaking in a warm, sincere voice. 'I want to know you as you really are. That's what I'm here for.'

'Well, what else! What else are you here for? Did you think it was for sex?' Her tone made him draw back, thrown off his usually very stable centre. She shrugged. 'Of course, it might happen, who knows. Though what idea could you have about someone like me? Only from books.'

Irascible by nature, he was himself surprised by his mildly facetious response: 'In the course of a not uneventful career, I have met one or two women. I might even say more than one or two ... Plus I've been married for fifteen years.'

'Not to someone like me.'

He laughed at that, and it made her say, 'I like the way you laugh – as if you haven't done it for a hundred years.' Now it was she who moved closer – actually, physically, to trace a finger along his high white brow. 'But it would be interesting to know what goes on behind this.'

Again mistaking the stage they had reached, he came forward with his lips poised towards hers. She took her finger from his forehead to push it against his chest. 'Let's have a first draft first, OK? And proceed from there.' Her finger was like a lily stalk, but it felt like steel against his chest to hold him back.

It was late when he left, long past the time when Eileen would have been serving her stew. Walking home across the Park, Theo was impassioned. Snowflakes were falling; he raised his face to them, looked up at the veiled moon. When he was halfway home, he turned back. Patty's household was wide awake and she herself still in the room where he had left her – no longer on the floor but in a chair, with Simon kneeling in front of her, holding one of her feet to massage it.

She didn't seem surprised when Theo returned; people were always coming back to her. She laughed at his appearance – snowflakes on his fur collar, his cheeks flushed with cold and excitement. She said, 'Take his coat, Simon'; to Theo she said as before, 'If you can find somewhere to sit.' Simon offered him the place on the floor where he had been kneeling. Theo, who knew how to deal with impudence, turned his back to let Simon divest him of his majestic overcoat.

Now Theo sat close to Patty and talked ardently. Ideas surged in him, and she received them. Simon walked in and out, so did several others of her staff. She gave orders, took calls on her phone, she put on horn-rimmed spectacles to check a bill in which she pointed out some errors – all without relaxing her attention on Theo. He took her hand and kissed it. How right she was! It was not some little piano student but a woman like her both he and the play needed – one whom only she could help him to create.

'Let me stay with you,' he said.

'What, tonight?'

'And every night.'

He had said this often before, but not as now. Icicles melted from around his heart; love and adoration flooded him. But he accepted it when she told him she had things she couldn't get out of. 'Come tomorrow,' she said. 'Or the day after. It's going to be fun.' Usually, at this time of departure, he had no difficulty taking a woman in his arms and looking into her eyes with promise. Here the whole air was filled with promise, and for a moment he was tempted to kneel in the place on the floor that Simon had offered him.

His elation lasted, even though the next day she couldn't see him, nor the day after. Before finishing his weekly column, he had opened a new file on his computer and begun work on his play. Now when he emerged for meals, the expression on his face made Eileen uneasy. It was the same as when he started on a new affair from which she would ultimately have to rescue him. Also, as happened at such times, she woke up at night to find him missing. But this time when she went down to the study, she found him working – though not as usual sitting upright at his computer with a small smile, as one vanquishing an enemy with ease. Now he appeared to be engaged in a strug-gle with himself, his hands deep inside his hair, making it stand up in anguish or ecstasy. She quickly shut the door before he could be aware of her intrusion.

Her mother-in-law was standing outside, a column of fire in her scarlet dressing gown. She laid a finger on her lips. 'He's working,' she said.

'At two in the morning? He ought to be asleep.'

'Poets never sleep,' Madame informed her with a smile.

Eileen tightened her mouth to prevent any disloyal word from escaping.

Another time Eileen found him pacing the study, muttering to himself. She told him, 'They called from the office.' She hardly recognised the face he turned to her nor the way in which he said, 'Tell them to go to hell, would you.' She complied in her own way – the same she used with women who had to be got rid of. The next day the call was more urgent, but when she told him, he waved her away dismissively: 'Tell them to get what's-his-name.' This was the second-string critic, who had never before been allowed to stand in for Theo.

Madame Sybille called Patty. 'He's working.'

'Fantastic,' Patty said.

'He's up all night. He's stopped sleeping. And eating,' she added, not quite truthfully but it seemed right.

'Perfect,' said Patty.

One night Madame concocted a special drink of coffee, hot milk, brandy and a dash of vermouth. When Eileen was in bed and presumably asleep, she carried it in to him. She found him slumped over his desk in exhaustion and she was proud of him. She peered at his computer but saw only the flickering logo of its pause. The printer was turned off, with sheets scattered from it all over the desk and the floor. 'Drink this, son,' she whispered into his ear and he half woke to take it from her.

She said, 'She called.'

It may have been the drink that roused him completely. 'What did she say?'

'She asked when you would have something to show her.'

He gave her the empty glass and she tiptoed out with it. Next day she telephoned Patty: 'He says he's almost ready to read to you.' Patty said she was excited.

Madame brought the same drink to him every night. Usually she found him asleep, and before waking him, she surreptitiously counted the number of sheets scattered from the printer. When she gave him the drink, she always said, 'She wants you to read to her.' But after emptying the glass, he slumped back on to the desk. She kissed the top of his head and went out with the empty glass.

One night Eileen stood outside the door. She took the glass and held it up against a lamp: 'What did you give him?'

'It's a special drink we had in the theatre. All the actors drank it, and the author and the director. Even the set designer.'

Eileen said, 'They called again from the office. This is the third column he is missing.'

'You'll have to make them understand. If you like, I'll talk to them.'

Eileen thanked her without taking up the offer – making people understand had always been her prerogative.

Madame found it to be more difficult to wake Theo with her drink. It also began to happen that, when she counted the number of pages, they had not increased; instead more of them lay crumpled in the waste basket. Nevertheless, she continued to report splendid progress to Patty, and Patty continued to declare herself excited.

Then there came the night when the waste basket was completely full. Instead of waking her sleeping son, Madame put down the glass and picked the discarded pages out of the basket. She carried them through the silent house until she came to her own room. Here she locked the door and spread the pages on her bed. There were twenty-four of them, and some were so crumpled they appeared to have been flung away in anger or despair. She smoothed them – most of them were revisions, repetitions and rewrites of the same text. She selected several different versions and began to read them, whispering to herself with expression, like an actress preparing for an audition.

It was not yet dawn when she wrapped the purloined pages in a beautiful old shawl she had brought with her from Budapest. She walked across the Park, oblivious of the dark, the snow, the howling wind. Patty's building was ablaze with all its lights and mirrors, and up in her triplex she was giving a party. Guests lay on the stairs, they ate from over-full plates and drank from over-full glasses, they slumped in chairs and across beds, entwined in twos or more. Music played, someone sang, someone else had climbed halfway up a curtain and pretended to be an acrobat suspended in mid-air.

Madame found Patty in the penthouse. This was walled entirely in glass and shone like crystal mirrors. There were flowers in glazed pots all around, and Simon, like a watchful gardener, was watering them out of a can. Unlike the rest of the triplex, it was very quiet here. Patty was reclining alone on a gilded sofa. She was wearing a long dress of cream lace over cream velvet that sparkled with what were surely real diamonds; more diamonds were scattered over her hair.

She unwrapped the parcel Madame had brought, but before looking at the pages, she admired the shawl. Madame said, 'It is for you.' In her will, she had bequeathed it to Eileen, whom she truly loved for her goodness; but Patty's position in her heart was of a different order. Anyway, Patty had already wrapped the gift around her shoulders and was regarding her reflection in the surrounding glass.

Patty couldn't read the pages without her spectacles; her poor eyesight was the only flaw in her perfection. 'You read it,' she said. Madame intoned them the way she had rehearsed at home, and Patty and Simon listened attentively. Her voice was deep and trained in declamation, and it seemed to rise from a more profound, a more passionate past. None of them, including herself, noticed that after a while she was no longer reading the text but was declaiming from memory in a foreign language. Was it Racine in French? Patty, draped in her new shawl, said it was wonderful and that she could listen to Madame forever.

At the same time, on the other side of the Park, Eileen was checking up on Theo in his study. He was asleep; the full glass stood at his elbow and she sniffed it, suspicious of its contents. When she managed to wake him, he stretched out his hand for it. She wouldn't give it to him. She said, 'Come to bed, dear.'

He got up obedient as a child, and she took his hand as though he were one. When he saw the waste basket, he said, 'Good. You emptied it.'

She helped him into his pyjamas and, lying in their twin beds, talking of this and that, she told him about the screening scheduled for the next day. He was pleased. It was the new film from a woman director he disliked, and he had been waiting to demonstrate how her work, while appearing to be pregnant with cultural significance, was finally as fecund as a hysterical pregnancy. Eileen looked across at him, at his face lit up by the night-light she kept on for him (he had never liked the dark). He was pale from his weeks of seclusion, but he looked relieved, released, and as glad to be in his bed next to hers as she was to have him there.

The New Messiah

Rita met Nathan Silveira at a time of low ebb: for her, and for him too. This was in London, three years ago. He had come there looking for finance for his new film – to London of all places, where everyone who had anything to do with film was mostly unemployed, including Rita herself. Her last job had been with a producer who couldn't get his project going and had returned to advertising. It had been that way for the past several years – she had managed to get quite enviable jobs and then they collapsed and she had to keep herself going with free-lance word-processing. There was also her brother Kris to look after. She was excited when she was sent to Nathan Silveira, who had asked for a temporary secretary in London. Although his last two films had been failures and he hadn't made one for the last three years, his first film (about a Faustian painter) was considered an underground classic. While in London, he was living at the Savoy – in a state of chaotic disorder, which Rita managed to straighten out for him. When he returned to New York, his hopes in London disappointed, he invited her to join him. She considered it the break she had been waiting for; she was in her thirties by then and did not feel London had anything more to offer them – that is, herself and Kris.

When she arrived, Nathan arranged a room for her in the huge gilded Fifth Avenue apartment of his eighty-year-old aunt. It was convenient because it was only a few blocks from where he lived in the equally huge and gilded apartment that he had inherited from his mother. When Rita found that the aunt expected her to act as *her* secretary-companion as well as Nathan's, she moved to a sublet where she was only asked to look after a canary and a bowl of goldfish. After that, she made a similar arrangement elsewhere; her one aim was to find a place of her own where Kris could come to live with her. Meanwhile, she spent money calling him in London; mostly she had to leave a message on the answering machine, asking him to call her back collect. He always did, though sometimes not till several days later, during which she worried about him. She knew she didn't need to; without her, there were plenty of others prepared to look after him. But maybe it was about that she worried.

At last she found something she could afford, and he was happy to come the moment she sent him the fare. He missed her, and he had never been to New York. The apartment she brought him to was shabby – a three-flight walk-up in an old brownstone waiting to be sold and torn down – but they were both used to that; also to having only one bedroom between them. Rita began to live a double life, physically between Nathan Silveira's apartment and her own, and socially between Nathan and Kris. But not emotionally, for while she liked Nathan, she loved Kris. She kept them apart for as long as possible, for she knew how susceptible Nathan was. She didn't even tell him about Kris; she didn't need to, he hardly asked about her personal circumstances. It wasn't that he was cold or indifferent – not at all – but that he had such a full life of his own.

He had to attend many social events: premieres, black-tie fundraisers, private dinner parties; it was necessary for him to be in the company of very rich people who were the potential financiers for his current film project. But anyway he loved parties – he became very excited as the evening wore on and two pink spots appeared on his white cheeks, so that people began to suspect him of using rouge. Altogether he appeared very feminine when he was enjoying himself, his big loose body shaking with laughter inside his evening jacket. He wore some jewellery, and his hair, which was balding on top but still thick around the sides, hung in long curly locks, almost like ringlets. Glamorous society women surrounded him; they adored him and he played at adoring them. Of course everyone knew that he was looking for finance, and next morning he would be making some very serious phone calls – not always taken and rarely returned – to the people he had met the night before. His social training had conditioned him always to have a lady to escort, and he had plenty to choose from. If one of them failed him, he would turn to Rita: 'Could you wear something lovely and come with me tonight? A bore for you of course, but thanks.'

Kris was on her mind throughout the parties she attended. She thought of his wistful smile when she left; he was happy for her, though he longed to go with her. Instead he had to stay alone in their cramped little place, sitting on the sofa with the broken spring someone had handed down to them, looking at their hired television set.

Kris did not complain, except about himself: that he didn't have a job, wasn't helping Rita with the money. She said it didn't matter, and that anyway he couldn't work without a green card. But she knew that he would only have to show himself in the right places – or just go to a gallery or sit in a coffee bar – for interesting contacts to present themselves. Already once or twice, when she had to go with Nathan, she saw that Kris too was dressing up. When she asked, 'Where are you going?' he said, 'Oh nothing much, just someone I met in the video place.' It began to happen some evenings that he had somewhere to go and she didn't; but if she said she had a headache, he cheerfully stayed home and massaged it for her. They cooked a little meal together, each producing a special gourmet dish, and then each insisting the other's was better.

She knew this could not last for ever: that she could not much longer leave him to pursue a social life of his own. So one day, when Nathan invited her to one of his evening events, she said, 'May I bring my brother?' He said, 'Your brother? I didn't know you had one.' Then he made one of his expansive gestures: 'Of course. Of course.' He loved pleasing people, doing them favours.

Kris of course was enchanted. He hadn't once worn the evening suit he had brought from London and now he quickly pressed it up on the kitchen table. She tied his black tie for him – he insisted she did it much better than he could, better than anyone in the world. She looked at his face as he raised his chin for her; as so often, instead of pride, she was full of misgivings. He was too perfect. They were already on the staircase when he remembered something and had to go back; waiting for him outside the door, she could hear him on the telephone – he spoke in a low sweet voice, full of apologies, breaking a date with someone who was pleading not to have it broken.

The evening evolved as she had expected, and maybe feared. Nathan was struck dumb by Kris – and being struck dumb took the opposite effect with him, it made him babble incessantly all the way in the limousine, not to Kris but to Rita and the chauffeur. He hardly addressed a word to Kris, but from time to time passed his eyes swiftly over his face, shy even inside the dark car. And when they arrived at their destination – a cinema bright for a premiere – he extended his hand to help Kris out as tenderly as for a child or a woman. The photographers yelled, 'Nat! Nat, this way!' and he smiled and obligingly posed; and as he did so, he laid his hand on Kris's sleeve, drawing him into the flashlight, the limelight with himself, as if he were his new star.

In the months before Kris's arrival, when Rita had been with Nathan all day, he had found out very little about her. Now he wanted to know everything. 'Tell me about you and Christopher,' he said when she came to work in his apartment the morning after the premiere.

'His name isn't Christopher. It's Krishna.'

'Krishna!' cried Nathan, in rapture and surprise.

Their Indian father had been a press officer at the Indian embassy in London; their English mother a typist in the same office. The father had been charming and good-looking – 'Like Krishna?' smiled Nathan.

'No, not like Kris,' Rita said. 'He wasn't a responsible person like Kris is. He drank and chased after girls and made our mother's life hell for ten years. Then he went back to India, when Kris was three months old. Two children was too much for him. There's a message here from that person at ICM – you want me to answer it?'

'In a minute. And your mother? Was she responsible?'

'She should have been – she was from one of those hardworking, completely teetotal, nonconformist families, but he made her drink with him and then she did it on her own because she couldn't stand it without. She was killed in a car accident, run over. There was no insurance money because she was walking against the red light, dead drunk probably.'

'So you and Krishna – Kris – are alone?'

'No. Not alone. He's always had me and I've always had him.'

She looked at Nathan, almost in hostility. She knew he wanted to say (others had said it), 'And now you both have me,' and it would be gratuitous. They didn't need him, except as an employer.

But she allowed him to invite Kris along every time he invited her; at least this way she would always know where Kris was and with whom. They became a threesome. Kris was often photographed with Nathan, the two of them walking over a red carpet together. They participated in opening nights and auctions and charity events in crimson and gold ballrooms. They celebrated the birthday of a studio head and praised and toasted him with the colleagues who would be ousting him the next day. At a museum gala Kris and Nathan both danced in the Impressionist gallery with an ancient trustee, skeletal but bare-backed, who was expected to donate her collection of Sisleys and Monets. Kris enjoyed everything and Nathan enjoyed watching him and Rita felt more or less safe. Nathan continued tender and respectful with Kris, almost holding his breath in his presence as if he didn't believe his good luck. All this time – several months – he made no new young friends, brought home no attractive waiters. He worked hard on his project and made Rita work hard; their calls to financiers were endlessly persistent. The project itself, however, was in flux, with Nathan revising all the treatments he had been working on.

Nathan's genealogy was as hybrid as that of Rita and Kris. His mother was American, from a family of Midwestern newspaper owners, very rich and very crazy. His mother herself had not been crazy. She had had a conventional upbringing, in refined boarding and finishing schools, and had worked hard at keeping up her transmitted conventions – in everything except her marriage to Nathan's father. He too came from a prominent family, but a very different one from hers. Originally from the Middle East, they had partly settled in New York; some of them may have assimilated but these did not include Nathan's father. Plump, dark, somewhat oily with curly black hair – Nathan took after him exactly – he had an exotic ancestry: a reputed descent from the family of a seventeenth-century mystic who had laid claim to being the Messiah.

It was this fantastic figure whom Nathan had chosen to be the subject of his film. There were only a few crude etchings in existence of his hero, and when he looked at them Nathan felt he was looking at his father, but as the years passed – for this project met with many vicissitudes – he recognised himself. Both he and his father were fleshy men, the very opposite of ascetic – but so was the Messiah. It had in fact been his mission to supersede all the restraints of the rabbinic law and inaugurate a new order where prohibitions gave way to licence. He himself had set the example by eating pork and marrying several wives; his marriages were reputed to have been uncon-summated, so that Nathan surmised his ancestor's tastes had coincided with his own. He had been subject to wild mood-swings – it was in his manic phase that he had thrown himself into every kind of forbidden joy, whereas in the depressive one he crouched in a corner and nibbled his beard.

It had always seemed right to Nathan that *his* Messiah should be like the original – a man of crude appetites and guilty of outrageous behaviour. But after he met Kris, his conception changed drastically. There were days when Rita, arriving at his apartment, found Nathan bleary-eyed after working till the early hours of the morning. He was revising his entire script, writing new treatments with a new central figure. He didn't work in secret but shared his thoughts with everyone he met.

He might be at some fundraiser in a hotel or club of Titian splendour seated at a donor's table for ten, eating in the rather frenzied way he had – he perspired a lot when he ate and his black tie came undone. Telling his fellow guests about his new Messiah, he spoke with a passion that made him lay his hand on his heart to prevent it from brimming over. 'Oh, you're so wonderful, Nathan,' they said. They really meant it. He was inspiring, and it was a marvellous sensation for everyone at that table to be inspired by something chaste and pure for an evening (though next morning they might not be returning his calls).

It became a conversation piece at social events to cast Nathan's new Messiah. The old one had been easy – there were any number of character actors or fat ageing stars who could have played him. But it was impossibly difficult to envisage the new Messiah in any actor – in any person, really. For the way Nathan described him was not like an embodied person at all but one who was – and this was a phrase he constantly used about him – 'clothed in light'; and when he said this, Nathan shut his eyes as if himself flooded with light. His fellow guests teased him: 'You're in love, Nathan!' He admitted it; yes, he was in love with the ideal of someone who walked the earth completely untouched and untarnished by its earthiness. 'Whoever will you get to play him?' they wondered, but went on to call out the names of several hot young actors. Nathan waved them away: all these young men had the wrong physical attributes – one had thick lips, another short legs – and they had also been tainted by ugly divorces, tax evasions, paternity suits, getting into fights and drugs. And even if there were some actor (though he himself couldn't think of one) who had both physical and moral perfection, he would be disqualified by the fact that he *was* an actor – had been sullied by newsprint and the gaze of thousands eating popcorn. Nathan cited the precedent of other directors who had had to cast difficult parts. One, searching for a prophet in the wilderness, had found a young French aristocrat who had never left his family's estate in Normandy; another, for the Virgin Mary, had chosen an English debutante fresh from her first London season.

Kris had a piece of news. 'I'll make your drink first; you must be *so tired*, poor Rita.' After she had drunk it, and they were eating the meal he had prepared: 'I've got a job.' She said, 'Oh no. Oh why?' He laughed. 'Think of the money! Five hundred a week. Fabulous, what? A fortune.' He kept this up all evening, trying to laugh and tease her out of her distress. He was used to having to do this whenever he took up some new employment. This one was in a very smart men's outfitter where she knew he would be exposed to the eyes of every customer walking in off the street; and they would be exposed to his charm, which he could not help exuding.

Although usually she went to sleep long before him, that night she lay awake. Their walk-up apartment was noisy, there was a diner downstairs and the kitchen workers clattered and shouted till after midnight, and Kris was watching a late show in the other room, which was partitioned from the bedroom by a cardboard-thin wall. When his programme was finished, he turned it off and came into the bedroom. They had always slept together in twin beds side by side, since he was eight years old; before that, he had shared her bed and couldn't sleep except curled up against her. She watched him now changing into his pyjamas. After some time, when they were both lying very still in their two beds, he stretched out his hand for her to take; and that was how she finally managed to fall asleep, not comforted but at least with his hand lying lightly in hers.

The next evening, Rita, having accepted Nathan's invitation for herself and Kris, turned up alone. Nathan seemed to crumple up in his evening clothes. 'Oh no!' he cried, stamping his patent-leather pump, completely forgetting his usual courtesy and Rita's feelings. She made an excuse – Kris had a headache. 'He could have taken an aspirin or something,' Nathan said. The two of them went alone and it was a depressing evening for Nathan; he didn't notice it was for Rita too, that in fact she had arrived in such a mood, with her eyes red-rimmed. And soon there was another evening that Nathan had arranged for the three of them when again she came alone, again claiming a headache for Kris. But when it happened a third time, she had to tell him the truth – that Kris had an engagement with someone else. Nathan questioned her more closely than he might have done if he had been interested in keeping up the least pretence of indifference. And Rita too showed more of her feelings than she usually did when she told Nathan that Kris now had a job, which had inevitably widened his social contacts.

Nathan hardly ever got up in time to make lunch appointments, so when Rita saw him at eleven o'clock in the morning dressing up in a pearl pinstripe suit with a pale pink shirt and a tie with gold crowns on it, she could easily guess where he was going. She had gone there herself, on the second day that Kris had started work. Nathan arrived home carrying a package containing a cashmere sweater. The next time he came back with an Italian robe. He proudly showed off his purchases to Rita, but otherwise he was secretive about his morning's activity – in so far as he could be secretive, for as usual his plump, white face expressed his inner feelings as though they had been plastered on in greasepaint.

Kris, on the other hand, could be secretive, if he wanted to. On this occasion he didn't want to. Although he said nothing about Nathan's first visit, when she asked him on the second day, 'Did Nathan come to see you at the store?' he replied: 'Yes, wasn't that kind of him? He bought a silk robe, Italian, very expensive, and he's asked me for lunch tomorrow. I told him I only get forty-five minutes so he said we'd go somewhere nearby. He's awfully nice.'

They went out to lunch three days in succession, and three times Nathan told Rita nothing and Kris described exactly, without her having to ask, where they had gone, what they had eaten and what Nathan had said.

On the third day Kris reported that Nathan wanted him to leave his job. 'And do what?' Rita asked.

'You'll never guess.' Kris laughed.

She guessed at once. 'You're not an actor.'

'That's why: he says he doesn't want an actor.'

'Then what does he want?'

Kris laughed again. 'He wants me.'

When she arrived for work, she told Nathan, before even taking off her coat, that she was going back to England. Nathan was still half asleep in his enormous bed, amid fleur-de-lys sheets. 'Kris and I both, of course,' she added.

Without waiting for his reaction, she went straight out to sort the papers he had left lying about for her in his study, which was also their workroom. This was no more worklike than the bedroom; Nathan had surrounded himself with exquisite and valuable objects, scattered about and so numerous that one was apt to stumble over them. Fortunately, not much could break because there were soft surfaces everywhere, cushions and carpets and upholstered chaises longues.

He had followed her, tying the robe he had bought from Kris. He tried to sound reasonable, even paternal. 'What will you go to London and *do*?'

'Why, you think I'm not good enough to get another job?'

'My dear, I know better than anyone how good, how very good you are.'

'Thank you,' she said tightly. She was aware of the way Nathan was looking at her. Rita had a good figure – she was tall and slim – and pretty dark brown hair; but she was used to people thinking, and even hinting, what a pity it was that the brother should have all the beauty. Even their mother had said it, when drunk and angry.

Nathan said, 'No one understands the project better than you, and you know how close we are now to getting it off the ground.'

'You don't have a star.'

'I don't need a star. I've explained that to you and I thought you understood.'

'Oh yes. I've understood.' She began to tremble and then to accuse him: 'Who are you to tell him what to do? He was so proud to have found work all by himself and to help me with our expenses. He's always done that. I wanted him to have more education, but he left school at sixteen to go out and find work.'

'And do you like him going out to work?'

'Yes. Because *he* likes it.'

She had been through this before: men like Nathan, and women too, wanting Kris to leave whatever job he had and come to work for them in something they had concocted for him. Sometimes Kris did and sometimes he didn't – but whatever his decision, it was always his own, reached for reasons of his own that he shared with no one.

'Can we talk?' Nathan said. 'The three of us?'

'Kris and I have talked. It's all settled.'

This was far from the truth, but that was not for Nathan to know – any more than he needed to know that she was as much in the dark as he was. Kris's nature was as clear as his countenance. Yet there was one area in him, one secret unknown place where even she could not penetrate. It wasn't

166

that it was deliberately shut off from her but that he seemed unable to reveal it: as if it were as much a secret place to him as to her, where his intentions formed themselves almost without his knowledge.

Kris liked working in the store, and everyone, colleagues and customers, liked him. Some of them loved him, which always happened, and though he preferred it when they only liked him, he did his best to deal gently with the others. He was very sensitive to people's feelings, probably because of always being careful with his sister, who was easily hurt. He himself was immune in that respect: his attachments were light enough never to chafe him – including that to his sister, though he wouldn't have admitted it. What he liked best was to be alone; one might have said alone with his thoughts except that he didn't have that many, or as far as he knew any very deep ones. He was also fortunate in that he could be alone while – for instance – joking around with the other young salesmen and dealing with customers (or clients, as they were called in his high-class establishment). It was rare for anyone on whom he attended to leave the store without the purchase he had recommended. This was because he genuinely felt the client's need for a particular item, and also because he himself admired it so much, stroking the luxurious silk of a scarf or necktie and making it irresistible by modelling it himself. All the time, though, he remained inside himself, detached and alone. The same when he was walking in the streets, which he enjoyed doing (but actually, he enjoyed everything). Often he would walk home instead of taking the subway, not to save money but to have an hour or so to himself. It didn't matter to him whether he was in New York or in London, or in Rome or Paris, where he was sometimes taken to stay in villas and grand hotels. The streets, the buildings were everywhere beautiful to him, so were the parks and monuments, though everything he passed or passed through was no more than a scrim covering something else even better. The sky in all its times and seasons was the best of all to him, and he experienced it so intensely that it seemed to remain inside him, transformed into a flowering garden. At night, lying in the bed next to Rita's and holding her hand, he lingered in that garden, staying awake much longer than she suspected – tranquil but also expectant not for anything in particular, not for a person, but for a call, a mission that might come to him provided he remained patient enough to wait for it.

Whenever the three of them attended some gala dinner, Rita would be placed at the same table with Nathan, as a pair, while Kris was accommodated wherever a single man might be required between two ladies. But on one occasion it happened that Kris too was seated at their table, exactly opposite Nathan. It was in one of the grandest clubs in New York and was to honour the scion of one of the oldest families of New York State for his work in preserving a well-known city landmark.

The dinner for two hundred and fifty guests was held in the main hall, which reached five storeys up to the glassed-in roof supported by cast-iron trusses. Granite staircases swept in two wings to the second floor where a small orchestra was seated under oil paintings of former donors and committee members. These were the ancestors of many of the guests assembled there, who were wry among themselves about the ways their money had been made – not in the railways and coal mines on which earlier family fortunes had been founded but in humbler products of domestic use. However, it was these families who were now the oldest aristocracy, and one already on the point of extinction. Everyone there was old, very very old; if they had children and grandchildren, these did not frequent the club but had taken a different direction – some to become carpenters, or to join spiritual groups, or make documentary films, fleeing every vestige of family tradition as though it were a curse. Sometimes it was a curse, and one that, if it hadn't been generally known, would have been a dark secret – alcoholism, suicides, even a suspected murder: declines that it had taken European aristocracies centuries to reach had here been achieved within a couple of generations.

Nathan's mother had come from a similar background, but his own blood had been refreshed by its exotic infusion. Also, he was an artist, adding to the sense of superiority he felt towards this company. When the speeches carried on too long – and they all did – he didn't disguise his boredom. He leaned back in his chair, rolled breadcrumbs on the table, and smiled across at Kris. Both Kris and Rita were listening with the zealous attention of outsiders. Along with everyone else, they applauded each reference lauding the dedication of the guest of honour. They smiled at humorous recollections of past events – if the guests hadn't been at school together, they had been at the same debutante dances, polo matches and university football games. But there was general relief when the last speaker – the guest of honour himself, an erect old gentleman whom everyone called Freddy – sat down and the steward signalled to his team of waiters to begin circling with the desserts.

The entire room was laden with billionaires, most of them in their seventies or eighties. Nathan had arranged for his party to be seated with the president of an international investment company, the heir to a supermarket chain and the descendant of a cosmetics empire. It may have been the presence of so much money that inspired Nathan, or it may have been the presence of Kris. Cutting across the pleasant interchange between old acquaintances about their diets and surgical procedures, he spoke as usual about his film; he had been doing that for years – everyone had heard him – but now in such a way that he induced these mighty men and women to silent introspection. The granite of their faces unexpectedly softened while Nathan offered a hope they had not thought to hope for. He seemed to be making them all extras in his film, metamorphosing these excessively endowed New Yorkers into seventeenth-century Middle-Eastern Jews – rabbis and moneylenders, small traders and thieves – who, after centuries of oppression and suffering, were suddenly told that the Messiah was on his way to them. He admitted freely that at first he had supported a false Messiah, one who had expounded a doctrine of redemption through being steeped in sin. But far from being steeped in it, the true Messiah had no conception of sin. Have you done insidious deeds such as manipulating the stock exchange, falsifying tax returns, for-nicating with teenage girls? The new Messiah would come and redeem you with his purity. Because he is innocent, he will make you innocent. The heiress seated next to Kris put her hand on his. Nathan nodded at him in smiling encour-agement, and shy though he was, reticent, self-effacing, Kris took that old hand and pressed it as in promise to a humble child. It wasn't going to be an expensive film, Nathan said; ten million, fifteen, twenty at the most – what was that in these days of inflated budgets? There weren't enough ladies to go around at that table, so on his other side Kris was seated next to the hereditary cosmetics king, heavy and hardened with his own money. This man too put his hand on Kris's; and now it was as though the entire table were holding hands, all of them united, like a circle of disciples or dervishes, in a promise and a pledge.

Shortly after that evening, and largely as a result of it, Nathan got his finance together. A period of tremendous activity followed.

He went from meeting to meeting all over town – always running late, constantly telephoning Rita with new instructions, urging her not to go home before he returned. He told her to ask the housekeeper to prepare supper for her as well as for himself – 'And for Kris, if he's around,' he added, casually, before hanging up.

She was never entirely sure whether Kris would be around. They usually left their apartment together in the mornings – he to take the subway to his place of work, she the bus to hers; from the moment she got up, she plotted how to ask him what he was doing in the evening, but often she couldn't manage it until the last moment before he descended into the subway. She knew he wouldn't tell her a lie, and sometimes he did say he had a date with someone from work, but mostly he said he wasn't sure – and it was the truth, she knew, and also knew he was keeping his options open, whatever these might be. So like Nathan she too was in suspense; and when, at the end of the day, Kris did show up at Nathan's, she couldn't hide her relief and joy, not even from Nathan – she met him at the door when he came in and said, 'He's here.'

Once Nathan came home so late that Kris had fallen asleep on the living-room sofa. Rita had covered him with a blanket. She tried to wake him, but Nathan said, 'No, don't.' He went into his bedroom and came out with an Indian shawl; this he substituted for the blanket – so gently that Kris never stirred. Nathan stood gazing down at him. Then he said, 'Why is he so tired?'

'Well, naturally, he's been working all day at his store.'

'And last night – where did he go last night?' Rita hesitated, and Nathan stopped looking at the brother to look at the sister: 'Did he get home very late?'

Now Rita replied promptly: 'Oh no. He was home by the time I got there.'

Unlike Kris, she didn't mind telling a lie when necessary. But it was she herself who was very tired, having waited up for Kris till three o'clock in the morning. And when he came, he kept her up longer while he undressed and lay down next to her, telling her about his evening – he told her in detail, leaving out, she presumed, nothing.

Again she made to wake him and again Nathan restrained her. 'Why don't you leave him here for the night?' he said. 'You stay too. You could be in Mother's old room – why don't you? You'll like it. It's so pretty and it gets the morning sun.'

'We're going home.' She called Kris's name and put out her hand to shake him; Nathan caught it, and when she struggled to free herself, he gripped it tighter. For a moment they stood glaring at each other.

Nathan let go; he said, 'No. Let's do this in a nice way.' Then he said, 'This thing has gotten very big, you know that.'

'Big for you, not for us.'

Although they were no longer trying to keep their voices down, Kris went on sleeping under the soft Indian shawl.

Nathan said, 'I'm taking him away. No no, not from you, of course not, I would never try that. I mean take him away with me on the location scout. He has to see all these places – all his former haunts.' Nathan smiled.

'If you think he cares for travel or luxury hotels or your first-class plane seats, if you think you can seduce him with any of that—'

'Seduce?' Nathan said, and repeated it as if he didn't believe his ears.

And she repeated it too, so loudly that Kris woke and sat up and rubbed his eyes. He looked from one to the other. He said, 'I'm hungry.'

Nathan shouted: 'Of course you are! We all are! Starving! Ravenous! We're on the point of devouring each other!'

'We'll pick something up on the way home,' Rita said. 'That chicken barbecue place is open till after midnight.'

She went out to get both their coats, leaving the two men alone. She took a moment to fix her hair in the mirror on the hallstand – standing there listening for what they might be saying to each other. But she heard nothing. When she returned, Kris was putting on his shoes, ready for departure, and trying to prevent Nathan from kneeling down to help him.

Next day Rita didn't leave for her job. She spent the day alone in their apartment – that ugly little place, with a hole of a kitchen in which she often had to kill cockroaches (Kris couldn't kill anything) and occasionally mice, well fed from the restaurant downstairs. Although she wished they could have afforded better accommodation, she didn't really mind and neither did Kris; they were used to shabby places and never contrasted them unfavourably with the way people like Nathan lived.

But now Kris said he wanted them to move. This was while they were eating the little meal she had cooked for the two of them. 'Is that your idea?' she asked, putting down her knife and fork. She ate in a very nice way, the English way, and she had taught him to do the same.

'Well, it's Nathan's actually, but I think so too. I mean, look what happened last night, it's ridiculous and I feel stupid, falling asleep like that, on the sofa . . . '

'You want us to move in with Nathan?' When he was silent, she said: 'Did he come to see you at the store today?'

'He came to take me out to lunch. He sends you his love and hopes your cold is better – I had to tell him that, you know, to explain why you stayed home.' He blushed, ashamed to have resorted to a lie on her behalf. It made him the more determined to be absolutely candid with her: 'I think Nathan's right, and it'd be much more convenient for everyone—'

'For him?'

'Yes, and for you and me. You and I?' he queried, for she was careful of his grammar, also of his accent which she had carefully pruned of any influence from the immigrant and other poor London children he had gone to school with.

'You and me is all right. But aren't you and I – see, here it's the subject, see the difference? – aren't we leaving, going back home?'

'Rita, Rita,' he reproached her.

Both got up though they hadn't quite finished eating. He began to clear the dishes, and when she tried to help him, he said, 'No, don't – you must be tired.'

'From what? From my cold? . . . I don't see why you had to tell him a lie. Why couldn't you say straight out that we're leaving? That's no secret. I told him long ago; he should have got used to the idea by now.'

They had been there before: whenever she had to get him away from someone who was laying too large a claim on him. Each time he had resisted – always because he couldn't understand what it was she had against that person. 'But he's so kind,' he would argue. 'Such a good friend.' She invented every kind of calumny against this friend, and though he made no pretence of believing her, he gave in to her – for her sake, because he saw how unhappy she was. But this time, with Nathan, he didn't argue; he said nothing.

Rita no longer went to work for Nathan and he made no attempt to call her back. She rarely went out but stayed alone all day, pounded by street and kitchen noises from below. The telephone stood dumb. No one called her, and she refrained from calling the only person she wanted to talk to because she knew Kris was embarrassed to be called at work. But he came home to her every night and was as frank as ever about his activities. So she learned that Nathan, though frantically busy, came punctually every day to take Kris out during his lunch break. She was also fully informed what they talked about – the film of course, and how Nathan was still trying to persuade them to give up their apartment and move into his. Kris continued to think this a good idea. 'He says you can have his mother's room – it's so pretty and gets the morning sun.' The third time he said this, Rita put her hands over her ears. Then he quietly dropped the subject, and next day he told Nathan to drop it too.

'He was so nice about it,' Kris told Rita. 'He said if that's the way Rita feels, it's all right, we'll do exactly what she wants.'

'We? Who's we?'

'Oh gosh, Rita,' he said but smiling. 'You and I of course.'

'That's right: you and I,' she said, determined, grim.

It was easy for Nathan to let go of that plan because now he and Kris were discussing their location scout. This too Kris reported to Rita: how they would go to all the places where the film was to be shot. Lebanon, Jordan, the Holy Land – 'Rita, imagine!' She realised that this situation was not like the others from which she had had to disengage him, because this time she had come up not only against a person – not only Nathan, or even his film, or all the exotic ancient countries of their itinerary – but against Kris himself: that place in him to which neither she nor anyone had access.

She said, 'What about me?' in a voice she made small and weak, though ashamed of using this tactic.

His reaction was instantaneous. 'You? But you're coming with us!'

She said she was going back to London. She wanted to sound positive, unyielding, but knew she didn't because she wasn't. She was pliant with supplication, needing all his love for her. He knelt to put his arms around her waist, his head in her lap.

He begged her not to go – but he did not say that he would go with her nor, if she didn't change her plan, that he would change one iota of his.

Next day just before his lunch break, she went to see Kris at the men's store. The place was hushed and sacred with good taste; beautiful young salesmen stood discreetly at the sides, waiting to be selected by one of the customers who entered with the air of hunters on the scent of new attire. Rita felt like an intruder – she *was* one, but although Kris was engaged in selling a cravat, bestowing his grace and courtesy on his client, he took a second off to reassure her with a flick of his smiling eyes.

He did the same to Nathan when he came in; and Nathan greeted Rita warmly and consulted her on the potential purchase of an Italian robe. She gave her advice, not reminding him how he had quite recently bought one from Kris; and when they left for lunch, it was taken for granted that she would be of their party.

Obviously they were expected – their table was ready, and a third place was quickly added. It was a famous restaurant, over-burdened with decorations as luxurious as the gateaux and soufflés being wheeled around on carts. It was the favourite lunch resort for ranking people in the film industry: top agents and studio executives just flown in from the Coast. The seating hierarchy was as strictly observed as at a court, or in their offices; the upholstered booths along the sides belonged to the top echelons, that is, those with ultimate decision over the cash flow. As an independent producer, Nathan rated a table within shouting distance of the royal booths. A lot of shouting did go on, from table to table, not for actual communication but as proof that one knew and was known. It also mattered how many and who stopped to chat at whose table, and how loudly everyone laughed; for the conversation consisted of joshing and joking, as in a locker room. They were mostly men – the older ones short and stocky like Nathan, the younger ones smooth, tall and blond, hand-fed on vitamins. There were a few women who told scatological jokes and knocked back Bloody Marys. There was the occasional famous face – an actor being entertained by his agent – and once a very famous actress wafted her way along a row of tables, tall under an immensely tall hairdo, as effulgent as the sun and wearing the self-effacing smile of someone who could never be effaced.

Nathan greeted, shouted, played the game along with the rest; but what was going on at their table for three was of a different order. Although it was an actual journey he was proposing to Rita and Kris, in using the antique names – Aleppo, Smyrna, Adrianople – he conjured up their past with ships in their harbours and the sultan at his court; and from there he penetrated into the heart of their ghettos, which was also the heart of his film, where devout shopkeepers felt a stirring of the soul that told them the Messiah was coming.

'*He* was coming,' Nathan said, pointing at Kris, who lowered his eyes and smiled in a charmingly deprecating way.

'He's not an actor,' Rita repeated stubbornly.

'Nobody would believe an actor,' Nathan said.

'But they'd believe him?'

'They'd believe *in* him,' Nathan answered her. He leaned forward and spoke in the intimate, passionate way he used whenever he wanted to fire financiers up about his project. Now it was to Rita that he described the lives of the believers, humble, despised, persecuted, forced to practise their faith in secret – and then, in their darkest hour, that promise, whispered from shop to shop and alley to alley, that the Redeemer was on his way.

'People want to see him. They need to see him,' Nathan said.

'Who do you mean? Kris? Or the character in your film?'

Just then someone beckoned to Nathan, who, excusing himself, got up to join him. It was an actors' agent, in the process of negotiating a contract with Nathan for a client; but now he had called him to tell him the latest joke that was making the rounds of the studios about a recently fired executive. When they had finished laughing, Nathan directed the other's attention towards Kris.

The agent looked, appreciated. He said, 'Who's his agent?'

Nathan said, 'You are.'

Left alone for a moment of privacy, Kris and Rita exchanged – not words, not even glances, they didn't have to do that. Kris was fully alive to her doubts and fears and wanted only to still them. 'It'll be OK,' he said. 'It'll be fun, Rita. A fun trip.'

But what she surmised in him had nothing to do with a fun trip. She realised that whatever Nathan believed, or pretended to, Kris *truly* believed.

'I can't do this without you. It's a big job, Rita. A terrific responsibility – I mean, all these *people*.' He waved his slender hand around the restaurant, indicating to her all that gross luxury and the sinners in it making deals. 'I've got to help them because, you see, really in their hearts they want something different; like they're waiting for it; like they've been promised.'

She had never seen him so worked up. He was fervent, inspired – not from outside, but as from that inner source that had, up till now, remained secret and hidden. He was pleading with her: 'I can't let them down, Rita.'

She kissed his cheek (it was burning). She didn't understand or believe in his mission, but she knew that she had to be by his side for whatever it was he felt called upon to do. She persuaded herself that she was necessary to him, that he needed her. But really she knew it was the other way around, and that it was she who needed him, just as much as did all the others who so passionately desired him. She already surmised that soon these would no longer be counted as individuals but in their tens of thousands. This was confirmed for her when Nathan and the agent joined them, each of them laying a hand on Kris's shoulders, each of them smiling – as delicately reverent as though touching a golden idol capable of fulfilling every promise, every wish.

Pagans

Brigitte: calm, large-limbed and golden as a pagan goddess, she loved to lie spreadeagled on the beach or by her swimming pool, in communication with the sun. Los Angeles had been good to her. When she was young, at the time of her marriage, she had been a successful model. Her husband, Louis Morgenstern, was a small wizened shrewd little man, thirty years older than herself but a studio head, a powerful producer, a very rich man. It had been a relief for her to give up her career. She preferred to swim, to sunbathe, to give dinner parties for Louis (studded with stars but as dull, in their different way, as those her sister Frances gave in New York for her banker husband); also to travel in Europe and occasionally take lovers – wry intellectuals who taught her what to read and confirmed her contempt for the sorts of films made by the studios, including her husband's.

Her sister Frances had been very sceptical about the marriage to Louis. She was wrong. In spite of the lovers – kept secret, discreet – it lasted almost thirty years and so did Brigitte's respect and liking for her husband. While Frances had married conventionally within their own circle settled in the US for several generations, Louis was the first in his family to be born here and still had a grandmother who spoke no English. Frances and her husband Marshall were ashamed of what they considered their sister's misalliance. They felt themselves to tower over Louis and his family – socially of course, culturally, and physically too, as was clear at the wedding when tiny Morgensterns scurried among the lofty trees of bankers and real estate developers. Afterwards Marshall joked about the ill-matched couple and how Brigitte would be crushing Louis on their wedding night between her mighty thighs.

Brigitte was in her fifties when Louis died, and Frances, for whom Los Angeles was a wasteland, said, 'Now perhaps you'll come back to civilisation.' Brigitte sold her house – the Hollywood mansion of indoor and outdoor pools, patios and screening rooms – while Frances searched for a suitable apartment in New York for her. Meanwhile Brigitte moved into a suite in a hotel, and although Frances found one Upper East Side apartment and then another, all close to herself and Marshall, Brigitte kept making excuses not to move into them. She liked Los Angeles; unlike New York, it was lightweight and undemanding. From one hotel window, she could see pretty houses frail as plywood scattered over the wooded hillside. From another, she had a view over the city of Los Angeles spread flat as far as the horizon; at night it was transformed into a field of shimmering flickering glow-worms fenced by the cut-out silhouettes of high-rise buildings. And the trees – the tall straight palm trees with their sparse foliage brushing a sky that was sometimes Renaissance blue and sometimes silver with pollution but all day held the sun to pour down on the ocean, the golden beach and Brigitte herself, past menopause but still golden and firm in her designer swimsuit, and pads on her large smooth lids luxuriantly shut.

Frances was getting impatient. I suppose she has a new lover out there, she thought to herself; and she said it to Brigitte over the phone: 'Who is it now, another of those foreigners filling your head with clever rubbish.'

Brigitte laughed; she had always laughed at Frances's disapproval, whether it was of Louis, of her lovers or of her indolence. Brigitte still had male friends – she needed them to tell her what to read – but she had long since reached a stage where she could admit that sex was boring for her. With Louis, she had enjoyed sitting beside him while he explained their stocks and shares and other holdings to her. By the time he died, he had been ill for some years but was only semi-retired, for his successors at the studio continued to need his experience and his financial clout. Twice a year he and Brigitte still gave their dinner parties where the agents and the money men mixed with the stars. Louis had little respect for most of the stars; he mocked their pretensions and perversions, their physical beauty which he said was the work of plastic surgeons and monkey glands. After each dinner party and the departure of the famous guests, he kissed Brigitte in gratitude for what she was: full-figured and naturally tanned, almost Nordic, God knew how and it was not only the hairdresser and the beautician. Louis had grown-up children from a previous marriage, and when it turned out that Brigitte couldn't have any, he was glad, wanting to keep her perfect, unmarred. Actually, Brigitte was not sorry either; she didn't think she had time for children. Frances said anyway she was too slothful and untidy ever to be able to bring them up. Frances had untold trouble with her own now grown-up son and daughter, who had gone the unstable way of the young and too rich.

*

Two years after selling her house, Brigitte was still in Los Angeles. By this time she had met Shoki, a young Indian, and an interesting relationship had developed. It may have appeared a classic case of older woman with impoverished young immigrant, but that was not the way it was at all. It was true that he was young, very young; it was also true that he was poor, insofar as he had no money, but the word impoverished was inapplicable. He had the refinement of someone born rich – not so much in money as in inherited culture. This expressed itself in him physically in fine features and limbs; culturally in his manners, his almost feminine courtesy; and spiritually – so Brigitte liked to think – in his eyes, as of a soul that yearned for higher being. These eyes were often downcast, the lashes brushing his cheeks, for he was shy – out of modesty not lack of confidence. As far as confidence was concerned, he reposed as on a rock of ancestral privilege, so that it never mattered to him that he had to take all kinds of lowly jobs to keep himself going. Brigitte had met him while he was doing valet parking at her hotel; he had been filling in for another boy and left after a few weeks to work in a restaurant, again filling in for someone else. There were always these jobs available in a shifting population of unemployed or temporarily unemployed actors and other aspirants to film and television careers.

He himself wanted to become a writer-director, which was why he was here so far from home. He informed Brigitte that film was the medium of expression for his generation – he said it as though it were an idea completely original to himself. He carried a very bulky manuscript from agent to agent, or rather to their secretaries, and was always ready to read from it. Encouraged by Brigitte, he sat in her suite and read to her, while she watched rather than listened to him. Maybe it was all nonsense; but maybe it wasn't, or no more than the films on which Louis had grown so immensely rich; and she wanted him to be successful, so that he wouldn't go away, or wouldn't sink along with the other young people for whom he filled in on an endless round of temporary jobs.

She introduced him to Ralph, who had started off as a producer and now had his own talent agency. He had often been among her and Louis's guests, the powerful locals who had been their friends or had considered themselves so. Actually, some of them had made a pass at her – as who did not, even when she had been beyond the age when any woman could have expected it. Usually she laughed at them, and the one she had laughed at the most had been Ralph: 'Come on, you don't mean it.' Finally he had to admit that he did not. His excuse was that she was irresistible. 'At fifty-five?' she asked. He was the only person ever to explain to her in what way, and of course it was easier for him, with his lack of taste for women, to be impersonal. He said that her attraction was her indifference – the fact that she just *was*, the way a pagan goddess is, Pallas Athene or someone, ready to accept worship but unconcerned whether it is given or not.

The introduction to Ralph was a success. Shoki came back enthusiastic about Ralph's kindness to him. When Brigitte phoned Ralph to thank him, Ralph said it was one's duty to help young talent. He sounded guarded; there was a silence, then she said, 'So what did you think?'

'About the screenplay? It's interesting. Different.'

'Yes, isn't it.'

Brigitte had hoped Ralph would have a more explicit opinion. She knew for herself that the work was different, and also difficult. The characters spoke in a poetic prose that was not easy to understand, but it sounded beautiful when Shoki read it to her, and every time he looked up for her appreciation, she had no difficulty giving it. Then he continued, satisfied – though really he did not need approval, he had the same confidence in his work as he did in himself.

When there was another crisis in his living arrangement, Brigitte solved it by taking a room for him in the hotel. He was concerned about the expense, but when she reassured him that it wasn't a suite, just a single room, he moved in with his small baggage. He liked it very much. It was on the second floor and overlooked the hotel garden with its cypress trees and silver fountain. It was also decided around this time that it was really not necessary for Shoki to take any more jobs when he could do so many helpful things for Brigitte.

Frances found the perfect New York apartment for her sister and Brigitte agreed to take it, pay a deposit, sign papers – 'Oh please, Frankie, whatever.' Frances was not satisfied; she knew she was being got rid of and asked herself, What's going on? Unfortunately she had no one with whom to share her doubts. Although she and her husband Marshall were known and seen everywhere as an indivisible couple – large and rich – the communication between them was not intimate. Whenever she tried to confide some deeper concerns to him, he answered her with an indifferent grunt or by rattling his newspaper at her in irritation.

'What's the matter with you?' she reproached Brigitte over the telephone. 'What's wrong? I thought you wanted to come.' Then she said, 'Do you have someone out there? A relationship?'

'Oh absolutely. He's sitting right here.' Brigitte smiled across the room at Shoki, who looked up inquiringly and smiled back.

'It's not a joke. And if you knew how I've been running around trying to find the right apartment for you, and at last I have.'

'Bless you,' Brigitte thanked her, but Frances remained dissatisfied.

A few days later, after a particularly annoying telephone conversation with Brigitte, Frances decided it would be best if she went herself to Los Angeles. She proposed this idea to Marshall who said at once, 'Impossible.' They were about to go out to someone's anniversary dinner – she had laid out his evening clothes and was putting on her jewellery.

'Only for a few days,' she said.

'Oh yes? And what about the hospital ball, the library, the God-knows-for-what fundraiser?' He was looking at himself in the mirror, adjusting his suspenders over his dress shirt. He was a big broad man carrying a load of stomach in front, but it gave him pleasure to dress up and see himself. She, on the other hand, inserted her earrings as though she were undergoing a disagreeable ritual.

'Why?' he said. As if he didn't know that her reason for going to Los Angeles could only be her sister. But she wasn't going to spell anything out for him: if Brigitte was to be mentioned, he would have to do it. 'You hate flying,' he said, holding out a sleeve for her to insert the cufflink. 'You sit there as if the pilot's one ambition is to crash the plane with you in it. You spoil every trip you take with me before it's even started ... I thought you told me she was moving to New York.'

Frances was now concentrating on tying his black tie, something he had had no cause to learn since she did it so expertly.

'Well, is she or isn't she?'

'I don't know.'

'You don't know. That's your sister all over – playing mystery, making everyone dance to her tune.'

But later, inside their chauffeured limousine, where they took up the entire back seat as they sat side by side in their party clothes: 'Call the office to book your seat; or remind me tomorrow, I'll tell them.'

Frances was querulous. The flight had been as horrible as she had expected, she already hated her room and it was all

Brigitte's fault for making her come here. 'Yes you did – I knew something was up, and who else is there to care except me?'

'Darling,' Brigitte acknowledged. She looked around the room. 'But it's charming, what's wrong with it?'

'It's cheap and gaudy, like a film set. And the light is giving me a headache.'

'I'll draw the curtain' – but Brigitte regretted having to exclude the sun, the bright view.

'Marshall thinks you have a lover, that's why you're sticking on here.'

'Did Marshall say that?'

'I'm sure it's what he's thinking.'

'I have a friend,' Brigitte said.

'A man?'

'God, Frances. What are you thinking?'

'Who knows, nowadays.' Frances was sad, thinking of her own children, about whose lives she could only speculate. 'How old is he?'

'Young. Very young, Frankie.'

Her sister was the only person left in the world to call her Frankie, and Frances's mood softened. She said, 'I suppose it happens, especially in this place. You'd be far better off in New York.'

'There are no young men there?'

'I'm there. We'd be together again, after so many years … We don't have to be lonely.'

With her cool lips, Brigitte kissed her sister's cheek. 'You must be dropping. I'll let you rest.'

Frances agreed meekly. She really was tired – certainly too tired to call Marshall and tell him she had arrived safely. Anyway, he would only say that, if she hadn't, he would have heard about it soon enough.

But it was he who called her. He even asked about her flight;

he also asked about her return booking, and would she and Brigitte be arriving together? She told him she was worried about the New York apartment for which she was negotiating – it was very desirable and others might preempt it – and in reply he did what she had hoped, asked for details, so she knew that he would be following them up and far more efficiently than she could. There was no reason after that not to hang up, but at the last moment he said, 'What's she tell you?'

'About what?'

'About being a crazy woman and getting herself in a mess back there.'

Brigitte was woken up by a phone call from Ralph, asking her if she knew where Shoki was. He was trying not to sound agitated. 'He's not in his room so I thought he'd be with you.'

'No, but he'll be here for breakfast.'

'Breakfast! Do you know what the time is? ... Anyway, he was supposed to be here; I'd set up a breakfast meeting for him. Remember? I'm his agent.'

Brigitte said, 'Of course.' But it was true – she really had forgotten about this connection between Shoki and Ralph. Maybe she had even forgotten that Shoki was here for any other purpose than to be with her. She asked, 'Do you and he often have breakfast meetings?'

'Well. Most days. I'm trying to help him, Brigitte.' She could hear Ralph trying to choke down his anxiety. He said, 'Have you any idea where he spends the night? You think he's in his room, don't you, but have you ever checked?' His voice rose. 'Don't you ever wonder?' he asked, angry with her now.

Actually, she did wonder sometimes – not as Ralph evidently did, with anguish, but with curiosity, even pleasure. She knew it was not possible for Shoki to restrict himself to people he liked but who, by virtue of their age, were barred from one whole potent side of his nature. For that he did need – she freely admitted it – those as young as himself, and as gay (possibly in both senses). But to Ralph she only said, 'What's happening with his screenplay?'

'It still needs work.' He swept aside the irrelevant subject. 'The fact is, he needs someone to take charge, be a bit strict with him.'

'You mean to make him work?'

'Yes yes, that too. Now listen, Brigitte, we need to talk—'

'Oh,' she said quickly, 'there's someone at the door. That may be he.'

But it was Frances. Brigitte went back to the phone. 'No, it's my sister. She's here from New York.'

'Do you realise he was not in his room, not at midnight, not early this morning?'

'My sister and I are going out now. This minute. We have a dental appointment.'

When Brigitte was off the phone, Frances said, 'I don't know why you have to tell people lies all the time.'

'That's not fair, Frankie.' But she reflected for a while. 'It's mostly to save their feelings.'

Frances was silent; she drew in her lips. 'Don't ever think you have to save mine.'

After a moment of surprise, 'Of course not!' Brigitte said. 'Why should I think that? Why should anyone?' But in her heart she thought, yours most of all. A rush of love and pity filled her, and she kissed her sister.

There was a very brief knock – for courtesy, not permission – and then Shoki came in. It was exactly the time he appeared every day. Wherever he might have been all night and this morning, now he was fresh, rested, smiling and terribly pleased to meet Brigitte's sister. As for Frances, whatever prejudice she might have had was entirely swept away: it was as if she herself was swept clean of all negative thinking. If she had come to assess the situation, she would have to start all over again with entirely different premises.

How to explain anything to Marshall? He had never in all their life together been so attentive with phone calls; and never had she been so negligent in return. It was the first time she had actually enjoyed Los Angeles. Before, on her visits to Brigitte, she had disliked being here, and so had Marshall, though he had insisted on coming with her. Everyone they met – the actors, agents, producers, publicists – appeared to them to be social flotsam. The town itself was flotsam, its houses ready to be razed as quickly as they had been put up, or collapsing into the earth quaking beneath them. But now that she was having fun with Brigitte and Shoki, all that was changed for Frances.

Shoki had accepted Frances completely. He loved the idea of family, and a sister was something almost sacred to him. With the intimacy that came so naturally to him, he at once adopted Frances and became the only other person besides Brigitte to call her Frankie. 'Doesn't Frankie look marvellous?' he would say about some new outfit. Between them, he and Brigitte had decided to change Frances's style; and although Brigitte herself loved brilliant orange and purples, for Frances they chose discreet and lighter colours, with a hint of California playfulness. Accompanying them to a boutique, Shoki sat outside the dressing rooms chatting up the sales girls; and when Frances emerged, he said, very thrilled, 'It *suits* you.' Then the years dropped away from Frances.

She confided to Brigitte that, with Shoki, it was like being with another sister – though at the same time he was so manly, in the best way. Unlike other men, he was not hard and insensitive but the opposite. 'He must have grown up with a lot of sisters,' she guessed, 'that's how he knows about women, what we have to put up with.'

Brigitte agreed, but she too was guessing. Although Shoki had a high regard for the notion of family, he hardly ever mentioned his own. When he did, it was with a wistful, almost sad air. They speculated with each other – perhaps he was too homesick, perhaps the subject was too sacred for him. But Ralph said it was because he was too damn secretive.

Ralph – for Frances he had become as disturbing an element as was Marshall with his constant phone calls. Ralph often turned up in one of the restaurants where they had booked a table for three. 'May I?' Ralph said, having already drawn out a chair for himself. He knew a lot of people there and sometimes he took Shoki away to introduce him to a useful contact. This was very irritating to Frances – 'Shoki is with *us*,' she complained. But Ralph was dissatisfied too, as if it wasn't enough for him to be professionally useful to Shoki. Shoki was always as nice to him as he was to the two sisters and seemed anxious that all of them should be comfortable and happy with one another. But Ralph rarely was. He talked too much, telling some insider anecdote, that made him laugh or sneer. He became brittle, malicious, assuming a role that perhaps belonged to his profession but was not in his nature. Sooner or later, and sometimes before he had even finished laughing at his anecdote, he became gloomy and was silent. When Shoki tried to cheer him up, Ralph brushed this good-natured attempt aside. Instead he said something that the two sisters could not and Shoki perhaps would not hear. Then all three avoided looking at Ralph, the way a squeamish person avoids looking at someone in pain.

Marshall asked questions over the telephone. 'So what's he like – the little friend? The lover?'

'There's nothing like that.'

'Come *on*.'

There was always some threat in his attitude to her that

prevented Frances from holding out when he wanted something. 'He's only a boy, Marshall.'

'A substitute son? I knew she'd pick one up sooner or later . . . What about you?'

'I have a son,' Frances said with dignity. Marshall hadn't spoken to their son for two years and gritted his teeth when he had to write out cheques for him and his dependants from various relationships.

In a thoroughly bad mood now, Marshall told her: 'Just get yourself back here. I don't want you hanging around there. In that *atmosphere*.'

Atmosphere! Frances thought to herself. What about the home, the heavy empty costly apartment he wanted her to come back to and live in with him? And as if guessing the new desire arising in her heart, that same day Shoki suggested: 'Wouldn't it be great if you stayed with us?' He turned to Brigitte: 'Wouldn't it?'

Brigitte said, 'Frankie's husband really needs her. They've been married for – how many years is it, Frankie?'

'Thirty-two,' Frances said, and Shoki made a gallant joke: 'I don't believe it. You're not a day over thirty-two yourself.'

'My son is thirty. And Gilberte, my daughter, is twenty-eight. They're both married. And divorced.'

Brigitte said, 'He twice, and now he's in Hong Kong with another girlfriend. And Gilberte? We don't know about Gilberte. The last time we heard she was in Buenos Aires, and that was almost six months ago. So at least she doesn't need money – unlike her brother who needs lots. He even comes to me for it.'

'I wish he wouldn't,' Frances said, speaking as freely before Shoki as when she and her sister were alone.

Brigitte laughed. 'He knows I'm loaded.'

'This is the family today,' Shoki commented. But although

they waited, he still did not speak about his own family. Instead he said, 'That is why everyone is making their own arrangements.'

As though aware of this subversive conversation, Marshall arrived the next day. He had taken an early flight and went straight to his wife's suite in the hotel. Brigitte and Shoki had started on their room-service orders – neither of them could ever wait for meals; that day it was not Frances who joined them but Marshall. 'What a surprise,' Brigitte said, calmly continuing to eat her croissant. But Shoki leaped to his feet, in deference to an older man. He appeared flustered, not emotionally but socially, like a hostess with an extra guest. 'Should we send for more coffee?' He lifted the lid to peer in. 'Frankie needs at least three cups.'

Marshall's eyebrows went right up. 'Frankie?' Then they went down again. 'Frances has a headache.'

'Then there's enough.' Shoki was already pouring for Marshall. 'But Brigitte has finished the entire bread basket. So *greedy*.'

'It's all right,' Brigitte said. 'Marshall has to watch his weight.'

Marshall was certainly a weighty man. This was never so obvious at home in New York, or in his office, or at his club lunches with other weighty men. But here in Brigitte's hotel suite, where the furniture was gilded and frail and the flowers seemed to float without support of vases in a cloud of petals, Marshall in his thick business suit imposed a heavy burden.

He didn't consider Shoki worth addressing, so it was Brigitte he asked: 'Is he an actor?'

Of course Brigitte knew that to identify anyone as a possible actor was, in Marshall's view and intention, to insult him. Shoki, however, answered as though he had been paid a compliment, and it was regretfully that he admitted he wasn't – although, he added, he had done some acting in college. 'What college?' Marshall said, asking an idle question to which no adequate answer was expected. Anyway, Shoki apparently didn't hear, he went straight on – 'Just smaller roles in student productions, but the experience was very helpful to me as a writer.'

'You're a writer?' Marshall spoke like one picking up an unattractive insect between pincers.

Shoki began to bubble over with enthusiasm. He spoke of his screenplay, which his agent was placing for him – at the moment it was with Fox, who were showing interest. Of course it was a difficult subject, he confided to Marshall, partly symbolic and partly historical. The history reflected contemporary events so it was very topical, though one did have to know something of India's past as well as of her not always perfect present. Marshall consulted his watch and shifted his big thighs where he sat. He tried to catch Brigitte's eye, the way he always did, had done through all their past together, to communicate the fact that he desired her and wished to be alone with her. Shoki appeared completely oblivious of this tension – he carried on expounding his story as though Marshall's sole intention in travelling to Los Angeles was to listen to it.

But sooner or later, Brigitte knew, Marshall would create the opportunity of being alone with her. He might give the impression of being unwieldy, but he was also subtle, at least in mental calculation. By next morning he had discovered the arrangement that his wife and sister-in-law had made with Shoki for their morning meal together. By the time Frances woke up, he was fully dressed and on the point of going out.

'I need fresh air,' he told her. 'A stroll by the ocean.' He didn't usually tell her his plans, so she didn't think it worth mentioning how far they actually were from the ocean. 'How's your headache?' he said. 'You had a headache. You'd better stay in bed and rest.'

'Who is he anyway? Your little friend?' was his first question to Brigitte. After opening the door to him, she had gone back to bed and he sat by the side of it, the vast hotel bed with the padded satin backrest.

'He's a prince. From one of those old Indian princely families. What do they call them? Maharajas.' She had only just thought of this but it made sense.

'Yes, and look at you: a Maharani.'

She did look royal, leaning against her pillows, one side of her silken nightie slipped down from her broad shoulder – divine even, a goddess emerging out of a flood of rumpled shiny satin sheets. He murmured to her in a voice that had gone thick, so that she knew soon he would be climbing in next to her, and she would let him. It had happened before in their many years together as in-laws, and the only thing surprising to her was that it should still be happening.

'Frankie will be here any minute,' she said afterwards to Marshall, who showed every indication of staying right where he was next to her.

'My wife has a headache and I advised her to rest.' But he was good-natured about letting her push him out of bed and smirked a bit as he climbed back into his trousers.

Then he became practical. He said he wanted her to return with them to New York – why wait? Everything was ready for her arrival.

'Oh, you bought it, did you? The apartment Frankie was talking about?'

'You don't need an apartment. We have one. It's enormous. It's big. Much too big for just two people now that the kids are – where are they?'

'In Hong Kong.'

'Yes and Buenos Aires. What are Frances and I supposed to do rattling around by ourselves in a place that size? It's ridiculous.' He frowned at the impracticality of it, and she laughed at his impudence.

'So you and I would be like this every day of our lives from now on?'

'It makes perfect sense. We shouldn't be wasting time, having to commute from one apartment to another, secret rendezvous and all that nonsense.' He spoke with the decision of a man of business, the chairman of the board. She smiled a bit, but she said, 'You really have to leave now.'

He took his time about it, strolled around the suite, stood at a window to frown at the city of Los Angeles and its giant billboards. 'I don't know how you can live in a place like this. No climate. No history.'

'I didn't know you cared about history.'

'Only my own. Grandmothers and so on. Great-grandmothers. New York.'

'What about Poland and Russia?'

'That's too far back. By the way, I saw him this morning – your princely friend.'

'He has a room in the hotel.'

'He doesn't seem to have spent the night in it. I'm just guessing of course – but he looked like someone sneaking in after a night on the tiles.'

'What would you know about tiles, Marshall?'

'Nothing. And I won't have to, if we make this arrangement I mentioned to you. No sneaking out, or back in.'

On his third and last evening in Los Angeles, Marshall hired a limousine to take his two ladies to dinner. The restaurant he had chosen was one known to other East Coast bankers and to West Coast attorneys from old-established family firms. It was very different from the ones Brigitte usually went to, but she didn't mind; it was Frances who said, 'Why do we have to come here? We might as well have stayed in New York.'

Brigitte was surprised; she had never heard a note of rebellion from Frances in the face of any decision made by Marshall. And what was also surprising was that Marshall did not wither her with one of his looks but concentrated on reading the menu.

'Don't you hate it?' Frances asked her sister. 'I hate it.' She was actually sulking, and still Marshall continued to read the menu.

The restaurant was a fantasy of an opulent New York eating place recreated by earlier settlers in the Californian desert. It was dark with antique lamps throwing insufficient light and thick carpets and velvet drapes shutting out the rest of it. There was a buffet table overloaded with silver dishes and with giant fruits and flowers that appeared to be a replica of those in the varnished still-lifes on the walls.

'Lobster,' Marshall said, returning the menu to the waiter. This waiter was no out-of-work actor but an elderly professional, Italian or Swiss, who had been with the restaurant for over forty years and would soon be mourning its closing. He hovered over Frances, who was unable to make a choice of dishes, but when Marshall said, 'You could have the lobster too,' she quickly ordered a green salad with a light dressing.

'You know what?' she said to Brigitte. 'He's let that apartment go. And it would have been so perfect for you! Now where are you supposed to live in New York? In another hotel? Then you might as well stay in Beverly Hills – I should think you'd want to stay here. My goodness, who wouldn't. And I don't suppose it's occurred to anyone that I'd like to be near my sister. That I'm sick of having her live at the opposite end of the world.'

'Not the world, darling,' Brigitte said. 'Just the country.'

'Frances has always been a dunce in geography,' Marshall said. He tried to sound playful but was too saturnine. He had tucked his table napkin under his chin and was expertly excavating the meat from a lobster claw. He ate and drank the way he had done throughout his life and would continue till he could do so no more. It was natural for a man like him to be companioned by a handsome woman, even by two of them.

These two were no longer discussing the pros and cons of living in New York or Los Angeles but whether Shoki was a prince. Brigitte had raised the question and Frances had taken it up with such pleasure that Marshall felt he had at once to squash it. He said, 'They don't have princes any more. They've been abolished. They're all democratic now, whatever that might mean. And they're all poor. No more jewels and elephants.'

'Money's got nothing to do with it,' Frances said. 'Anyone can have money. Anyone. But look at the graceful way he moves.'

'And the delicate way he eats.'

Marshall wiped the butter from his chin. He said, 'It's time I took you two back to New York.'

'I found a lovely apartment for Brigitte and you let it go.'

Brigitte felt Marshall nudge her knee under the table. She was used to this gesture from him, though today it was another kind of plea. She denied it in her usual way, by moving her knee out of his reach. But she said, 'Why don't you tell her your grand plan?'

'It's simple common sense,' Marshall said, losing no ounce of authority. 'Our apartment is big enough for ten people, let alone three.'

After a moment of shock, 'You're completely insane,' Frances told him. She turned on her sister. 'And you listened to him? You sat and listened and didn't say a word to me?'

She pushed back her chair, rushed from the table. No one looked up from their plates; even when she stumbled against their chairs, the diners carried on dining. The waiters too kept their eyes lowered, so did the maitre d' while guiding her towards the ladies' room, where he opened and held the door for her.

'Ah, the pièce de résistance,' Marshall said as their waiter came towards them bearing the chocolate soufflé. The critical moment of its departure from the oven had now been reached and it rose above its dish in a splendidly browned dome.

Brigitte said, 'You are a fool, Marshall.'

'Today is not my lucky day,' Marshall said. 'She calls me crazy, you call me a fool. Why fool? How fool? She's always telling me how she misses you, and you I guess miss her. Sisters, after all ... I wonder how they get it to this consistency; I suppose that's why it has to be ordered in advance.'

Brigitte too was enjoying every bit of the soufflé, but she said, 'I'm going to see how she's doing.'

'Explain it to her – how it's best for everyone.'

'Best for you.' Under the table she moved her knee further away. 'I'll explain that to her; after all these years maybe she ought to know.'

'Did you ever tell Louis?'

'Tell on you? He'd have laughed. He knew how I wouldn't give you the time of day.'

'Sometimes you give it to me. The time of day.' Over the table his lips curved in a smile, under it his knee went in pursuit of hers.

'I'd better go. This table is not big enough for you and me.'

'But the apartment is enormous, as I keep saying. Have a second helping, be a devil. Well, I will then,' he said and was already digging his spoon in when she left.

A tiny old oriental attendant welcomed Brigitte into her pink kingdom. Brigitte could see Frances's elegant shoes and ankles under a stall so she took an adjoining one. She said, 'It's me.'

'I know. I can see your feet, and I wish you wouldn't wear those kinds of teenage sandals.' Frances's voice was steady; she had not been crying but she had been thinking, and now she announced her decision. 'I'm not going back with him. I'm staying with you.' But when Brigitte said nothing, Frances's voice was less firm. 'I'm staying with you and Shoki.' She pulled the lever in her stall and went out.

Brigitte lingered inside; she could hear the excited birdlike voice of the attendant communicating with Frances in what sounded like Chinese but could not have been for Frances was able to respond. When Brigitte emerged, the attendant addressed her in the same birdsong, offering fragrant soap and towel. Frances was already wiping her hands on hers, and since neither of them spoke, the little attendant took over the conversation. They gathered that she was distressed about her job, which she had held for twenty years, and now they had been informed by the management that the restaurant was closing. Suddenly she was crying; tiny tears ran down her wizened cheeks, slightly rouged. Brigitte made comforting noises at her.

Frances was staring at herself in the mirror. Her eyes were dry, her face was set. She said, 'You can't send me back with him because I won't go.'

'Who's sending you back?'

'I haven't heard you say stay.'

Brigitte was using her towel to wipe away the attendant's tears. She told her, 'You'll find another job. Anyone would like to have you in their home.'

The attendant praised Brigitte for her kindness. She went on to explain that she was not weeping for herself but for the others, the old men whom no one would ever again want to employ. She herself had a son and a daughter, both of whom did not want her to work any more. She took the towel wet with her own tears and gave Brigitte a fresh one.

'You don't need to feel sorry for the whole world,' Frances said. 'And you heard her – she has a son and a daughter who care for her.'

'Of course I want you to stay,' Brigitte said. 'I don't know what gave you the idea I don't. Shall we go back now?'

'I don't want to see him.'

'I mean go back to the hotel. He's all right. He's having another helping of chocolate soufflé.' She found a fifty-dollar bill in her purse and put it in the tactful little saucer. 'That's too much,' Frances said outside, though she herself, usually more careful, overtipped the valet who whistled up a cab for them.

One evening a few weeks later Shoki gave Brigitte a lovely surprise. He came to her suite dressed up in a high-collared jacket of raw silk – Indian, but he had had it made in Beverly Hills. 'I showed them exactly what to do, how to cut it – you really like it?'

'Love it, love it; love you,' and she kissed his cheek in the beautiful way of friendship they had with each other.

He had been invited to a charity premiere and he asked her to come along. He assured her his host had taken a table for twelve.

'Ralph?'

'No, someone else, another friend.' There was sure to be room, someone or other always dropped out.

'What about Frankie?'

'Of course; let's take Frankie.'

Frances said she was waiting for a call but might join them later. Her call came exactly when she was expecting it.

Marshall telephoned the same time every evening. It was always when he was home from the office or a board meeting and was having his martini by the fireplace in the smaller drawing room (called the library, though they had never had many books). She imagined him wearing slippers and maybe his velvet housecoat; or if he was going out, he might have begun to dress.

'Isn't tonight the Hospital Benefit?' When he yawned and said he didn't feel like going, she urged, 'Marshall, you have to. You're on the board.'

'I guess I have to. But to turn up there by myself –' He always left such sentences unfinished. She waited; perhaps tonight he would say more. Instead he became more irritated. 'Marie can't find any of my dress shirts – do you think she drinks?'

'Marie! After all this time!'

'Who knows? Servants need supervision. Someone to make them toe the line.' Perhaps suspecting that she had begun to preen herself, he said, 'I'll send from the office to buy some new ones. What about you? You want any of your stuff sent out there?'

She hesitated; it was true she was running short of the underclothes that were specially made for her by a Swiss lady in New York. But the subject of her underclothes was not one she ever intruded on her husband, so she murmured, 'I'm all right for now.'

'For now? What's that supposed to mean?' She was silent, and then he almost asked, though grudgingly, what she was waiting to hear: 'Are you intending to stay out there forever or what?'

He sounded so put out – so fed up – and it was her fault. She said, 'What can I do, Marshall? Brigitte just likes it better here.'

'She thinks she does. She's from New York. She was born here like the rest of us, why would she want to be in that joke place out there? Where is she, by the way?'

'She's gone out. It's a premiere. A big event. She wants me to join her later. Do you think I should?'

'You should do what you want, not what she wants. Though why anyone would want to go to a thing like that. "A Premiere. A Big Event." Tcha. You'd be better off at the benefit with me.'

'Marshall? You know my dresser? In the last drawer there are some bits and pieces I might need. If it's not too much trouble. Just some bras. And girdles.'

'I didn't know you wore girdles.'

'They look like panties but actually they're tummy control.' She was glad he couldn't see her face – it was the most intimate exchange they had had in years. 'Marie can pack them.'

'If she's not too drunk.'

'Marie is practically a teetotaller.'

'You're the easiest person in the world to fool,' he said.

Shoki had been right and there were two empty places at his host's table. This host was a powerful studio head but a far more modern type than Louis had been. He was from the Midwest and had been to some good schools in the east; still in his thirties, he was well groomed, well informed, *smart*. The guests at his table were there for their fame, their money or their youth and beauty. Brigitte's celebrity was in the past but that gave her an aura of historical tradition, and she kept having to raise her cheek for the tribute offered to her by other guests. Each table was ornamented by someone like Shoki, with no claim whatsoever to celebrity. Some were girls, others young men or almost boys, some were very lively, some totally silent – it didn't seem to matter as long as they were visibly there and known to be attached to a powerful member at the table. Shoki and his host hardly acknowledged one another, except that from time to time the older man's eyes stabbed towards the younger, maybe just in an instinctive gesture of checking on the security of possession. He could be entirely relaxed – Shoki gave all his attention to Brigitte next to him and to the matron on his other side, a former star. He was lightheartedly laughing and making them laugh.

But there *was* tension – not emanating from their table but from elsewhere. Her eyes roaming around the room, Brigitte soon discovered Ralph. He was craning in their direction and even half rose in his chair as though intending to leave his place and make his way towards theirs. But it was impossible – the room was packed, each table crowded and the spaces between them thronged with guests still trying to find their place or changing it for a more desirable one, while the servers weaved and dodged among them with their platters and wine bottles.

Although without an invitation card, Frances looked too distinguished not to be let in. But once inside, she had no idea which way to turn to locate Brigitte among this crowd of strangers, strange beings who all knew or knew of one another. She stood there, dazed by the din and glitter. Then she heard her name called: 'Are you all right?'

It was Ralph. He settled her into an empty chair beside him and tried to revive her with wine. She preferred water. 'For my aspirin,' she said, taking her pill box out of her evening purse.

He laughed. 'Are you sure that's what it is?'

'It may be Disprin. For my headache. It's so terribly noisy. How can anyone enjoy being in such a noisy place?'

'At least one doesn't have to hear what's going on in one's own head. They're over there. No, you're looking in the wrong direction.'

The reason it took her so long to find Brigitte's table was that all the eighty-four tables crammed into that space appeared very much the same. Everyone there sat as in a burnished cast of wealth, of costly ornament. It was she, Frances, who was out of place. Although her hair too was professionally dyed, it had a discreet touch of silver; and her jewellery was not like that of others, women and some men, who displayed diamonds and rubies and pearls of a size and quantity that, if this had been any other place, would have been taken for paste. And maybe it was paste, she thought; it couldn't be safe to walk around loaded with such immeasurable riches.

'They're waiting for me,' she told Ralph.

'I've been trying to get through myself, but there's such a crush. Maybe after they've served the dessert. Why didn't you come with them?'

'I was on the phone with my husband. He wants me to come back to New York.' Again looking around the room, she thought of Marshall at his fundraiser. He too would be with the powerful and rich, but his would be not only physically less brilliant but much more glum than these surrounding her, who were laughing, chatting, shouting and outshouting one another as though placed on a stage to impersonate characters having a festive time.

'Brigitte doesn't want to leave. But he wants both of us. They've been having sex together.' She found it difficult to say – the words, that is; to herself she still thought of it as 'sleeping together'. 'It's been going on for years. I don't blame her for not wanting to come live with us. She doesn't even like Marshall.'

'No. Not the way she likes Shoki. As a friend, that is. They're friends.'

'Yes, he's my friend too. But I really think I must go home. Of course Marshall will be angry if I come without her. But he's angry at me anyway. It's just that he needs someone with him where he can be any mood he wants. That's the only way he feels comfortable.'

Dessert had been served. A master of ceremonies tapped a microphone. Speeches were about to start. Ralph suggested

206

they should try and squeeze through the crowd to the other table. He led the way, and when Shoki looked up, he saw them cleaving a path towards them. Shoki told Brigitte that it was very hot inside and maybe they should try to catch some fresh air? She got up at once and he took her elbow to guide her. Their host rose in his chair, but they did not appear to see him, or to hear him when he called after them.

Unimaginably, outside the noisy room there was an empty terrace hovering over an expanse of ocean and moonless sky. Although a crowd of brilliant figures could be seen agitating inside, no sound reached through the double glazing of the windows. Two faces were pressed against the glass, trying to peer out into the darkness. Shoki said, 'There's Ralph.'

'Yes, and Frankie.'

They sighed as though something was difficult for them. But it wasn't. Nothing was difficult for them. Shoki knew a way down from the terrace to the beach and soon he and Brigitte were walking there, their hands lightly linked. He told her about Bombay, where he had also walked on the beach, but it was not the same. For one thing, the sun was too hot, and then, always, there was Bombay – right there on the beach with the coconut sellers, the boy acrobats, and others seeking money for food; and beyond, the whole city of Bombay with its traffic, its slums, its huge heavy Victorian buildings pressing down on the earth and the human spirit. He didn't have to explain much to Brigitte, because somehow it was how she felt about New York, where everything was just as oppressive. But here, now, the ocean was very calm and very dark and all that could be seen of it were the white fringes of its waves gliding into the sand. There was absolutely nothing, no world at all between water and sky, and it was inconceivable that, with such fullness available, anyone could be troubled about anything – apartments, desires, attachments, anything.

THE LAST DECADES

Death of an English Hero

This happened in 1970. His name was Paul Lord, but various people knew him by various other names. Fortunately, when he was found, he had his British passport on him, otherwise it might have been difficult to identify a body found in a broken-down guesthouse in the bazaar of an insignificant Indian border town. It was during a sweltering summer, and in that part of the world bodies have to be disposed of on the same day; so that by the time his next of kin had been informed, Paul had already been cremated.

The reports on the manner of his death were unclear. Some said he had been shot in the head, others that he was stabbed in the chest. There were no witnesses; nothing could be proved or revised since the body was long since cremated. There were also conflicting reports whether he had been killed where he was found lying on the bed, or whether his body had been carried there afterwards. Everyone agreed there were no signs of struggle in the room. The proprietor of the derelict little guest house swore he had seen and heard nothing; the only other occupant (a long-distance truck driver) had been dead drunk and remained in a stupor even after the police arrived and tried to slap him awake.

The dead man's next of kin appeared to be his mother, Catherine Lord; the address found on him was not hers but that of a flat in London. She was aware that he had rented this place more than twenty years ago, but she had not seen it until now when she was asked to clear out his possessions. It was off the Marylebone Road in an Edwardian house subdivided into four rental units, all of them except Paul's small businesses. His flat was at the rear of the second floor and it was dark, bleak and almost empty. The only personal items included some books, in a script that may have been Arabic or Urdu. There were also a few books of poetry. The most personal items were the certificate of his marriage to a woman called Phoebe, spinster, aged thirty-five, of Stockbridge, Mass., USA, and a bundle of love letters from a woman in India called Leela. His mother felt it to be her duty to inform both of them, and both arrived within a very short time.

Mrs Lord travelled up to London to meet them at the Marylebone flat, and while she and Phoebe were exactly on time, Leela was three-quarters of an hour late, which Paul could have told them was typical of her. She at once broke down in a very dramatic way. She appeared beyond consolation, which anyway the other two, unaccustomed to so much emotion, were unable to offer. But Leela recovered on being shown her own letters. She even laughed with amazement and some pride: 'He *kept* them, can you imagine!' It was hard to imagine, for Paul was known to destroy every scrap of paper, along with all else that might have given anything away.

His mother was less surprised by the revelation of a mistress than of a wife. Like any mother of a middle-aged bachelor son – Paul died at forty-five – she had sometimes asked him about marriage; he had usually answered her flippantly, saying who would have a penniless, homeless fellow like himself? She knew that he had always had many girlfriends, she had even met some of them – all of them English, young, dashing and self-confident. Neither Phoebe nor Leela was anything like that. Phoebe was American, with a long Yankee face that had in middle age taken on an archetypal quality. But Leela had even now in her forties retained her bounce and vitality, her rich black hair touched up only a little bit, her radiant eyes, and her full figure, still splendid though by now over-full. Paul had kept both these women secret, one for twenty years, the other for ten.

His mother was used to being uninformed about him. Even as a boy he had always had his own agenda, which he didn't share with her. There had been only the two of them – Paul had never known his father, a naval officer who had died in a submarine accident. At that time Mrs Lord held an important post in the civil service, and she and Paul had lived together in a flat in central London. His school was in London too, but when he was thirteen he insisted on being admitted as a boarder, and from that time on she knew less and less about him. He began to spend his holidays either with friends or by himself, only vaguely informing her where he was and with whom. He became even more vague when he went up to Oxford, but at least she knew he was there, taking a degree; and afterwards, when he joined the foreign office and was sent on postings to various countries, she still had at least some idea of his whereabouts. It was later, when he left the diplomatic service, that she no longer had any notion of his activities. All she knew was that he was constantly somewhere else, and his visits to her were short and irregular.

After her retirement from the civil service, Mrs Lord had

moved to a town famous for an ancient battle, about two hours from London. Here she lived in a semi-detached Victorian brick house by the river; probably it had once housed fishermen and barge captains employed on what had been a thriving river traffic. The house was very narrow with a downstairs living room and, at the top of a ladderlike staircase, two very small bedrooms. She slept in one of them and kept the other always ready for Paul, for the visits she lived for. His was as bare as every room he ever had. Even when he was young there had never been any clutter: no boy's paraphernalia, no pictures of film or rock stars on the wall. Not even a bed – on his visits, Paul slept on a mat on the floor, because of a back injury he had sustained, he said, while playing some sport (though he had not been known to play any sport).

She was aware that every embassy had some less important attaché whose official role was a front for other activities. This may have been why Paul was never promoted but kept in a position where he could operate more freely. Maybe these operations had been discovered, and he was asked to leave the country to which he was accredited. But such cases were usually reported and the expelled diplomat might even be shown boarding a plane home. No such report was ever seen about Paul. But he was not a person who would ever be caught – he just would not be!

She had long ago tried to put it out of her mind, but occasionally she couldn't help recalling something that had happened when he was fifteen. She was still living in London then and he was a weekly boarder at his school. There was a scandal. Some of his classmates were caught at night robbing the house of a parent known to be away for the weekend. A servant had caught them in the act – he had switched on the light in the master bedroom and found the boys crouched over jewel boxes that had been prised open, spilling their contents. Only one boy was quick enough to make his escape; the rest were locked into the room while the parent was summoned home. Two pieces were found to be missing; the school was quietly alerted, the boys questioned and some of them expelled. Although they were all Paul's friends, he himself was not implicated.

A few days later she was putting away his laundry when she discovered two pieces of jewellery tucked among his undervests. She replaced them and sat on his bed, deciding what to do. As usual she was expecting him over the weekend and would confront him then; but that Saturday, when she again opened the drawer, the two pieces had gone. Arriving just as she was standing by the open drawer, he asked her if she had seen his blue and grey jersey. He had forgotten to pack it and had intended to come home a day earlier to get it. But he had been held up –

'So you haven't been here?' she asked.

'I told you, I didn't have the time. Did you find it? My jersey? Great. You saved the day.'

Until the end of her life, and years beyond his, Mrs Lord continued to be active. In the summer she gardened till the last hours of daylight. All the seeds she put into the earth grew into an abundance of flowers and vegetables. But at night, alone in her house, she had doubts she couldn't suppress. She sat by her empty fireplace, gazing into imaginary flames as into thoughts that at first flickered and then leaped into fears. It was not only her doubts about his reasons for leaving the diplomatic service; maybe he never had left but was working secretly for his government on what was known as special duties. Or if not his own, some other country in need of his services; or not even a country but an insurgency working within it. He was away for months and years in places he had never identified. She always heard from him, he regularly wrote for Christmas or her birthday; but his letters arrived weeks late and with a postmark that failed to show who had posted it or from where. She knew that some of the countries were those he knew well from his foreign postings; probably he spoke the local language and would have been useful for someone wishing to employ him for purposes of their own. But if his business was illegal, he would surely have been a rich man. No bank accounts were found after his death, only the post office savings book she had started for him when he was a schoolboy, and this had remained at almost the original amount. She must have imagined the two pieces of jewellery hidden between his undervests, for no trace of them, or any profit derived from them, ever showed up.

Phoebe had met Paul in London, on her first visit there after the death of her mother. In earlier years, she and her mother had travelled together, staying in the grand hotels that her mother loved. Now on her own, Phoebe took a room in a bed-and-breakfast place, which was dingy and cheap. Not that she needed to economise any more than when her mother was alive, but it was in Phoebe's nature not to want to spend money. At home she had moved out of their family house, and her lawyer had arranged to rent it out. Phoebe now lived in a cabin on the estate, which had formerly housed the handyman. She no longer needed a handyman, nor any of the other employees who had been necessary to run the house and care for her mother.

On previous visits to London, there had been an active social life, with dinner parties in town and weekends in the country. The mother had known everybody but Phoebe knew nobody. She wandered by herself around the streets and bought theatre tickets for plays she couldn't wait to end. She often went to the National Gallery to see medieval angels, and that was where she met Paul, who had a taste for the same angels. Though after a while he stopped looking at them and became interested in Phoebe instead. He knew she was American before he even spoke to her – a sort of early American, austere, thin-lipped, her ancestors emigrated from Scotland in the seventeenth century. This turned out to be exactly what she was. Although he was not at all a person to act impulsively, he asked her to marry him after knowing her for only a week. She was surprised but she didn't question his motive. Even then she was aware that everything with him had its purpose, and she guessed that maybe he *needed* to be married to an American for a type of visa he couldn't obtain on his own.

He had proposed to her at her boarding house in Earls Court, where she had invited him to breakfast. While her breakfast was included in the price of the room, she had to pay extra for him, and he saw her signing a chit, after checking the total. When he asked her to marry him, her nose reddened, which was a sign with her – the only sign – of volcanic interior heavings. But she spoke calmly. 'We can't, can we. To get married, you need an address in London where you've lived for at least six months.'

Her knowledge of this practical difficulty was unexpected, but he solved it immediately. 'I have an address. It's in Marylebone, so we can go to the register office there perfectly legitimately.' He never took her to his flat, and she saw it only after his death when it was opened up and she met his mother there and Leela.

For their wedding night she and Paul had taken a double room in the Earls Court boarding house. Now his breakfast was also free, but that was not the only satisfaction she had. She was a thirty-five-year-old virgin and sex was entirely new and astonishing to her. Her ardour too was astonishing, the sexual feelings she harboured unknown to herself and undiscovered till he discovered them. He was away for almost a year and the only address she had for him was a poste restante in Brussels.

She never asked why he was there – or if not there, then where, and what he was doing. She totally accepted the fact that his work was secret; also that they would not meet very often.

Although Phoebe knew that all his expeditions were hazardous, she suffered no fears during his absences. His cause was unknown to her, but hers was absolutely clear. Her ordeal was simply to wait, and she did so back home in America, in her cabin in the woods of the old estate. She had got used to being alone and she loved it – the cabin itself, and she only had to step over its threshold to be among huge trees, maple and locust and copper beech, all of them ancient. Even those that were dying still had some green boughs and birds living inside them and squirrels hiding nuts in the hollowed trunks. Everything around her was stirring and murmuring, shot through with the trickling of the little brook that was choked in some places and in others so clear that stones could be seen shining inside it.

There were no friends or suitors for her and never had been. When she was young and living with her mother in the main house, the house itself had been her companion. She loved its walls and its ancient furniture and hangings as much as she loved the trees surrounding it. She spent her days up in the attic, while her mother paced restlessly downstairs. Phoebe engrossed herself in the books she found among the lumber in the attic; they were old and tattered and crumbled away bit by bit in her hands. A Union soldier from the Civil War haunted an upstairs bedroom. She had always known he existed and she spoke about him to Paul. Although himself swept clean of such beliefs, he liked them in Phoebe. He told her that, behind her mild appearance, there lived a fearful and fearing New World; her sexual ardour was part of it, it was a dead witch still smouldering inside her. When she asked if she had been burned at the stake, he said no, her New England ancestors had been more merciful and had merely hanged their witches.

She knew he moved about in many parts of the world, all of them ones she had only read about. But she did read about them – he merely had to mention a place name and, as soon as she was alone again, she went to the public library to study everything she could about it. She became fascinated by certain desolate areas – deserts or inaccessible mountain passes in Central Asia, not in their present but in their nineteenth-century past when British adventurers had criss-crossed one another's paths and lives, and often deaths. Poring over their photographs, she saw Paul in all of them – lean, tanned, with light eyes – although they were mostly disguised as horse-traders or holy men. Paul had shown her a photograph of himself in such disguise; he said it was for a fancy dress ball. She believed him, she knew he was very social and attended all sorts of smart parties. She watched him dress up in his dinner jacket (it was the only article of clothing they found when they had to clear out his Marylebone flat) and she kept awake in bed in one of those London boarding houses they always stayed in whenever they met. He was never too tired after his long social evening to amuse Phoebe with accounts of it, especially of the party games that had been played. There was one game where you had to tell something very personal about yourself, the deepest secret of your heart. She wondered what he might have told – might it have been about her? Was she his deepest secret? She doubted it; and even if she were, she was sure that he would never have revealed her, any more than anything else he wanted to keep hidden.

Leela had met him when he was a young Second Secretary at the High Commission in New Delhi. He was not her first lover. Her husband was many years older than she, very rich, very busy with his affairs and fast asleep when he was not. She had plenty of money to spend, plenty of time and a lot of energy. She first saw Paul at a reception at the Nigerian embassy where he was together with his First Secretary; he seemed in no way different from this other very British diplomat. He surprised her by phoning her later that same evening – in fact, the phone was ringing when she got home from the reception. She had had no indication that he had even caught her name, and when he said – his first words – 'Remember me?' she actually couldn't or wasn't sure. But that didn't bother him. He at once suggested a meeting and had already decided on the place and time.

Her previous lovers had been Indian, friends of her brothers or cousins with whom she spoke in their familiar jokey mixed-up Hindi. Paul was her first Englishman. She loved his looks: not very tall, he was slim and spare with light grey eyes in a face that was tanned by un-English suns. She was thrilled with him, and it was very difficult for her to keep silent about him. With earlier affairs, she had adored confessions – cross-your-heart, giggly secrets that she knew would not be kept. But this time, due to the nature of Paul's work, they had to be kept. Of course, as always in India, everyone knew at least vaguely about him and didn't believe her weak denials. When her two children were small, they wept when she left on her sudden journeys to meet him. Later they suspected her in the same way as everyone else did, and they were angry with her. Then it was she who wept and implored them to forgive her, though she didn't tell them for what. Feeling guilty before her children was the hardest part for her, but she could do nothing about it. When her son was ten years old, he contracted typhoid fever. Day and night she sat by his bedside, she sponged and kissed his face, she promised God that, if he made her son well, she would give up Paul. The son did get well quite soon, with antibiotics, so it may not have been her promise; anyway, she didn't keep it.

From her first acquaintance with Paul, his comings and goings had been mysterious to her. There was something that had happened on his first diplomatic posting in New Delhi that had remained inexplicable, so that over the years she wondered whether it actually had happened. Leela never lost touch with her servants after they had become too old to work; and if she heard they were sick or in need, she would descend on them wherever they were living. This was how she came to visit an old bearer called Mohan, who was staying with his son in a makeshift colony of shacks about thirty miles outside the city limits. Like all the rest, the son's house too was assembled from old planks and asbestos sheets, though he was prosperous enough to add another storey; this was so flimsily built that, while she was talking to the sick man downstairs, voices could be distinctly heard from above. The old man beckoned her to come closer; glancing up nervously towards the ceiling, he whispered to her about his son. The boy was rich, Mohan said, he always had money, bundles of cash notes. Once the police had come, but they left again, maybe they had been paid off with some of that cash. Other people visited upstairs, strangers whom Mohan suspected of leading the son into doing bad work. Hearing the voices raised, the father sank back on to his pallet, shutting his eyes to show that nothing had been seen or heard or said. But one of the voices Leela heard was Paul's – wouldn't she have recognised it anywhere? Except that this voice was not speaking in Paul's broken Sahib-Hindi: it was colloquial, racy, freely mixed with Punjabi curse words. She felt she had to leave before she was discovered, as though it were she who was on a suspect mission.

Her car and driver were waiting where she had left them on the outskirts of the colony, a desert no-man's-land of scrub and abandoned planks and tyres. On their way home, the driver informed her: 'Bibiji, I saw Paul Sahib going in there.'

Leela said at once: 'He too came all this way to visit poor old Mohan, wasn't that kind of him?' The driver agreed, and together they praised Paul's kindness for a while.

Afterwards Paul said the driver had been dreaming; probably some opium dream, didn't they all take opium? He engaged her in a lively discussion of drugs and their problems, so that she had no opportunity to ask him anything else, such as his ability to speak and curse so freely in the local language. And in fact she never heard him speak again in anything except his Sahib-Hindi; and he let her continue to correct his pronunciation of certain consonants while continuing to get them wrong. It had been an amusing game between them, but afterwards she didn't care to play it so much.

During the twenty years of their attachment, Paul had sent for her whenever he came to India or its neighbouring countries on some business of his own. Sometimes he was in a big city, but more often in a far-off place that was difficult to reach. There was no way she could prepare for her journey in secret, but she was used to the oblique glances and the grim faces that met her whenever she went off on one of her meetings with Paul.

Her son continued to suffer more than anyone else from her adultery. Once, when he was nineteen, he tried to stop her. He gripped her arm and said, 'Why are you doing this to us?' Impatient at the delay, she tried to shake him off; finally she said, 'All right, now listen – supposing I were going off on a pilgrimage, you'd want me to, wouldn't you? To Amarnath, to Shiva's lingam?' The comparison made her laugh – she was anyway in such high spirits with anticipation. But he, a pious boy shocked at the blasphemy, was so infuriated that he raised his hand and slapped her face. They stood staring at each other. She said, 'May God forgive you.' But then, seeing the tears welling up in his young eyes, she said, 'It's all right, darling, I forgive you.'

That time Paul had summoned her to a small town tucked

away among mountains where a pass led further north towards Ladakh. Already too soft and fat to get up on a horse, Leela had to have herself carried up by coolies in a palanquin. At first she could think only of her son: she knew it would be a long time before he could forgive himself, and she felt sorry for him. But then they went higher, the coolies chanted, the palanquin swayed and so did the crowns of the tall trees lining their ascent; water sprang from rocks on all sides, it splattered and foamed and was cool, and ice-cold the white mountain peaks rising on the glass-blue horizon.

The place was the usual collection of shacks, with a bazaar selling the things the poor sell to the poor. The hotel where Paul was waiting for her was at the end of the bazaar and somewhat set back from it, one of a row of crumbling buildings with a sagging balcony. He appeared to be the only resident, and really it was difficult to think what business anyone could have in that place to stay in its hotel. Leela had no thoughts to waste on that. She remained three days with him, fiery food came to them from the bazaar in little clay pots, each covered with a leaf held in place with a twig. She came to know that room very well, what there was of it: a pink-washed wall with what may have been blood from crushed insects or spatterings of red betel juice; a clay water jug with arabesques from the potter's wheel; a cotton mat, a narrow string cot on which they spent some of their time. At night only she slept on it – he needed to sleep on the floor, for his back. The floor sloped along with the hillside on which the hotel was perched; he arranged the mat on it and was perfectly comfortable. She let her hand dangle over the side of the bed, and whenever she woke, she found him holding it.

After Paul's death, the landlord of the empty Marylebone flat was impatient to rent it out at its market value, depressed so long by Paul's tenacious tenancy. To lock the place up and return the key, Mrs Lord travelled once more on the coach to London. She found the house dark and deserted and the timer on the stairs went off before she could reach Paul's door; inside, the only light was shed by a bulb dimmed with the dust collected on it. She opened the closet door – but she knew it was empty except for one wire hanger, from which they had removed the only garment they had found. She poked in further, hoping to find something they had overlooked; but there was only a cobweb with a dead fly in it high up in a corner. It was the same in the rest of the flat – only cobwebs too high for her to reach.

She heard footsteps on the stairs of the empty house. Leela had already left for India so she knew it could only be Phoebe – like herself wanting to be one more time in the place that had been his so long.

Phoebe paced the tiny rooms in the same way as Mrs Lord had done. Her footsteps rang on the bare linoleum; she pressed her face against the window as though there was something to see other than the trash cans of an adjoining courtyard. She too opened the closet door. She knew it would be empty; she had herself taken his dinner jacket to carry back with her to America. She saw the cobweb; she was taller than Mrs Lord but she too couldn't reach it without something to stand on. Of course there was nothing; they had disposed of the few sticks of furniture they had found there.

'He had this place for more than twenty years,' Mrs Lord said, in wonder at its emptiness.

'Yes, it's so full of him, isn't it,' Phoebe said, radiant at whatever it was she had discovered there.

Mrs Lord decided to ask Phoebe a question. It took her some time – she walked away from Phoebe and then back again; at last she said, 'Did he ever tell you anything?'

Phoebe replied immediately: 'That's what it was about, wasn't it – it was secret, secret work, something you're not supposed to tell anyone.'

'But didn't you ever wonder what it was he did?'

'Why should I? I knew it was noble. For a noble cause.' She smiled at Mrs Lord, but she was also blushing a bit, embarrassed at being outspoken about something so private and sacred.

Phoebe thought he would have felt at home in her American cabin. She too had only a few necessary items of furniture and not even a curtain to shut out the sky. She didn't miss the things that had been auctioned off from the family house – pictures and carpets and gold clocks. It seemed to her that she had brought them to live with her and that they crowded her memory, together with the Civil War ghost and all the other ghosts she had read about among the lumber of the attic. Now Paul had joined them.

She looked on a map for the approximate place where he had been found. It was some satisfaction for her to locate it somewhere within the region populated by those other British adventurers she had read about in the Victorian books she found crumbling in her American attic. She had always identified Paul with the heroes who had disguised themselves in weird costumes to penetrate places no European had ever seen. Some had returned home and been knighted and honoured with the gold medal of the Royal Geographical Society. Others were lost in the desert, or in deep gorges or swollen rivers. Some of their deaths were ignoble, their heads displayed on the carts of kebab-sellers. But whatever the manner of their deaths, their cause had always been noble. So it was for her with Paul.

Yet she knew that his heroes were not the same as hers. He had spoken to her about them only once. They too were part of the nineteenth-century empire, though they were Indian: hill-men selected for their intelligence and trained for the same dangerous work as Phoebe's British soldiers and explorers. They travelled as Buddhist pilgrims or Himalayan traders, secretly to survey and map deserts and mountain passes. They carried rosaries of a hundred beads to count the number of their paces; they replaced the Buddhist prayer scrolls inside their prayer wheels with logbooks recording their secret findings. Their journeys were long, they were often not heard from for years; some of them were never heard from at all. Their disappearances or deaths, when these were known, were not as embarrassing to their employers as those of British subjects, for whom protests had to be delivered followed by costly punitive action. Some of the hillmen were caught by Turkoman traders and sold in the slave market of Khiva, though even here they probably fetched a lower price than a plump Caucasian. Some may have died of natural causes, though this was unlikely. The fate of most of them was never known; they had no name, only numbers or cryptograms, and that was what may have appealed to Paul: their invisibility, the forever undiscovered secrecy and anonymity in which they lived and died.

When Phoebe had returned to America and Leela to India, Mrs Lord hardly ever thought about either of them. Her memories remained only with Paul, and the hours she had spent waiting for him. She had always tried to make the most of his presence; she sat close to him, told him everything she could think of. She wasn't used to talking so much and that, together with old age and her anxiety about his leaving, exhausted her, and she fell asleep right there where they sat together. When she started awake, she found him looking at her as though imprinting her in his mind. If she had hung a picture in a different spot, he always noticed and put it back the way it had been. It seemed that he wanted to find everything exactly the same in this one familiar place on earth where he was always expected. She knew he loved the town, its gabled houses and the grey stone walls and whitewashed interior of the thirteenth-century church; and the churchyard where she would lie and maybe, if they were lucky, he too. It was here that he belonged; under the mild sky and by the river that was the same light grey as his eyes, though sometimes shadowed by clouds shifting overhead.

After his death, she kept gazing into her empty fireplace as before, with the same thoughts as before, except that now she no longer expected him to return. When she hauled herself up the ladderlike stairs to her bedroom, she glanced out of habit into his, which she had kept unchanged. There was really nothing to change. In her bedroom too everything was the same, a glass of water on her bedside table, a vase of wild flowers on her dresser. She lay in her bed under her blanket and her feet on a hot-water bottle. Light played on the ceiling, from a streetlamp or the sky, so she was not in complete darkness. No ghosts had ever lived with her, or ever could, she thought. But again and again, every night, she suddenly sat up, her fist by her mouth in fright. It was not her fright but his that she imagined when she thought – as she did constantly – of the manner of his death. She imagined him lying as she was now lying on her bed; only not like that because she was alive with her thoughts and her heart pounding, while he had lain with blood oozing no one knew whether from his head or from his chest.

Leela knew that Englishmen had often died in places far away from home, and for the sake of an alien people who did not always appreciate their sacrifice. India was full of them. Not far from her house there was a cemetery where British heroes of the 1857 Mutiny had been laid to rest; now there were plans to dig up those graves to make way for a new underground transport system. The names of some of the heroes would remain commemorated in books; the rest of them would vanish with the memories of those who had themselves died long ago.

Even in her lifetime – and Leela lived to be very old – her Englishman had faded in her mind and finally disappeared, along with everything else. Yet in the first years after his death she had thought of him often. She had brought her letters to him home with her, and when she was alone, she took them out of the inlaid ivory box where she kept them hidden. They made her laugh, and she quickly clapped her hand over her mouth so as not to be heard by anyone in her large household. It was her own schoolgirl fun she laughed about – 'Hi there! BIG Surprise! I've cut my hair! Ha-ha, just kidding, it's all still there for you to wrap around *you know what*!' She and Paul were together for twenty years, but her childish playfulness and his amusement at it remained till the end.

One day while she was enjoying her letters, she forgot to lock the door, so that suddenly her daughter-in-law came in with her little boy. Leela quickly replaced the letters in their box and concentrated on her grandson climbing all over her, kissing her and she kissing him back. He tired of her when she began to argue with his mother, so he shifted his attention to the pretty ivory box. He admired it from the outside, then lifted the lid. By the time Leela noticed what he was doing, he had pulled out the contents and was crumpling them and tossing them like a ball. Leela took it all away from him and shut the box, while consoling him with the promise of a brand-new bright blue ball that would bounce properly.

Her daughter-in-law said, 'I hope it was nothing important?'

'No no, just some old household accounts. I have no idea why I'm still keeping them.'

Afterwards she smoothed the crumpled papers and replaced them with the rest. But she knew she couldn't keep them much longer. What if her grandson had been old enough to read them? In a few years he would be, and then they must no longer remain in the house; they must no longer exist. To dispose of them, she had to wait till very late at night with everyone in the house asleep. She went to the bottom of the garden and scraped together a pile of sticks and dry leaves. She lit a match, and although at first the flame was very small, it leaped up when she laid the first of the letters on top, and then it was easy to feed in the rest.

'Whose corpse are you cremating there?'

She saw her son approaching; he had just come from the cantonment and was in his army uniform. She didn't answer him, she saw him smile.

'Is it something very secret and private?'

'Oh my darling, what could there be secret and private now?'

The fire was dying down, the last of the letters had crumbled into ash. She tucked her arm into her son's and they walked together towards the house. He told her he would be spending the night at home, and the whole of the next day, but then he would be leaving, for an unknown destination. His destinations were always unknown and always made her fearful: 'There's not going to be a war, is there?'

'That's what we're here for,' he said. She loved his solemn patriotism. He had recently been promoted and his new stars glittered on his shoulders. How handsome he was, how tall and brave; and how romantic to walk together arm in arm, and the air sweet with the flowering scent of Queen of the Night.

'You won't do anything dangerous, will you?' she begged him.

He laughed as though at flying bullets. 'I can look after myself. It's you I worry about.' He looked severe – quite often he took on the part of father with her. 'You haven't been smoking again, have you?'

She assured him no – he had always hated her smoking,

though he had never seen her with the cigars she had smoked with Paul.

'And chocolates?' he asked. She lied that she never ate them, and he warned: 'You know what the doctor said about your cholesterol. So you'll be careful, promise? Even when I'm not here.'

She promised. There were tears in her eyes, and she reached up to kiss his cheek. 'My star. My hero. My Indian hero.'

The Teacher

It was the girls who first brought him here. I call them girls because of their girlish temperaments, though they were almost middle-aged. Maeve was by far the more emotional of the two, with a habit of turning her pale blue eyes upwards like a saint or a martyr. Betty was sturdier, with a square muscular body to anchor both of them. They shared an old house in the town, one of those run-down peeling places that smell of mould inside. During the two or three years I had known them, their goodness made them take up needy causes in the town: pregnant teens, deserted families, boys stealing for drugs. One time they had sheltered a sex offender, which had made them very unpopular; when he turned out to be guilty, they remained unrepentant, unshaken in their faith of having done the right thing.

They worked at home to make their living; Maeve copied scripts on a computer, Betty read manuscripts for a publisher. That was how they had met Dr Chacko, by way of his manuscript, which he had submitted for publication. Betty's own publishers had been too conventional to understand it, and so were several others whom she tried. She decided that the appearance of the manuscript may have been at fault – it seemed the product of a very old typewriter, with some letters too faded to be read. In her spare time, Maeve put the entire work on her computer; it was over seven hundred pages when printed out, but she was as inspired as Betty, and it became their cause, along with Dr Chacko himself.

They tried to explain his work to me, and it made them laugh when I didn't understand it. To them it was so simple – it was life itself, they said, life *and* death, which I said didn't sound all that simple to me. For them, they admitted, it was not the work but Dr Chacko himself who was difficult to understand. But wasn't it always like that, with rare human beings? They tried to describe him to me but they couldn't even say what nationality he was. At first they had taken him for an Italian, a Sicilian, until they discovered that he was partly Indian, the name Chacko from a Syrian Christian community in the south of India. They thought he was also partly Russian – or had he only said he had lived in Russia? He had travelled in many far places, but it was in England that he had started his first work-shop. This had been dissolved, and so had some subsequent ones elsewhere; now they had high hopes for the workshop they had started for him in New York City, about two hours away from our upstate town.

They were searching for a suitable place for him to live. Accommodation had been found in a partly converted loft in the city, but he longed for trees, open sky, water if possible, and so did the girls for him. Of course I knew what they had in mind, and not only for him. I lived by myself in my house; it was set in several acres of ground and with a separate cottage, which was unoccupied. The girls knew I had been left alone here after ten years of what I had considered a satisfactory marriage, and in proposing Dr Chacko for my cottage they also thought of relieving my loneliness. What they didn't know was that solitude had become natural and pleasant to me. Of course it had been different once, when my husband and I came here at weekends with car-loads of guests. That was before a cluster of modest homes had been built at the back of the property – not for visitors from the city but for residents with jobs in town, which itself had crept nearer with a diner and a realtor's office. It was really no longer suitable for the people who had been our friends, and maybe still were his and his young wife's.

I'm not sure now how it happened that Dr Chacko moved into the cottage. I have a memory of him riding past on his bicycle, but there are so many later memories of him and his bicycle, which remained his only mode of transport. It was a very old model tied here and there with string and not quite big enough for him so that it wobbled underneath him. I think it was this sight – of this thin grey-haired man mounted on an inadequate nag – that made me offer him the cottage. He moved in the same afternoon. I had been keeping it as a sort of storage dump so there were some old pieces of furniture in there, which the girls helped him rearrange. Afterwards they came up to the house to assure me that I had done a good deed for which I would receive a great reward. I assumed they meant that Dr Chacko's proximity itself would be rewarding. But I had already begun to worry that he might visit me more often than I would have wished, and also impose his philosophy or his mission on me, or whatever it was that made the girls admire him so extravagantly.

This fear turned out to be unfounded. I only saw him when he rode past on his bicycle, presumably on his way to the station. The girls had told me that he travelled to New York for his work with a group who paid his fare and a small fee. That appeared to be his only source of income while everyone waited for his manuscript to be published and make him famous. Meanwhile the girls came every day to bring meals for him in little covered dishes, only waving to me as they drove past in their pick-up. So his presence really should not have disturbed me – except that it did. Maybe because I had become used to being there all by myself; or the thought of him working in the cottage, as the girls told me he did, refining and extending his ideas, gave the place a sort of potency. It was at some distance from the house and shielded from it by a mass of old trees, and the fact that it was invisible increased its hold on my imagination.

I drove myself to the city to attend one of his workshops. New York held too many memories of the sort of life I used to live, so the only times I went there now were to visit my doctor or the salon for my hair. However, the place for which I was bound was very different from those I had known before. The house was in midtown, in a row of brownstones from the 1870s, now run-down and in the last stage of their existence. The only signs of life were here and there an air conditioner dripping into the street, or a windowbox planted with modest flowers that had not flourished. When I found the right number, it looked like a house that had lost all its tenants, for there was only one name beside the cluster of bells. I had to press it twice before a woman came down to open the door. She informed me that Dr Chacko had begun his work; cutting short my apology, she sold me a fifteen-dollar ticket and told me to follow her. The stairs were worn and steep, but it was not too long a climb before she opened a door and ushered me inside.

There were about twenty people in that small room, more women than men. Most of them were squatting on the floor, but I was given a folding chair beside two elderly people and a cripple. With so many people crowded together, the room was very hot and the air somewhat fetid – partly maybe because of the indifference to health and hygiene of those who have gone beyond worldly satisfactions. The women there reminded me of Betty and Maeve: the same age, the same homespun dresses and their hair in a fringe or a bun; and also, shining under this plain appearance, the same glow of aspiration. This was shared even by the one young person there, a teenaged girl with long blonde unkempt hair, who kept her eyes upturned in the same way as Maeve. What was he telling them that left them all so breathless, in fear of missing a word? He spoke for several stretches of five or ten minutes, and when he paused, everyone shut their eyes to concentrate. When they opened them again, he asked them to explain what they had understood. Some of them seemed to have understood better than others. The blonde girl had got it all wrong, and laughed along with the rest on having her error exposed; the cripple had understood so well that he went into a lengthy exegesis that made Dr Chacko invite him to take charge of the class. This too made everyone laugh – altogether there was a friendly atmosphere, emanating from Dr Chacko himself, who behaved the way a very good teacher does with his favourite students. Although for some of them it might not have been easy to spare the fifteen-dollar entrance fee, they all contributed another four dollars for the mug of herbal tea and the cookie that allowed them to stay in his presence for a half-hour longer. I couldn't help feeling out of place, partly because I had kept my shoes on, my high-heeled summer sandals, while everyone else's were left outside the door – a heap of shoes like those of pilgrims who had walked many dusty miles to reach their destination.

He accepted my offer of a ride back home. He was mostly asleep, slumped in the front seat with his legs stretched out as far as they would go. Only sometimes he briefly woke up, not to talk but to sing snatches of song, gesturing with one hand as though scooping out some beautiful melody that hovered above him. When I asked him what it was he was singing, his answer was to linger around a particularly lovely passage, making me a gift of it.

After that, I only saw him when he wobbled past on his bicycle. Until one day, at the height of that first summer, I almost literally stumbled across him. I had spent the day in my cooled house, venturing out only into the evening air when the sky was veiled in its dying light and the remains of a yellowed heat-haze. It was almost eight o'clock, but even the birds were still stirring uncomfortably in their nests, like sleepers tossing to find rest. It was in looking up to sight these restless birds in a tree that I stumbled on Dr Chacko lying underneath it. I had a shock but he did not; he remained stretched out full-length with his arms under his head. 'It's cool here,' he said. 'Cool and beautiful.' And he patted the place beside him for me to join him.

Well, he was not young, and neither was I, and I should have thought nothing of it. And actually, when I did lie down, there was no awkwardness. Like him, I looked up into the roof of leaves; though thick, it had holes in it to let in what from here didn't look like a heat-exhausted sky but stretches of pure cool silver. And the birds were not restless but glad to have our company, and one of them began to sing before being reminded that it was still far from dawn. Dr Chacko and I lay side by side, both of us gazing upwards with the innocent pleasure of children or even angels – he seemed to think more of the latter, for he said, 'Yes, this is my evening paradise.' When he added, 'Especially after a day like we've had,' I realised that this didn't refer to mine in my air conditioned house but to his in the cottage where there wasn't even a fan.

I didn't stay long under the tree but went home to search out a table fan for him. At first I thought of returning to give it to him, but I felt shy or embarrassed to do so, in case my return might be misinterpreted. (By whom? By him? Or, more likely, by myself.) Instead I waited for the next day and for the girls to take it to him. They thanked me so profusely that I realised that it was less for the fan than for what they took as a hopeful sign of my increased admiration for him.

So far they hadn't succeeded in placing his manuscript, and they had now decided that the only way was to publish it themselves. They had brought me a copy of it, together with a flyer they had put together to send to people who might be able to afford the book; and since there weren't many of these in their own acquaintance, they had come to ask me for a list of possible subscribers. This request made, the girls left to deliver their little cooked dishes to him before they grew cold. I took out my old address book with all the names I had thought never to contact or need again. And now when I saw those names – and thought of the life I had spent for so many years, the fundraiser banquets in hotel ballrooms, the catered dinners and the ladies' lunches – and then looked at the handbill designed on Maeve's computer with a passport-like photograph of him, I was struck by the incompatibility of that past with this present. At the same time, I couldn't help being amused by the idea of the recipients of the flyer, or their social secretaries, who would be discarding it in the waste basket along with other crazy mail. And if they were to read the text, what would they make of it? No more than I could. Here I stopped transcribing names to leaf through the manuscript itself, which the girls had left with me. I looked through it in the hope of some glimmer of understanding. There was none; it remained turgid and incomprehensible and in no way reflected the man I had seen lying indolently under a tree.

I put the list in an envelope with a note to say I hoped this would be useful to him. I knocked on his door and, receiving no answer, pushed it open. The cottage was empty, not only of him but of any presence whatsoever. There was nothing except the few pieces of my abandoned furniture and the fan I had given him – no photographs, no pictures, nothing personal. I put the envelope on the table and left quickly, as though I had done something I didn't wish to be detected.

My instinct turned out to be correct. Next day Betty came to see me, looking grave and holding the list in her hand. 'Where's Maeve?' I asked, for it was unusual for one to come without the other. Betty smiled at me, though sadly: 'Maeve is as grateful to you as I am, for the list. But she's hurt ... She so loves to do things for him. Sometimes at night she makes me drive her here, only so she can leave a little gift for him.'

I said, 'And now she's hurt because the gift of the list is mine and not hers?'

'Poor Maeve, her heart's too full of love. She's an orphan, you know, she was found on the steps of one of the Sister Marie-Jo Homes. She has no idea who left her there. And after the orphanage, foster homes; I won't tell you about those, why should you hear such things ... Maeve has these strong feelings, maybe they're wrong, probably they are. What she's always loved best is to leave anonymous gifts for him, it was the sweetest thought for her that he wouldn't know –'

'That you're helping him with the manuscript?'

'But now he does know. He's seen your list so he knows we're looking for subscribers.'

She appeared to accept my apology, but it was from that time that something changed between me and the two girls. This was true principally of Maeve, who seemed no longer quite to trust me – or was it trust me with him? It was on the evening of that same day that I entered into a new relationship with Dr Chacko. For the first time, he came to the porch where I sat with my evening drink. When I invited him to join me, he did so at once. He settled into a porch chair, and when I offered him a lemonade, he indicated my silver cocktail shaker. When I told him what was in it, he said he'd have that. It was quite a potent martini but seemed nothing new to him. And I was again surprised when he thanked me for the list I had compiled.

'I thought you didn't know about the subscription,' I said. '*They* think you don't know.'

'Like those chocolate bars they leave? ... But it's different with the manuscript.'

'Won't you like having it published?' He made a vague gesture – of an indifference that seemed to express something of his personality. I asked, 'Don't you think it ought to be published?'

'What do *you* think?'

He had turned fully towards me. If he was, as I had been told, part Indian and part Russian, I couldn't see anything to suggest either. He was too dark to be Anglo-Saxon, and his teeth were not Anglo-Saxon, they were very strong and very white, the most alive thing in his lean face. He spoke English fluently – more than fluently. Under the layers acquired through much moving around in the world, there remained – like a canal still alive in the oldest part of a city – the flat accent of the English Midlands. I had only noticed this at his lecture in the workshop where he had deliberately stressed it – as though its homely and provincial sound would bring his message closer to the earth.

When he felt he had waited long enough for my opinion of his manuscript, he interpreted my silence as unfavourable. He admitted that it was hard labour for him to write, like birth pangs – 'Thoughts trying to get themselves born – except I don't have many thoughts.'

He laughed with those magnificent teeth, at himself and at me, as if I might not believe him. But I did believe him. I'd seen him at his workshop, where he seemed to operate not by thoughts or words or ideas but just by being as he was.

For the rest of that summer, he joined me several times more for drinks on the porch. When the season changed, we sat by the fireplace in my living room, and we carried on this practice throughout that year and the beginning of the next. But it wasn't until the second summer that he joined me for a meal. Unlike the girls and probably many others I had seen in the workshop, he wasn't a vegetarian but thoroughly enjoyed a veal cutlet and the wine to drink with it; also the candles in my silver candelabra and their reflection on the mahogany table.

Even on the days when he ate with me, I saw the girls going to the cottage with their covered dishes. At the end of one of our meals, I asked him what he did with the food they had cooked for him. He said he got up at night and ate it. 'If I didn't,' he explained, 'they'd discover it next day when they come to bring more. It's their kind nature. There's nothing I can do about it.'

One evening, finding the cottage empty, they came up to the house to see if I knew where he was. They stood silent in the doorway, holding their covered dishes. At first we didn't notice them, and as soon as we did, he took charge like a good host. He drew out chairs for them, he gestured towards the table. 'There are some wicked things here that you won't want, but what if –' he turned to me – 'two more plates, would it be possible?' And it was he who uncovered their dishes and served them on the plates I had brought. 'What delicious smells, and may I?' He dipped in a fork and, tasting, confirmed that it was indeed delicious. With all this, he didn't quite succeed in overcoming my embarrassment and whatever were their much stronger feelings. After a while, I managed to contribute some small talk, and so did Betty, both of us half-heartedly. As for Maeve, she remained looking down at her plate, maybe trying to hide the tears trickling into her untouched food.

Later in that second summer, Betty told me that my list of potential subscribers had proved useless. Now she had a new suggestion, which was that I should underwrite the publication of the manuscript. She made it sound like a good business proposition, pointing out that in no time royalties would be coming in, whereupon I would be the first person to be reimbursed. Maeve didn't say anything; she only traced her toe over the floor, looking down at it so as not to look at my face or let me look at hers. Ever since that evening meal, this had been Maeve's way with me; and it continued on subsequent visits when Betty went over the details of the publication. Maeve was always with her, but she wandered off outside by herself, making it clear that she wanted no part in any discussion with me.

During these summer months my evening walk sometimes took me as far as the waterfall at the edge of my property. The precipitous climb to the rock from which it fell was no longer easy for me; but I enjoyed the solitude here, the moss-covered stones, the trees bending towards the arc of the water. One day I saw a figure within that arc, sheathed in its iridescence and turning in its spray: it was Dr Chacko, naked and singing as he soaped himself. His towel and a pair of rubber flip-flops lay on a rocky ledge far enough not to get wet. Before I could leave, he emerged, still singing and naked; if he saw me, he gave no sign until he reached his towel to wrap around himself.

Nimbly, on naked feet, carrying his shoes, he climbed the rocky ledge that separated us. He sat beside me, drops still sparkling on his thighs and his chest. As far as I could make out over the roar of the water, he was telling me how much he enjoyed coming here for his shower – though of course he didn't feel the same in the winter. I wondered then was he intending to spend another winter with us, or were we only his refuge from the summer heat of the city? When I thought 'we', I meant those of us who were united in our care for him – except now apparently I stood accused of having taken more than my fair share of him. It was so ridiculous! And, seemingly prompted by the same thought, he said the same word – 'Ridiculous' – as we got up to walk together towards the house. 'But it's always happening,' he went on, 'and it's always my fault. I should have told them, why wouldn't I have told them? There's nothing wrong in it.'

'You mean in eating meat?'

'And your being my friend. Careful.' He lifted a prickly branch nodding over our narrow path. I hadn't mentioned Maeve, but in that way he had of taking up one's unspoken thoughts, he continued, 'It's sad that she's an orphan, but there are some orphans who grow up quite happy and carefree. When I was younger, very young, I used to look in the mirror: "Who is this?" I didn't even know my name – Chacko were the parents who adopted me for a while. They were Indian, but they lived in the UK, in a very dull town, and at seventeen I made my way elsewhere. I'd been reading the old Russian authors, and I thought all Russians were saints or else gamblers and swindlers; but when I went there, I found no one like that; so I worked my way to Baku, and from there further east ... A long story; a long odyssey.' He didn't tell me any more of it that day (or any other day, now I come to think of it). Instead he plucked one of his melodies out of the air, some strange tune from far away.

He did stay through the winter, and through the spring, and then another year had passed and it was summer again. In the meantime Betty had seen his book through production and had made it into a very handsome volume. She watched me examining it, while Maeve stood by, gazing at her own toe circling the carpet. That evening I sat down seriously with the book, but I still understood very little; actually nothing.

Carrying the book, I went to see him next morning. He was sitting on the threshold of the cottage, carving a piece of wood. He invited me to sit next to him, and when I did, I had again that feeling of intimacy I'd had lying next to him under the tree. An innocent intimacy, enhanced by the way he was carving, like a boy whittling a stick. He showed it to me, a simple little figure that could have been a man or woman or, most likely, a symbol. But he said it was a piece of wood he found that looked good for carving. Woodwork was just a hobby for him now, but once it had been useful when he had fixed shelves and done minor repairs. It was his only skill, he said, since he hadn't had much education. Then I did ask about the book, pointing at the title page where his name was printed – with 'Ph.D.' attached to it.

'I bought it,' he said. 'Not actually I, but a lady who liked to hear me talk. There's a small college in India that sells Ph.Ds. BA and MA too, if that's all you want … It never earned me a living, for that I had to do other things – when I really needed money, for a wife and kids.' He was silent for a while and so was I. Then he went on, 'Three of them, all grown up now. I miss them, but they're doing all right. Some of them are married, they may even have children of their own. I miss my wife too, occasionally. She's with someone else now. I liked her, I still do, though she never understood a word of anything I said or wrote … Do you?' he asked me, but I didn't have to answer, for he had opened the book, was leafing through it, reading a sentence here and there as if he had never seen it before. Then he shook his head and laughed. He had a rather whinnying laugh, like a horse; I liked his singing better. 'Probably only God knows what it's all about . . . But there are others – others,' he said, for just then the girls' car drew up, 'others who think it's me who understands, and so I must be God.' He whinnied again and waved at them and Betty waved back. But Maeve was looking at me, where I sat close beside him on the narrow doorstep; and from that day her hostility to me entered a new phase.

Those were days of such unpleasant heat that it became impossible, Betty told me, to continue the workshop in its present quarters. She had worked out a solution. The first part consisted of a collection from the members to hire a coach to bring them to the country, into the balmy summer air, the spacious grounds. The second part of Betty's solution involved me, or rather my grounds, where the workshop was to be held, under my trees. 'They needn't come in the house at all,' Betty promised, adding in her truthful way, 'Except to use the toilet.' I asked, 'What about Maeve?' But Betty hadn't come here to make unnecessary excuses for Maeve. She said, 'They'll come in the coach after work – they'll be tired at first from their long day – but then they'll sit under the trees – he'll talk to them – they'll revive, they'll be happy, peaceful.'

This was more or less how it happened. They arrived in the late afternoon, the same people as in the New York workshop. They fanned out after getting down from their coach, they wandered around, admired the flowering trees, breathed in the fragrant air. By the time he came out to talk to them, the shadows were longer and cool. He made them sit under one of the trees, the same under which he often lay and looked into the leaves. They looked only at him – though without the intensity there had been in that rented room where they had been squashed close together. Now each had space to breathe in, to inhale his message. I watched from the porch. For me, there was something almost legendary about the scene – the earnest seekers around their teacher, drawing inspiration from him and their surroundings. Lively households rustled and stirred within the trees, a chipmunk scurried across a path with a nut in its mouth. There was the sound of the waterfall and, as the sun contracted, a deer came out of the distant woods and stood, shy but fearless, against the sky that was partly rose-tinted and partly gold. Everyone was, as Betty had predicted, peaceful, serene. No one seemed to be aware that Maeve had got up from the group and was circling it, the way a wasp would.

They didn't come again. The workshops resumed in New York, but not for long. I learned about the great upheaval after it happened by piecing together Betty's reluctant account. It was easy to imagine how in that cramped and overcrowded room, simmering in dog-day heat, the smallest spark could have caused an explosion. Betty admitted that she had known from early morning that Maeve was not herself. Or rather, that it was one of the days when she was only part of herself, the part that early trauma had drained of her natural sweetness. At first Betty had tried to dissuade her from going, but Maeve had insisted with that stubborn, closed face I had begun to think character-istic of her. Betty settled her on a chair among the disabled, but it was only a few moments into the lecture that Maeve began her disturbance. At first all she shouted was 'No!' Then, 'Lies! Lies and fakery!' Maybe if at this stage Betty could have suc-ceeded in taking her away, the others might have settled back into their concentration. But wedged between others on the floor, Betty couldn't reach her, and Maeve went further out of control, shouting, 'Ask him! Why doesn't anyone ask him!' Disconcerted by these wild shouts, the disciples turned their attention from their teacher towards Maeve. Jerked out of a deep tranquillity, they reacted violently, in shock and frustration. And Maeve worked them up along with herself: 'Ask him!' she shouted. 'Ask him about the one he drinks with and eats meat!' Then the room erupted – the cripple raised his crutch at her, others tried to pull her off her chair; by the time Betty managed to reach her, her frock was torn at the shoulder. She struggled against Betty too – maybe she didn't recognise her, confused her with the rest; although, Betty admitted, Maeve had sometimes fought against her in this way. Betty put her arms around her to lead her out. Already halfway down the stairs, Maeve was still struggling to free herself, sobbing and yelling, 'Ask him what else he does with her!' No one followed them; the door upstairs was shut against them while the lecture continued, as maybe it had continued throughout that angry scene.

The girls no longer brought covered dishes for him and he no longer cycled to the station for the train to New York. This made me suspect that the ugly uproar may have caused a split among the members; or he himself, for reasons of his own, had terminated the workshop, like those in England and other places. I realised that this had always been on my mind: that everything with him was transient.

Now on my evening walk I didn't stumble over him under his tree because I had learned to expect him there; I never again lay down but sat beside him and we talked a bit. Strangely, I had become more shy of him than before. I even hesitated now to ask him for a meal; instead I brought him dishes I had cooked and sometimes left little treats on his doorstep. He never asked where they came from. He may have taken it for granted that there would always be someone to leave things for him.

One day Betty drove up to my house. She had brought all the unsold copies of Dr Chacko's books, which was almost the entire edition. Only a few copies had been bought by some workshop students who had been able to come up with the price; efforts to place them on consignment in bookstores had been unsuccessful. 'Where shall I put them?' Betty said, staggering with armfuls of them up the steps of the porch. It's not easy to accommodate over five hundred books without prior arrangement, so they had to be piled on chairs, sofas, tables, wherever there was a surface. I helped her carry them in, and when we had finished, she accepted a fresh lemonade. She became more relaxed than she had been on arrival with her load and I ventured to ask about Maeve.

Her face softened as always at mention of Maeve. 'We're past the worst of it, thank the Lord ... Put yourself in her place – someone who's been betrayed so bitterly in the past.'

I said, 'I suppose everyone has been, at some point in their past.' This was as far as I ever went in speaking to her about mine.

Anyway, it wasn't me she wanted to talk about. 'Maeve loved and trusted him and shouldn't have. What do we know about him? Only what he's told us ... Are you going to let him stay in the cottage?'

I said, 'He's no trouble to me.'

She clamped her lips tight for a moment before continuing: 'Not that I listen to gossip, though they say he was in prison in Bangkok for two years before being deported. But people will say anything, so who knows what to believe or not to believe ... Well, thanks for the lemonade, it was a real treat on a day like this.'

'And thank you for the books.'

'Oh no. Those are yours. You paid for them.'

That day I overcame my embarrassment or whatever it was

that had prevented me from inviting him to dinner. He laughed when he saw his books piled around the house; he said, 'It looks like I've really taken you over here.' But that was so untrue – he had never encroached on me or asked for anything.

Since my table and chairs were occupied, we sat on the porch with plates on our laps and glasses at our feet. For the first time I asked him about the workshop. He said, 'People move on. *I* move on too.' As so often, he answered my question before I had asked it. 'There's always somewhere. One gets used to it.'

I said, 'But wouldn't you rather stay?'

'If there are people who wish me to stay.'

Evidently he didn't intend to carry on this conversation, and I also realised there was no need. It was cool outside now, in the night air. Glow worms glittered below, stars above. Instead of talking, he had begun to hum one of his songs. Was this his teaching? To say nothing, to want and need nothing? All the same, I couldn't help myself, I had to ask. 'So you think you won't want the cottage much longer?'

He stopped humming. 'Why? Are you looking for a new tenant? If so, hope he'll pay you better than I.'

'You're not my tenant.'

'No, of course not. Tenants pay rent. But I should do something for you. Look at this –' and he held up an early autumn leaf that had fluttered on to the porch. 'You won't be able to sit out here much longer – with luck another month, and after that you'll need your chairs and tables back. You'll have to get rid of the books. They're useless anyway if you don't understand them.'

'One day I shall.'

'And till then? Are you going to eat and sleep with them? I tell you what I'll do. I'll build you shelves for them so then they won't be in your way and you can have your house back from all this intrusion.'

Did he mean my house or the cottage? Again I couldn't ask; and this time he provided no answer but went on talking about the shelves and how we would need to buy wood – good quality, he said, to go with the rest of the house.

He came to take measurements, and then we drove to a building supply depot in town. He heaped two huge shopping carts, he pushed one and gave me the other; when it came time to pay, he wouldn't let me sign my credit card slip before he had checked all the amounts. Next day he set up the trestle table we had bought under a tree, and there he worked with his shirt off and singing. I carried out sandwiches for us at lunchtime, and we ate them under the tree with the trestle table. The air was filled with the scent of sawdust, of grass and the wilted leaves that had begun to fall, and also the whiff of perspiration rising from the tangled hair on his naked chest. It was the last, the very last days of summer, already in its decline with dusty drooping trees, and flowers going to seed, and flying insects fierce in their final throes.

I was eager to pay him for his work, and while I was still wondering how to raise the subject, he presented me with a bill. He had itemised all the hours he had spent working for me, and it came to a substantial amount. But anyway, whatever I paid was worth it for me. I continued to make sandwiches for his lunch and to join him in eating them. More and more leaves had begun to fall, some on his naked back and some on his hair where they remained like Bacchanalian vine leaves. Sometimes a stronger breeze brought down a shower of them which fell on both of us, veiling us in gold.

One day he said: 'Betty came to ask when I would be moving out of the cottage.'

'What did you say?'

'I said I have a job to finish here.'

Several days of rain followed, and since he could no longer work outdoors, we carried the shelves into the house. The woodwork was almost finished and he had begun to varnish and polish. As I realised the work was drawing to a close, I thought up more jobs for him: a spice rack in the kitchen, towel rails in the laundry room. Although he was always agreeable, I began to worry that, to oblige me, he was postponing other plans. But I kept on finding things I needed to have done around the house, including some I didn't need at all.

When I had almost run out of ideas, he himself brought a suggestion. He said it made him uneasy to see my silver so insecure in the breakfront where any intruder could smash the glass. In the dining room there was a niche large enough, he told me, for a cabinet that he could build for me with several shelves and also a lock to secure my silver inside. We went out to buy more wood, and he set to work at once. He explained the kind of lock he needed, and as I drove myself to the store, I thought that maybe not only I but he too was trying to prolong his stay – if, that is, he intended to stay.

On my way back, I drove past the girls' house. It was thrown wide open, windows and doors flowing out into the front yard, which was full of toys, and playing with them were the usual children the girls gathered up from the town – orphans, or fugitives from bad homes. The girls had set up a swing and Maeve was sitting on it, shouting 'Higher!' while two laughing children pushed her. Betty saw me in my car outside; she waved and called, 'Isn't this fun!'

But when she came out to talk to me through the car window, the first thing she said was, 'Is he still in the cottage?'

'He's working on my bookshelves.'

'If he's working for you, why don't you let him stay in the

house? There's plenty of room for just the two of you. He hardly needs a whole cottage to himself.'

'Then who else would stay there?'

'You've seen our kids, how happy they are just in that inch of space we have for them. And on your place, in that air, those trees – and then the seasons! Rain and wind and snow! Beautiful.'

I started the car, and when I revved the engine, she had to talk louder: 'It's not good for people to stay alone. I know what I was before I met Maeve, and I know what she was, but together –' here she shouted after the moving car – 'the two of us together, that's a life!'

The cabinet took longer than the other jobs he had done for me. He became so involved in the work that he continued after our supper and after I had gone to bed. I listened to him hammering downstairs, and one night I got up to see how he was getting on. He was concentrating on fitting in the shelves but was dissatisfied and took them out again to plane them. I stood silently watching him. When he turned around, he looked at me in the doorway in my long nightdress, which was of delicate silk, fit for a bride. I remembered the thoughts Betty had tried to put in my head – had actually put there; and the idea that he could read them, as he so often could, both embarrassed and excited me. I went back upstairs and continued to lie in bed listening to his hammering. When it stopped, I heard him moving around downstairs and, wondering what he was doing, wanted to go see for myself. But the same embarrassment overcame me, and I continued lying in bed listening; that too was nice, to hear him moving inside my house.

When I woke in the morning, the sun was pouring a sea of sparkling autumn light into the room. I wore a robe and tied it as I hurried down the stairs, thinking I might still find him there. But he had gone; he had completed his work, and swept up the wood shavings, and altogether left everything completely neat. The cabinet was finished; it sat in its niche. The lock was on, so I knew he had moved the silver inside and locked it up for security, taking the key to give me in the morning. One of the books was lying on the dining table with a note on it that said, 'See page 420.' I opened it to that page and found the key inside. I scanned the page to see if there was a secret underlined message for me, but there was not. I read it again, but still detected no message. I tried the adjoining page and the following one, with the same result. But the key was definitely there. I unlocked the new cabinet and found I had been mistaken, and he had not yet moved the silver inside. But the breakfront was empty, and so were the drawers in my sideboard, in which I had kept my silverware.

The cottage too was empty and swept with a broom, which he had left leaning against the wall. The only thing missing here was the table fan. The first thing I wondered about was how he had managed to transport everything on that rickety mount of his. I imagined how he might have fastened the fan to the bike and then, like a real burglar, slung the silver in a sack over his shoulder; and so he would have stood at dawn on the highway to thumb a ride from long-distance trucks on their way to far-off, unknown, undiscoverable destinations.

The girls soon transformed the cottage into a playroom. The children painted fantastic murals of jungle animals and space-ships; Betty baked cookies while Maeve wove a rug on her loom, which had stood unused in the attic of their old house. As for me, I've been studying his book. I start at the beginning and read right through to the end; then, in the hope of getting to understand more, I go back and repeat the process. Maybe this is what he had in mind for me, in return for what he took.

So the loss of my silver may not be a loss at all but the fee charged for my education. Sometimes, though not always, I think it was worth it. Meanwhile, as Betty had anticipated, each season here brings us its own joys: ghosts in bedsheets at Halloween, stars and angels on the Christmas tree, and in the depths of winter, when the snow has fallen thick and fast, tobogganing down the slope behind the cottage into the hollow that in the spring will be covered in new grass and sprinkled with small flowers, bluebells and forget-me-nots.

At the End of the Century

Celia and Lily were half-sisters, but since both their fathers had long ago withdrawn, they were united by their one parent in common, their mother, Fay. Fay took them along with her – to France, South America – wherever she had a new marriage or liaison. Celia, who was ten years older than Lily, returned to New York as soon as she could. Educating herself through a series of semi-professional courses, she set up as a psychotherapist and became quite successful, while waiting for Lily to be old enough to join her.

Lily was sent to boarding school in Switzerland, where she was miserable. Celia advised patience; she knew Lily would be miserable anywhere except with herself. As soon as she had failed her last exam, Celia made arrangements for her to take art classes in New York, though she wasn't really surprised when Lily dropped out within a month. After that, Lily spent her days wandering around the streets carrying her sketching pad. This remained blank, but perhaps for the first time in her life Lily appeared to be entirely happy, living with her sister in their apartment in an Art Deco building on the East Side.

Celia was still there – immensely old, the only one left. Even Scipio was gone (killed when his racing car overturned at São Paulo), although his name remained as sole heir in Celia's will. Nowadays, all Celia could do was keep herself slightly mobile. When she managed to get up, she somehow dressed herself, usually askew, and shuffled off to the soup and salad place at the corner. Here she was served the same bowl of soup every day, which was all she seemed to need for nourishment. What was there left to nourish? The present was extinct for her, the past had vanished with all the people in it, even the dearest of them.

When Lily, at nineteen, had decided to get married, it had been unexpected: a shock. She simply produced Gavin, didn't even introduce him, murmured his name so softly that Celia failed to hear it and he had to say it himself, louder. Celia couldn't find out where and how they had met. 'I picked her up on the street,' Gavin said. He warned Celia: 'I've been telling her she really ought to be more careful about strangers.' He said it tongue-in-cheek, a joke, but afterwards, when she and Lily were alone, Celia was serious about the dangers of the street. Lily said mildly, 'I don't talk to many people and hardly anyone talks to me.' Celia believed her; there was something remote about Lily that would discourage strangers from addressing her.

Gavin's family liked and accepted her immediately. Gavin was a poet, and it seemed right for him to unite himself with his muse. Lily was fair to the point of evanescence, delicate, almost diaphanous – it was easy to think of her as a muse. She loved Gavin, everything about him. 'Why?' he would ask, amused, but she couldn't answer, she had no gift for words. She was an artist by temperament more than practice. She liked to trace

Gavin's features – not with a pencil or brush but with her finger, lightly feeling him. This also made him laugh, but he kept still for her.

He came from a large old American family, and the wedding was quite grand. It was held in the Hudson Valley mansion where Gavin's mother Elizabeth still lived with two old uncles. China Trade dinner services were taken out of cabinets where they had been shut up so long that they had to be soaked in tubs of water to wash the dust off. Faded tapestries were hung over wallpaper that was even more faded. But it was summer and the grounds were lush, the ancient trees loaded with foliage that looked too heavy for their broken limbs to carry. A fountain spouted rusty water out of the mouths of crumbling lions. There was a band and some of the guests danced, even some very old ones in very old long dresses that got wet in the grass.

The original idea had been for the newly wed couple to live in the house with the groom's mother. Gavin was the youngest of Elizabeth's five children and the only son; his sisters were all married with children, but he was over thirty and had not been expected to marry. Elizabeth prepared one of the bedrooms for him and Lily – it had been unoccupied for years, but all that was needed was to renew the curtains and the canopy over the four-poster. Elizabeth picked flowers and filled several vases so that youth and freshness permeated the ancient room, which held a harp and watercolours of mountain streams and a broken-down castle in the Catskills. It was enchanting, and at first Lily and Gavin were enchanted. It seemed so perfect for them, for him who wrote poetry and her who painted.

It turned out that both of them preferred the city. Lily saw plenty of sky from the terrace of Celia's apartment, and birds, and buildings as fantastic as trees and more ornate; this was as much landscape as she needed. Gavin had spent his childhood in the country, but after he went to boarding school, he didn't look forward to going home; school was far more exciting to him (he made deep friendships) and even during vacations he preferred to take up invitations from friends whose parents lived on Park Avenue and had season tickets to the opera.

Six months into their marriage, Gavin and Lily were mostly with Celia in the city. At least Lily was – Gavin spent much of his time elsewhere, with friends in their studios and their weekend houses on Fire Island or the Cape. It didn't occur to him to take his wife with him on these visits; she too appeared to think it natural that she should be mostly alone or with her sister. Marriage for her meant waiting for Gavin and being very happy when he was there. And because Lily was happy, Celia too complied with the situation, at least to the extent of not commenting on it.

Then their mother Fay showed up. She did this every now and again, whenever a liaison broke down, or she had to see her lawyer about increasing her remittances. She was bored easily, loved to travel, loved to meet new people. She was very skinny and very lively and dressed with tasteful flamboyance, wound around with Parisian scarves and Italian costume jewellery; her hair was a metallic red, cut like a boy's.

It was the first time she had visited her daughters since Lily's marriage. She had been living in Paris just then and was unable to attend the wedding because of undergoing an unspecified procedure. All she told them about it now was: 'You don't want to know all that ... But guess what: I'm a widow.' They didn't understand which husband she had lost, till she revealed that it was Celia's father. They hadn't heard her refer to him as anything but 'that loser', but now she became sentimental, remembered early days – 'Fay and Harry! Crazy kids!' – and then felt sorry for Celia, for being fatherless, orphaned. 'You're still here,' Celia pointed out, which irritated her mother; those two never could be together for long without irritation.

Now they had to live together, for although Fay felt most at home in hotels, she couldn't for the moment afford to move into one. Celia's apartment was large – the same one in which she remained for the rest of her life – but, with Fay there, it was no longer large enough. Fay suggested that the front part, Celia's office where she saw patients, could be made into a charming bed-sitting room for herself. 'You don't see your crazies all day,' she argued, promising to make herself scarce during office hours. Failing that, she felt it to be appropriate to move into the bedroom now given over to Gavin and Lily. 'They should have a place of their own,' she said. 'It's working class for a young married couple to be living with their families.'

'They're looking,' Celia lied. But they weren't, and she even suspected that Gavin had kept his old apartment and continued to live there the way he had done before his marriage.

Lily agreed that it was a waste for the married couple to have the larger bedroom when she herself was mostly alone in it. One morning, while Celia was busy with her patients, Lily helped Fay carry her load of possessions into the room she willingly vacated. Even Gavin, arriving from one of his excursions, didn't seem to mind that his clothes were now scattered over various closets. Also, since their new room was too small for two of them, he made himself comfortable on the living-room sofa. He kept the light on all night to read, while playing records very softly, so as not to disturb anyone. He was always considerate, more like a house-guest than a husband.

The second Sunday after Fay's arrival was the day they drove her to meet Gavin's family in the country. A traditional Anglo-Saxon lunch of roast lamb had been cooked by Elizabeth,

Gavin's mother. Her kitchen still had its old appliances, which had become antiques, but Elizabeth coped very efficiently, even providing a special dish for Lily, who was vegetarian. The cavernous dining room had been opened up, and as far as possible the dust wiped out of the convoluted furniture. Only its smell remained pervading the air. There was no smell of food, since the family usually ate in the kitchen.

In outward appearance and manner, this family now seated around the table was also more or less traditional. Besides Elizabeth, who sat at the head, there were two uncles, her brothers-in-law who lived in the house with her; both wore three-piece suits, their waistcoats and bow-ties slightly spotted with food. The visiting guests were three of Gavin's sisters, two of them with husbands and some children, and a few relatives introduced as cousins. All spoke in the same loud voices, guttural with good breeding and unchallenged opinions. The conversation consisted mostly of amusing family anecdotes recounted by the two uncles. At the punchline, each uncle rapped the table and coughed with laughter, which made tears rise to their sorrowful, faded eyes. Elizabeth too laughed as at something she had never heard before; and she looked around at her guests to make sure they absorbed this family history, which it would one day be their turn to pass on.

At the end of the meal, when the sisters and cousins had driven off to visit other relatives embedded in the neighbourhood, Elizabeth invited Fay on a house tour. Several rooms had to be kept shut up because of the cost of heating and the lack of domestic staff, and here the furniture – New York State and valuable – was shrouded to protect it against bat droppings. The paintings and the statuary testified mostly to the taste of the ancestors whose portraits hung all around the house they had built and rebuilt. They featured the same type of men and women through the generations, the original tall bony merchants and farmers – they operated gravel pits and flour mills – still visible in the later portraits of New York clubmen living on trust funds.

These portraits were the only part of the house tour of any interest to Fay. While hardly listening to Elizabeth's detailed biographies, she stepped close to examine them; but none of them in the least resembled fair slender Gavin. At last she asked Elizabeth, 'I suppose he takes after your family?' But no – Elizabeth's family, professional people from an adjoining county, were mostly, like herself, short and sturdy. Gavin was the first to look like – well, what he was: a poet.

As they crossed an upper landing, they saw him on the stairs; he was arguing with Celia, who called to them, 'Gavin says he's going back to New York!' They walked up together to join their two mothers on the landing. Celia was angry; she said, 'He has to meet some writer from Poland.'

'Fixed up weeks ago,' he regretted. 'Just the sort of stupid thing I do. It's not even a writer, it's a critic. But I'm not going to spoil your fun. I know Mother has a whole programme for you this afternoon. The Shaker Museum; the old almshouses. It's just my bad luck ... Don't look at me like that, Celia, as if you're seeing right through me. You scare me.'

'I wish I did. Maybe then you'd be nicer to Lily.'

'Oh my Lord! Ask Lily who, *who* could be nicer to her than I?' He pecked her cheek as though grateful to her for her compliance, and she watched him, lithe in his linen suit, run lightly down the stairs.

Later, Fay and Celia were standing by the window in the bedroom allotted to them. It was a bright gold afternoon, but they looked only at the figure sitting on an ornamental bench under the largest maple, which was still magnificent though half destroyed by storms.

'She's sketching,' Celia said.

'Have you ever actually seen . . . ?'

'Gavin says she has talent.'

Lily was sitting very still. Perhaps she was taking in the scene to interpret it later. She could often be observed sitting this way, gazing in front of her, her hands folded on the sketchbook in her lap: maybe watching, maybe waiting, definitely patient.

Fay turned away impatiently. 'I couldn't bear to stay the night in this creepy room. No doubt they all died in that *bed*. Let's go: I don't need to be entertained any more. And surely the Shaker Museum is a joke.'

'No. And neither are the almshouses.'

'You just love to torment me, Celia, you've always loved to do that.'

But she wasn't serious – she was relieved to have Celia with her. Although so different in every way, she and her daughter were both out of their element here. Unlike Gavin's ancestors, theirs hadn't tilled this land nor built their houses on it. Their great-grandmothers and grandmothers had long since looked to Europe for their sustenance; this was evident in both Fay and Celia, in the cast of their thoughts as well as their chic appearance.

Only Lily was a throwback to earlier, simpler, simply American girls. She came in, as so often barefoot, her white-blonde hair wind-blown; she was holding a branch with a few leaves on it. She said at once: 'Where's Gavin?'

'Doesn't he tell you *anything*?' Fay said, and Celia, eyebrows raised: 'The Polish critic?'

'I'm really stupid,' Lily said. 'I forget everything. Look, there's Elizabeth. She's pruning a rosebush. She's always busy; she does a million things. Can't you see her? I wish you'd wear your glasses, Mummy.'

'I don't need them. I don't need to see anything more. I did a house tour; I sat through an entire lunch. I'm starting a headache and I want to go back to New York.'

Lily didn't look at her but trailed the branch she was holding across the faded flower pattern of the carpet. She said, 'It wouldn't be fair to Elizabeth. If we left. It wouldn't even be polite. It would really be very rude. I mean, if it were me, I'd think these were really very rude people.' Still intent on her branch, she missed the look of wry resignation that passed between her mother and her sister.

Lily became pregnant. At first she said her stomach was upset, and as for her periods, they were always irregular. When Celia wanted to take her to a doctor, she didn't want to go because doctors always discovered something horrible. 'But supposing it's not horrible,' Celia said. 'Supposing it's something you'd like, you and Gavin?'

'Oh, you think it might be a baby? Well, why not. I *am* married.' She looked at her sister out of those very candid fairy-tale eyes that made people love and trust her.

On being informed: 'Is it possible?' Fay asked Celia.

'Of course it is,' Celia said. 'You hear about it all the time. I have friends you'd never think – and then suddenly they spring a grown-up son or daughter on you, visiting them over Christmas.'

Fay also had such friends with unsuspected offspring. But still she said, 'I can't imagine.'

'Can't imagine what,' Celia said, the more irritably because she also couldn't imagine: not about Gavin and, if it came to that, not about Lily herself. But there she was, pregnant, an indubitable fact.

Gavin's mother Elizabeth had no doubts at all. She came travelling up to the city and took Lily to her own gynaecologist, who confirmed that everything was fine, and also that the scan showed a boy. Elizabeth was delighted – another grandchild, and this time the son of her only son. She advised plenty of exercise for Lily, plenty of walking, plenty of good food and fresh air.

Lily did plenty of walking but the air she was taking in was not altogether fresh. It was what she liked best in the world – street smells, petrol fumes, leaking gas pipes, newly poured tar, pretzels, mangoes from Mexico, Chinese noodles, overblown flowers – the exhalations of the city, the densely populated streets that she traversed from one end to the other, walking lightly on sandals so flimsy her feet might have been bare and treading on grass. On warm days she wore a very light summer frock – no more than a shift – that blew with any breeze wafting up from the subway or from leaky steam pipes. She avoided parks and other open spaces unless they were from a building recently demolished; and if she sat for a moment to rest, it was on the steps of a Masonic temple or a store front, from which she was sometimes chased away. When it rained, she sheltered under an overbridge, though she liked to get wet – very wet, with the drops trickling from her hair down her face so that she flicked out her tongue to taste them and refresh herself. She stopped occasionally to sniff the flowers arranged in the front of a grocery store. On raising her eyes to the sky, she was perfectly satisfied that all she could see of it was a bright patch inserted among tall towers. If it was night – for she wandered around for many hours – there was sometimes a slice of moon and helicopters flitting and glittering around like fireflies.

Celia summoned Gavin to her office. 'I hate it,' she told him. 'The way she walks around everywhere by herself and at all hours. It's not safe. She's not safe.'

'Lily?' He was gentle and smiling, patient as no patient of hers ever was. 'But Lily is always safe. Don't you feel that about her – that nothing could happen to her?'

'Maybe it's happened already.' She was trembling a bit – at what she was saying, the danger to Lily, but also at his *calm*, the way he sat there, crosslegged and slightly swinging one foot in its narrow shoe. She said, 'You know how innocent she is, how trusting.'

'Yes.' He smiled in recognition of these qualities in his wife, and he assured Celia, 'I love and adore her as you do.'

'I'm her sister. I love and adore her in a different way. All I'm asking is that you should stop her from wandering around the streets. Or help me stop her. Please be home tonight so that we can talk to her together.'

'Yes, we should – but unfortunately, tonight, what a pity.'

'Tomorrow then?'

'Oh absolutely,' he promised. 'Definitely tomorrow.'

But it was on that same day that he met Lily to report on his talk with her sister. They met where they usually did, in a church in midtown. It was the place where they had first seen each other, amid a sea of empty pews with here and there a few bowed figures, some come to pray, others only to fall asleep for want of food or a home to go to. Everyone was alone, maybe lonely and certainly in deep need. If Gavin and Lily were in such need, it was at least partly satisfied that time when they first met each other.

On the day of Gavin's talk with Celia, they did not go in but sat on the steps of the church. He ran down for a moment to buy them two pretzels from a cart, and a drink to share. They picnicked there on the bank of a river of traffic, rushing and foaming in the street below. They sat close together at the side, undisturbed by people walking past them. Gavin informed her of everything that Celia had said to him and the way she had said it; he concluded, 'She thinks you may have been ... attacked? By someone. In the street?'

'No. No.'

'Then what happened? If you want to tell me, that is.'

She did – and it was relatively easy sitting so close and he listening with the sympathy and selfless love that he always showed her. 'It was raining,' she said. He nodded; he understood that she was sheltering somewhere. 'Yes, under the 59th Street bridge. The rain was coming down really hard and I only had this –' she indicated her diaphanous dress – 'I didn't want to stay there because you know what it's like under a bridge that people who don't have anywhere else use for their, you know, their toilet, and also to store whatever they have, from the trash or whatever. No one spoke to anyone, like they don't in church, because of having so much else to think about? Different things. Except there was one person, maybe he didn't have too many worries to consider, I mean he was maybe too young to have them.'

'How young?'

'Seventeen. He told me he'd come from – I've forgotten – some African country. He'd come here to start a restaurant. That was his dream. He was looking for a job to be a waiter where he could save enough money to open his own restaurant with the special food from his African country. He was very very hopeful that it would happen. I was the first girl he met to talk to since he'd come here. He did what you always do – touched my hair and then let it sort of run through his fingers. He was very sweet, gentle also, till he got excited. He got like ... frantic? No, I wasn't scared; I understood he got that way because he hadn't met any girl here, so it was my fault really, in a way. And afterward he was very nice again and said he wished he had something to give me to keep for myself. I didn't have anything either, so I told him I'd come back next day and bring him something.'

'And did you?' Gavin asked, playing with her hair the way she said the boy under the bridge had done.

266

After a moment she admitted it. And after another moment: 'I thought: maybe he'll never have the restaurant, maybe not even a job in one, nothing that he expects will happen, ever happen, such a lot of disappointment ... I gave him a silver chain Fay had brought me from Peru. I'd never liked wearing it, it was so heavy, like being put in irons. But he was glad to have it and to see me again. I think he thought I wouldn't come back.'

'But you did.'

She hung her head but raised it again before answering frankly: 'That time we didn't stay under the bridge. We walked to the Park; it wasn't raining that day but the ground was wet. It was chilly but much nicer than under the bridge. This was the day before you and I drove to the country with Fay and Celia, and all the time we were there, I kept thinking how he didn't have a sweater or anything, and what if he caught a cold and had nowhere to sleep except under the 59th Street bridge? So when we got back to New York, I went there with a blanket and a sweater, but he'd gone. And I keep hoping he went off to a job as a waiter in a restaurant but also I think – what if he got ill being out in the open? And it turned into pneumonia and he was taken to a hospital where they take poor people?'

'Boys of seventeen don't catch pneumonia,' Gavin affirmed clearly. 'He's working as a waiter and saving money for a restaurant. You have to believe me. I don't want you to worry in any way or have disturbing thoughts, because that's bad for our baby. OK? Promise. Only nice thoughts.'

'About you.'

'About me, if that's what you want.' He took her hand and kissed it.

Next day he took her to the country to stay with his mother. Lily liked to sleep late, and in the mornings, when Elizabeth

267

herself had already been up for many hours and completed many tasks, she sat beside her frail daughter-in-law and the precious unborn child where they lay in a deceased great-aunt's great bed. Elizabeth was nearing seventy, strong and stocky, with apple cheeks and bright blue eyes. Although her connection with the family was only through marriage, she was an expert on each degree of their convoluted relationships and of their convoluted stories. These stories, which she was passing on to her pregnant daughter-in-law, were mostly of domestic or social interest. No one had held high office or distinguished themselves in any wars. But they had involved themselves in local politics, built additions to the house, engaged in lawsuits with neighbours about boundary lines. There had been some scandals: divorces as long ago as the beginning of the century, also the stigma of gambling debts, and more than one case of temporary confinement in a mental institution. But mostly they had led long and uneventful lives, with several of them celebrating their hundredth birthday. They had done some travelling – honeymoons and study tours in Italy, safari in Africa – but they had all spent their last years at home and with each other. In the end family loyalties triumphed over everything, even property disputes between brothers and sisters.

Elizabeth encouraged Lily to walk around the grounds. It was the end of what had been a very wet summer, and the estate had become a wilderness of tall grass with trees sweeping down into it. The trees themselves had survived their centuries with hollowed trunks; some of them had split apart and had been kept from falling by iron chains that had grown rusty and appeared to be part of the trunks they were meant to hold. Besides age, storms had ransacked the land, and every winter one of the great trees – copper beech or red maple – had given way and crashed to the ground, to be cut up into firewood to feed the giant fireplaces inside the house and warm the chill bones of its inhabitants.

Although Lily traversed city streets in complete confidence, here she tramped through the grass with misgiving of what might be lurking there – poison ivy, or a snake she knew would not be harmless to herself. Passing two blighted apple trees – the remains of what had once been an orchard cultivated for profit – she picked up one of the apples that lay half hidden in the grass; soft and rotten, it split apart in her hand and maggots crawled out of it. She miserably counted the minutes until she could say she had had enough fresh air and return to the house to be near the telephone on which Gavin called her regularly, at the same time every day.

Celia, also calling every day, asked her, 'When are you coming home?' Lily was evasive – for Celia, this was something completely new in her. Lily said she needed the home-cooked meals Gavin's mother provided instead of the gourmet take-out Celia usually sent for. 'I thought you liked it,' Celia said, and Lily replied yes she did, when she had only herself to think of.

Celia told Fay: 'She's lying to us. They're both lying to us.'

'What if they're not?'

'I'll find out. We'll go there this weekend. She'll tell me the truth. She always does. Don't *you* want to know the truth?'

'Not always,' Fay said. 'Will Gavin be there with her, do you think?'

'Is Gavin ever with her,' Celia said in exasperation.

Suddenly Fay said with more energy than she usually produced, 'Whatever's happened has happened. So let it rest, Celia.'

But 'No,' Celia said. 'No.'

On the weekend, challenged about her husband's absence, Lily remained calm. 'He's trying to get away, but there's always something.' Her shy-violet eyes were large and solemn with truthfulness. 'Gavin knows a lot of interesting people. Everyone wants to meet him.' She sounded as proud and pleased as Gavin did when he spoke of her. 'He's so wonderful – different from everyone in the world. More wonderful,' she explained.

Celia said, 'That's what I'm saying: he *is* different; all right, more wonderful, if that's how you want it ... You don't have to go through with this,' she continued. 'It's a very easy thing to do nowadays, almost legal, certainly with someone as small as you ...' She tried to span her hands round Lily's waist not only to demonstrate its smallness but to touch her in affection.

Lily disengaged herself. She said, 'If you don't believe me, you don't love me. People don't love people they think are liars.'

She went out and took the only action she knew – she called Gavin, and from her voice he realised he could not delay any longer. He told her he would be there on Sunday morning and, confident that he would, she got up early and accompanied her mother-in-law to church.

So when Gavin drove up to the house, he met only Fay, unsuccessfully trying to make coffee for herself in the stone-age kitchen. He did it for her, and she thanked him, and then she said she was glad he had come, to help intervene in the situation that had arisen between her two daughters. The difficulty was, she told him frankly, that Celia couldn't stand the competition, always having had Lily completely to herself.

'And now you're here,' he said.

'Not for long. I'm going away. But you're not. And the baby is not, I presume.'

'Yes, he and I are here to stay.'

'Isn't it exciting? I'm excited.' She stroked his arm, lingering over the sleeve of his summer jacket; she had always appreciated good-looking men. She said, 'It was so kind of you to have married my little Lily.'

'No no, not at all; quite the contrary. It's Lily who is kind. Mother adores her. For her sweet temperament,' he explained, 'and for being so much part of the family. I hope when they've finished praying together, Mother will show her around the churchyard. It's full of us, going back two hundred years. Of course there've been ups and downs – two hundred years is no joke! – but that's how it goes. Kingdoms like the orchard flit russetly away, and all the rest of it.'

'But the name is still there,' Fay said. 'And you're carrying it on. You and my Lily. That's so mysterious and lovely.' She pressed his shoulder, massaging it a bit in affection.

The Sunday lunch Elizabeth served on her return was the same Fay and Celia remembered from their previous visit. So were the family anecdotes told around the table, and they seemed endless to Celia, leaving her tense with frustration. But afterwards she managed to manoeuvre herself and Fay to be alone with their hostess in the parlour. Elizabeth was embroidering a little muslin shirt, and she explained that the pattern – of birds, daisies, violets – was copied from a framed sampler with a faded signature and the date 1871. Beside it hung some watercolours of local scenes – a waterfall, a horse and cart in a field – painted years ago but still there, Elizabeth said, to be rendered by anyone with artistic talent. She herself had no such talent – which made her all the more thankful to have Lily in the family. Fay confirmed that Lily had always loved sketching and had gone to art school.

'She lasted a week,' Celia said. 'Lily is really too frail – physically and otherwise – to see anything through. That's why we're worried about her present condition: if she's strong enough to carry it full term.'

'Our Dr Williams said everything was perfectly normal,' Elizabeth said with satisfaction.

'Perfectly normal,' Celia repeated. She threw a swift glance at her mother, but despairing of help from there, rushed in on her own to tell Gavin's mother: 'We hardly see him. We have no idea where he is, with whom. All we know is he's not where he should be. At home, Lily never knew if her husband was on the sofa where he had chosen to sleep, or if he'd been out all night.'

Snipping off a thread, Elizabeth smiled in reply. 'Gavin has always been a nightbird. I suppose poets usually are, that's when they get their inspiration. Luckily dear Lily is an artist herself, she understands him perfectly. A perfectly matched couple.' She smiled again.

'A poet and his muse.' Fay smiled back.

Two slender figures in light clothes, Gavin and Lily wandered among trees and bushes in the grounds. When he lifted a branch to let her slip through, they appeared to vanish – tenuous as shadows, insubstantial. But for each other they were substantially there. They hardly touched; only sometimes he held her hand, or guided her by her elbow. The grounds were different for Lily when he was there. Now she saw that here and there the ancient and broken trees had sprouted new branches with leaves on them. He led her to where there was a fishpond with water lilies unfolded and goldfish swimming beneath them. They sat on a pile of stones forming a bank, and he lightly laid his arm across her shoulders while she traced his features with her finger, in silence and contentment.

It did not last very long; he looked at his watch. He had to go back to the city, an appointment.

She said, 'Let me come with you.'

He smiled and kissed her hair. 'Mother so loves having you here and she can look after you better and cook you all those dishes. I know you don't like them, neither do I, but you need them. The baby needs them.'

'And afterward? Do we have to live with Celia? Can't I come live with you?'

From his sad smile she realised how impossible this was. She knew he had a place where he needed to do things of his own, write his poetry and meet poets and other friends.

'Celia lives near the Park. You can take the baby there.'

'I don't like the Park.'

'Then walk in the street with the pram – I'll meet you every day and I'll push the pram. I'll love to do that.'

'Really?' She laughed out loud with pleasure.

'Oh yes. Yes. It'll be fun. Our own baby . . . I'm so much looking forward to it. We all are. Mother can hardly wait.'

They were silent. After a while he said, 'Mother will stay with you while he's being born. She did it for all my sisters. She'll be the first to see him.'

A leaf dropped from an overhanging tree; a frog croaked. Gavin said, 'Tell me about him again.'

She waved her hand before her face as though waving away something she did not want to see; but on the contrary, it was a gesture of conjuring up a vision that was imprinted on her mind. 'He was small, very small and skinny. Like those pictures you see of children starving in Africa? Only it was the way he was built, he wasn't exactly starving, though he was hungry. I could tell from the way he ate my pretzel and then asked for another and two hot dogs. It may be because teenagers can never get enough to eat. His hair was very curly and it sat on him like a cap, and his ears stuck out from his head like two handles. His eyes were the biggest thing about him, they were huge, huge, and they shone in the rest of his face – I mean his face being so dark and it was also dark under the bridge.'

'Yes,' Gavin said. 'I think I can see him. In fact, quite clearly.'

'I see him all the time and I'm scared.'

'Why should you be? I'm here. It's my son.'

'Scared that he may have gotten sick from being in the rain and having nowhere to dry his shirt. I don't think he had another one, and it was very thin cloth so you could see his shoulder blades sticking out.'

'I thought you trusted me,' Gavin said, sounding so sad that she gave a little cry of reassurance and for a brief moment laid her hand on the shoulder of his jacket.

'If you trust me, you have to believe me.'

'I do believe you, and last week I went around to all the Ethiopian restaurants I could find in New York, but he wasn't there. But maybe he wasn't Ethiopian.'

'No, maybe he was Nigerian, but you wouldn't want to go around to all the Nigerian restaurants. He's working and saving his tips for the restaurant. You have to believe me without proof. That's what faith is – believing without proof.'

They got up from the bank of stones. It was getting late, the shadows lay cool and lengthened on the grass and the tops of the trees had the stillness around them that means the end of the day and its liquidation in the setting sun. They retraced their steps back to the house where his car was parked, and when they passed through the blighted orchard, he picked up an apple for her and she ate it. She didn't even have to look; she knew it would be whole, without worms or decay.

Nevertheless, some of the things he had promised her did not happen. The baby was born and, as Gavin had predicted, Elizabeth was the first to see him emerge with his little cap of black hair. Gavin chose the name Scipio for him (after the Roman general Scipio Africanus, he explained to Lily). But Lily did not often push Scipio in his pram. Instead she pushed Gavin in his wheelchair through the streets they both loved. Poets traditionally die young – in the past often from consumption, but Gavin was an early victim of a new disease. He had been moved to Celia's apartment and stayed in the bedroom that he now shared with Lily, he alone in the bed and she on a folding cot placed at the foot of it. She cared for him entirely by herself, refusing to engage a nurse and only sometimes grudgingly accepting Celia's help. It was easy for her to carry him, he had become as light as a child, and he looked up at her with perfect trust in her ability to hold him.

A week after he died, she climbed up to the roof of an office building that Gavin had pointed out to her as a typical example of post-war commercial architecture. He had told her it was architecturally very boring, but it suited her purpose after she discovered that the fire-escape stairway leading to the roof was kept open during office hours. So it was by day that she took the long climb to arrive at the top. From here she gazed down over the city: the churches and the bridges and the ribbons of river, and the streets with their shoals of cars and glittering towers of museums and stores and theatres and restaurants and dreams of restaurants – dreams of glory and gold pouring down from the sky that, now she was so close to it, turned out to be much larger and brighter than she had anticipated.

While he was growing up, the orphaned Scipio mostly lived in the country in the family house permeated by the family history that his paternal grandmother transmitted to him day by day. He didn't listen to her stories very carefully; at this time his principal interest was in horses and he often accompanied his two great-uncles to the races at Saratoga. His ambition was to become a jockey, for which he was small and wiry enough, and even slightly bow-legged. But after spending a vacation with his grandmother Fay in Monte Carlo, where she had settled for tax reasons, he grew enthusiastic about motorcar racing. This led to his subsequent career as a racing-car driver. He became famous and was photographed for magazines, leaning against his car with his crash helmet under his arm, his radiant smile stretching up to his ears where they stuck out like two handles.

This photograph, and many others of him, stood in Celia's living room. She looked at him with pleasure, but as the years passed she began to be puzzled by these pictures of Scipio. She wondered what he was doing there among all the others, especially next to the photograph of Gavin and Lily on their wedding day. But after some more time she also couldn't remember who this couple was – she wiped the dust off the glass, but failed to make them or her memory any clearer. No one heard her mutter to herself; if she muttered some names, she had no faces to put to them, even though they were smiling all around her. There was a film over her eyes, and a film over her mind. Only sometimes there was a glimmer – a shimmer of two figures in light-coloured clothes on the verge of disappearing from sight, between trees or around a street corner, or simply fading into the ether. The ether! Even that – a poetic idea but a false hypothesis – has ceased to exist.

Ruth Prawer Jhabvala was born in Germany of Polish parents and came to England in 1939 at the age of twelve. She graduated from Queen Mary College, London University, and married the Indian architect C. S. H. Jhabvala. They lived in Delhi from 1951 to 1975. Since then they have divided their time between Delhi, New York and London.

As well as her numerous novels and short stories, in collaboration with James Ivory and Ismail Merchant, Ruth Prawer Jhabvala has written scripts for film and television, including *A Room with a View* and *Howards End*, both of which are Academy Award winners. She won the Booker Prize for *Heat and Dust* in 1975, the Neil Gunn International Fellowship in 1978, the MacArthur Foundation Fellowship in 1984 and was made a CBE in the 1998 New Year's Honours List.